Duncan McLean was born in Aberdeenshire and now lives in Orkney. His collection of stories, *Bucket of Tongues*, won a Somerset Maugham Award in 1993. He has also written for stage and television. He spent most of 1995 in Texas, in search of Western Swing hero Bob Wills; an account of his travels will be published in 1998.

BY DUNCAN McLEAN

Fiction

Bucket Of Tongues
Blackden
Bunker Man

Play

Julie Allardyce

BUNKER MAN

DUNCAN McLEAN

W. W. NORTON & COMPANY

NEW YORK • LONDON

First American edition 1997
First published 1997 by W. W. Norton by arrangement with Jonathan Cape Ltd.

Copyright © 1995 by Duncan McLean

The right of Duncan McLean to be identified as the
author of this work has been asserted by him in accordance
with the Copyright, Designs and Patents Act, 1988

Printed in the United States of America

First published in Great Britain
by Jonathan Cape Ltd.,1995

A CIP catalogue record for this book
is available from the British Library

ISBN 0-393-04121-2
ISBN 0-393-31616-5 pbk.

W. W. Norton & Company, Inc., 500 Fifth Avenue, New York, N.Y. 10110
W. W. Norton & Company Ltd., 10 Coptic Street, London WC1A 1PU

1 2 3 4 5 6 7 8 9 0

BUNKER MAN

Rob!

Mmm.

Robbie!

Eh?

Wake up!

What... He raised himself on one elbow and looked over to her side of the bed. What is it?

Shh! Listen.

He lay still, his ears straining into the dark. I can't hear anything, he said after a moment.

There's somebody in the house, she whispered, and there was panic in her voice.

He listened again, reached a hand out towards her. It landed on her bare arm, and she jolted.

I can't hear anything, he said.

It was there a minute ago. Somebody walking around. Doors opening. Drawers being pulled out. I heard it!

Jesus. He sat up. The house was silent, except for Karen's quick breathing and his own heart starting to thump in his chest.

Who is it Rob? Who is it?

How do I know?

She leant towards him, put one hand on his back. Go and see.

What!

Robbie, you have to.

1

Jesus. . .

He swung his feet out from under the downie and lowered them onto the carpet. Then he reached for his jeans, which were lying folded on the chair by the bed. He started to pull them on.

What are you doing?

I'm not going down there in the buff, he whispered back. How could I fight somebody off with my goolies dangling about?

There! Footsteps! And breathing, I can hear somebody breathing!

He paused, listened, then stood up and walked to the door of the bedroom. If I'm not back in half an hour, call the coastguards, he said. He opened the door and stepped out into the cool air of the lobby.

He stopped at the head of the stairs. Still he couldn't hear a thing, only the central heating timer humming in its box by the front door, and far away, impossible to place, a low low roaring that could've been wind or traffic or the sea, or blood roaring in his head.

He put his foot down on the first tread of the stairs, then drew it back again. There were two ways to do this: either creep down in the dark, silently, and have surprise on his side when he jumped whoever was down there, or else slam on the lights and thump down the stairs boldly, but slowly, and hope the intruder would've legged it by the time he reached the bottom.

He'd never been much good at the physical stuff. He'd go for the mental attack method.

The light switches for the stair and upstairs lobby were by his right shoulder. He clicked both of them on, blinked at the sudden brightness, then cleared his throat loudly and dunted his heel down on the first step of the stairs again. There was no sound of scurrying footsteps. He went down another step, letting all his weight fall on it. Nothing from below. He carried on all the way down to the landing where the stairs turned ninety degrees to the left, letting him see the hallway for the first time. The coats were hanging from the hooks, the vase of dried flowers was sitting on the electrics box, the door was closed – though impossible to know from here if it was locked.

He was getting fed up of this. If there was some bastard downstairs, why didn't the cunt make a move? He still hadn't heard a damn thing: no footsteps, no heavy breathing, sod all. Probably there was nobody and nothing down there in the first place.

He ran down the second half of the stairs, lunged for the switch that lit up the hallway, shoved wide the living-room door and jumped inside.

Nothing. The air was still and silent, with just a trace of the evening warmth left. He glanced down at the clock on front of the video. 03:30. Four hours till he had to leave for work.

He walked back through the hallway, relaxed and yawning now, stuck his head round the kitchen door, then went into the bathroom and took a pish. He hadn't bothered to switch the light on, and he could hear his aim wasn't too good: splashes and spirks were hitting the vinyl flooring. As the lavvy flushed, he trundled a length of paper off the holder and bent to swipe it round the base of the pan. Then he lifted the lid and dropped the tissue into the last roils of the flush.

Washing his hands, whistling under his breath, he remembered the locks on the doors. The front door was just across the hallway, he tried that first: double locked. The he stepped into the kitchen and gave the handle of the back door a yark: the door swung open, cold air rushing in over him.

For a second he just stood there. Then he leant outside, glanced up at the starry sky, then all round his patch of garden: dead, not even a blade of grass to be stirring. He'd have to get onto it. He banged the door shut, turned the key in the mortice, then headed out of the kitchen and quickly back up the stairs.

He slowed before pushing open the bedroom door, and called in a low spooky voice, Karen. . . Karen Catto. . . He walked in stiffly, arms stretched out in front of him, groaning.

There was a giggle from the bed. Robbie, I ken it's you.

Got me! He laughed. Are you disappointed?

Come to bed.

Too right I'm coming to bed, it's bloody starvation out here. He kicked off his breeks and got under the downie, immediately sliding over to cuddle onto Karen, who squeaked and jerked away, then settled in towards him, her backside into his groin, her back against his chest, her shoulder under his chin.

You're like ice, she said.

Come on and warm me up a bit then. He wrapped one arm round the front of her, laid it over both breasts, and squeezed.

Mmm. . .

There was nobody there, he said, shifting himself against her, feeling an erection starting to come.

I worked that out, she said. I heard you singing to yourself.

Singing?

Maybe I was dreaming the whole thing. It's funny. I really thought there was somebody down there.

I'll tell you something though, he said in her lug. The back door wasn't locked.

4

Was it not? I did lock it.

You can't have. And that's your job. I spend all my day locking and unlocking doors, I don't want to have to worry about them at home too. You know the deal.

I know Rob, I'm sorry. I must've forgotten.

You know what happens if you forget, don't you?

What?

He paused, then whispered. You'll get somebody coming in *your* back door in the middle of the night. . . He shoved his hips forward, so the bulb of his cock pushed in between the cheeks of her backside.

Is that right?

That's right.

He pushed harder, but she opened her legs slightly so he slipped forwards and into her cunt. She pressed back against him, circling her hips, and turned her face to one side to meet his mouth as it trailed over the bones of her shoulder and came searching for her lips and tongue and breath.

The talk in the bothy was all about the memo the rector's secretary had delivered after dinnertime.

It's shite, said Donald. That's not my job, that's not what I signed up for.

What was it then? said Billy. The foreign travel, the glamour of the uniform?

I just wanted something close to home, said Donald.

Rob nodded, looking serious. Aye, that way you can get out of your bed, round the corner, and in here with your feet up – all without ever coming awake.

Billy laughed till his face was dark red, then started coughing.

His face went purple, veins bulged out in his neck and in the hollows at each side of his forehead.

Keep talking Rob, said Donald. You'll kill the old bugger yet.

Billy wiped tears away from the corners of his eyes, still chuckling. You've touched a nerve there! he said at last. Cause it's true. On a good day Donald still hasn't come awake by lowsing time!

Shite.

That's really why you're a jannie: cause you reckoned it was the best skive available on a union wage, you workshy cunt!

Oi, Bill, said Rob. Watch the language. We don't want the kids to hear words like that, do we? *Union*, he mouthed.

Donald put down the paper he'd been pretending to read while Billy slagged him. Moran doesn't, anyroad. That's what I'm saying. He doesn't want them hearing things or saying things or doing things. Fair enough. But now he wants us to stop them saying and doing stuff. Like I said: no way! That's not in the job description. It doesn't say janitor brackets police!

Nothing wrong with the police, mind you, put in Billy. I served. . .

. . .twenty-four years, I ken, I ken! But the point is, that's not what you're employed as now, and Moran can't force you to do it.

Ach, you're getting too worked up about this, said Billy. Where is the damn thing? What does it say?

Rob shifted his coffee mug and piece box further along the bench, then brushed crumbs off the pink bit of A4 that had been lying underneath them. He read aloud: FAO All janitorial and cleaning staff. While realising blah blah blah other, primary duties. . .

Primary? said Donald. This is a secondary!

6

Shut up, said Billy.

. . .none the less, on occasion blah blah blah opportunities to uphold the moral standards of the school blah blah age old problems blah smoking, petting, blah blah new and more serious blah *drugs*. Blah blah ask you to exercise special vigilance blah blah blah don't hesitate to draw to my blah or take immediate action yourself if appropriate. . .

There! cried Donald.

. . . any queries. . . via Mr Catto in first instance blah blah B.L.J. Moran, dominie.

Does it really say dominie? said Billy.

No, said Rob, I made that up.

I don't ken how you can crack jokes, said Donald. This is serious stuff, guys, it changes our whole responsibilities. Taking immediate action! Exercising special vigilance! What are we, the effing SAS?

No, but you have to admit, said Billy. There is such a thing as school rules. If kids break them, it's just like somebody breaking the laws of the land: they have to get punished. That's the whole point of laws: if you break them, you get clobbered.

Aye, maybe, but what I'm saying is, it's not us that should be doing the clobbering. If Moran wants to clobber the bairns, fair enough: he gets paid five times what we do because he makes these decisions. All I'm saying is, I'm not going to do it for him, not at three sixty an hour.

But Donald, Donald, said Billy, leaning forward in his chair and spreading his hands. I don't think you've got a choice. The headmaster's ordered the head jannie, and now he's ordering us. You have to do it!

Hold on though, said Rob. I have to tell you what I'm told to tell you, but I haven't ordered anybody to do anything.

But he is *telling* us Comrade MacBain, said Billy, and winked at Donald.

But if you want my idea about what's actually to be done, Rob went on, I reckon the first thing is to write a memo back to Mr Moran saying that we have noted the contents of his, eh, communication, and that we will. . . fulfil his requests as diligently as opportunity allows.

Spot on! Without a script, too!

That's how you get to be a head jannie, instead of just a minion, said Donald.

Billy pointed at him. Bugger off, he said.

Donald turned back to Rob. And what's the second thing we should do? And mind it's not outwith the job description, or the union rep'll have to get involved. And I ken he won't like it.

Cause he's you, muttered Billy.

Exactly.

The second thing is, we don't put ourselves out to look for trouble. Enough comes our way without us raking for more. But if we do catch the wee bastards fucking about, we should do like Moran says and blooter them. Just think: their folks would do if they saw them, but they're not here.

In loco parentis, said Billy.

In a train with the parents, said Donald.

Exactly, said Rob. And we're the ticket collectors. If they're smoking in the corridors, or shagging in the bogs, we can't pretend we don't see it.

Who's been shagging in the bogs?

Rob sighed. Nobody Billy, it was just an example.

I'll be keeping an eye out for the likes of that, said Donald. Wouldn't want to miss anything exciting.

Fine, said Rob. That's my opinion in a oner, my head jannie's opinion: we keep our eyes open, see what we see. But we don't go looking for trouble. He glanced from one to the other; they both nodded. And here's another opinion, he went on, Billy should stick the kettle on again, Donald should pass me over my memo book from the tray.

He took a ballpoint from his coat pocket and pressed the button in and out a few times, then lifted it just in front of his eyes and examined the fibres and grains of muck gathered around the nib.

This is something you'll find out about me, he said as he wiped the tip of the pen with a scrap of paper. I don't like the dominie or the teachers hanging around my bothy. So I don't want Moran having to come inby the morn's morn to see if we got his message okay – like he did last week about the staffroom ashtray-wiping dispute. Therefore I fire a reply off to the bastard right away.

Dear Rectum, said Donald, and all three of them laughed.

There was a rap on the door, and a short man wearing a tracksuit sprang in.

Chaps!

Mr Jackson, said Billy.

Right to the point chaps. I've just been having a kick around with the S2s on the blaze pitch, and I was noticing the line markings are pretty rubbed out.

Is that right? said Rob.

Folk keep running all over them with big knobbly boots on, said Donald. That's the problem.

Not that it's urgent really, but just if you could find time over

9

the next day or two to lay some new ones down, I'd be saved a lot of arguments over throw-ins and penalty claims!

We'll get on to it right away.

No hurry, Mr Catto, none at all. Though I do happen to know it'll be free next period. I'm on volleyball in the hall, and Sylvia's outside – hockey with the S3 girls – but that's on the grass pitch.

Listen, Mr Jackson. . .

Brian!

Aye, don't worry Brian. I'll see to it right away. Rob stood up, and took a step towards the teacher. Tell you what, no extra charge, I'll give it a good raking too.

Champion, chaps! Knew you wouldn't let the side down. He rubbed his hands together, looked at each of the jannies in turn, then ducked back out the bothy door.

Rob waited a second, then turned to the others and said, See, if you're nice to them they fuck off twice as fast!

So you'll have another cup of tea afore you start? said Billy.

Where's the doughnuts gone? said Donald.

Rob stood there for a few seconds, gazing out the window at the car park and the trees beyond it. Actually, it's not a bad day, he said. I reckon I'll just head out and get on with it.

No fly? said David.

You have yours. But I won't bother, I feel like getting out. You have yours. Then just the usual afternoon routine, okay?

He left the bothy and headed down the short corridor to the car park. Then he went round the outside of the school towards the playing fields. The noise of hockey sticks banging against each other, and against legs and the turf and occasionally the ball, got louder as he approached the end of the school buildings. As Rob unlocked the toolshed at the edge of the pitch, he looked over and watched the game and the players for a few minutes. Then he went into the shed.

When she came back from the bar he didn't move along the bench, so their legs pressed together as she sat down. She kissed him on the cheekbone, then pushed his drink along in front of him, lifted hers to her lips.

They looked across at the band for a minute, him moving his head in time to the music, her rocking her feet on the floor. Very soon the friction of her thigh on his started getting to him; he could feel his cock beginning to stiffen. He turned to her, and she was just lifting her face to his. They kissed, then parted and looked at each other, then kissed again, longer this time. When they broke apart, her tongue wasn't all the way back in her mouth. He saw the pink tip of it, and immediately his cock went completely hard.

You're sweet tonight, he said.

It's the Coke in the rum.

No, it's you, he said. I'd like to drink you, drink your insides out.

Oh aye?

Aye. I've got a thirst for you.

I reckon you should stick to your Becks for now.

For now?

Aye, till we're out of here.

Are we leaving, like?

She shrugged. Do you want to stay?

Me? Nah. He took a long drink.

I mean, the band is good, she said.

Aye, they're fine.

11

But they're hell of a loud.

That's true.

I like to talk to you, see?

Aye.

Especially when I haven't seen you all day.

Aye.

So what's the point of sitting somewhere we can't hear each other speak?

Pardon?

She grinned. He lifted his glass and took another big swallow. Let's go then, he said, foam flecking his top lip.

She put her right hand up and brushed it over his mouth, at the same time patting him on the knee. What's your rush, laddie? she said. Then she slid her left hand up the inside of his leg and over the bulge of his erection, where she let it rest.

He leaned over and whispered in her ear, I'm away to come.

Ah. She nodded. So that's the rush! She lifted her hand up, took hold of her glass, and took a tiny sip. Then she put the glass down again and folded both hands together in her lap. Hey, she said. They're playing Sweet Home Chicago – your fave rave.

Oh yeah. He listened. Hold on, they've changed the words. Hear?

After a few seconds the band reached the chorus, and the singer bellowed out, Sweet Hame Auchenblae!

Rob and Karen laughed.

Is that where they're from? she said.

Could be. The bass player used to be at the school – maths. But he's teaching up at Stonehive now, so he could bide at Auchenblae. Donald at work was telling me about him.

Donald? He's the young one?

Aye. Ages with us, anyway. Does that count as young?

Hhm. I feel young. Do you not?

He shrugged. Aye, most of the time.

Thirty's no great age, she said.

It's just when I look at some of the kids coming running into the school in the morning – that energy! Then I feel like I'm ninety years old, never mind thirty!

Aw... She stroked his arm. Are you feeling worn out, honey? Do you need a wee lie down?

I wouldn't mind, he said. If it was on top of you.

Rob, you have got a one track mind.

Nuh.

You have!

No, *you* have. He leaned close towards her. Cause all you ever think about is my cock. I think about your cunt and your tits and your mouth. So there you go: a three track mind at least.

They looked at each other. Neither of them said anything. After a second they got up and left the pub. Walking along the High Street, they held hands, sweat trickling into the crevices where their fingers laced.

When they came to the junction, Karen turned away from the road that led up to their estate. She tugged at Rob and tried to pull him along the other way. He wouldn't budge to start with, but she kept tugging his hand till he gave in and let himself be pulled one step towards her.

Where are we going? he whispered. I want to fuck.

Aye, me too, she said. But we don't have to go home.

Where then? he said. Round to your folks and ask to borrow their settee for five minutes?

No, she said. I'll show you: somewhere I used to go when I was a kid. Come on.

He allowed himself to be yarked along, and within a few minutes they were through the far end of the town, past the school, and heading northwards out the path that ran along the top of the low cliffs there. Woods came down close to the shore, and soon the lights of the town were out of sight. But the clear pink sky had enough light left in it to show up the well-worn trail in front of them.

Suddenly Karen stopped, looked around for a moment, then jumped off the path, plunging into some gorse bushes and disappearing. He followed her. After ten seconds submerged in the bushes, he came out onto an open area of short grass, with water on either side: a narrow spit of land fifty metres long, edged with black rocks cragging down into the sea. There was a concrete ruin of some kind out at the far end, and halfway towards it Karen had laid her coat on the ground and was stepping out of her trousers.

He went running up to her. She let her pants fall to her ankles.

We can't do it here! he said.

Why not? We're married, we can do whatever we like to each other. She put one hand out to rest on his shoulder, and the other down to open his spaver.

Aye, but somebody might see!

Like who? Ships in the night? She pulled him in against her. Come on, fuck me.

He put his hands down to the skin of her arse. You want me to fuck you?

Come on!

He pressed his mouth against hers, kept pressing, pressed all his

14

weight against her face, till she folded to the ground, half on her coat and half on the grass, and he fell on top of her. His cock jabbed inside her and they banged against each other, her with both hands round the back of his head, him holding onto her backside, pulling her up towards him as he lunged into her, lunged again, lunged, and came. She shouted something in his ear, bucked against him several more times, then gave a grunt, froze, and finally relaxed underneath him.

They lay there for a moment, then he levered himself up off her and let his cock slip out to hang in the cool air. She lifted a hand, wrapped her fingers round the shaft, and moved it up and down a couple times.

Pleased to meet you, Mr One Eye, she said. I think we're going to be great friends.

He laughed, sprang to his feet, and tucked himself in. You're mad, he said.

Well you must be double mad.

How?

Kenning I'm mad and still getting married to me.

Mad with love, that's me. He took a couple steps away and looked over the edge of the taing, down at the dark sea cracking about the rocks.

Mad with lust, more like, she said.

Are you complaining?

She came up behind him, put her arms around his waist and her head on his shoulder. Do you ken what the happiest day of my life was? she said.

So far?

Aye.

The day we got married.

No, that was my mother's happiest day – my second happiest.
I give up then.

She breathed in his ear. It was the first time you stuck your cock
up me and wiggled it around. If I'd died that night I wouldn't've
been disappointed.

What, you wanted to die?

No, I wanted to fuck again! But if I had died, well, I would've
been happy to go out on such a glory.

He turned to face her. You shouldn't talk like that, he said.

Why not?

Cause it makes me want to stick it up you and wiggle it around
right now.

She raised her eyebrows. Hold that thought till we're back on
our nice soft bed, she said. I've had enough grass jagging my bum
for one night.

Shame, he said. Can I whip your tits with thistles instead?

She laughed, and they headed home.

In the afternoon they drove to the supermarket at the edge of
town and filled a trolley with paint and rollers as well as food.
They looked for a long time at a display of different seed packs and
bulbs, but ended up not taking any of those; all the packets were
printed with complicated information about suitable soil types
and ideal mixtures of shelter and exposure, and Karen said they
should check what their garden conditions were before grabbing a
lot of unsuitable plants. Rob nodded, then suggested that they
should buy a load of packets anyway, chuck the seeds in the bin,
and glue the colour pictures to canes stuck in the earth all around
the garden. Guaranteed spectacular results, with much less
digging. Karen laughed, and they headed for the checkout.

16

As Rob wheeled the trolley through the busy car park towards their Fiesta, Karen reached into her coat pocket. Then she frowned, and stuck a hand into the other pocket. She stopped in the middle of an exitway and started going through her inside pockets, then checking the outside ones again. A car honked its horn behind her. She jumped, and ran a few steps to catch up with Rob.

Go and open the boot, he said as she came alongside him.

I can't.

Eh?

I've lost my keys.

He stuck his hand in his jeans pocket. Here, use mine, he said.

She fumbled with them for a moment, then got the hatchback up. But listen, she said. I've lost them. She started feeling all her pockets again. And my wallet! My wee wallet with the cashcard and stuff! That's gone too! Shite!

Rob was putting tins of paint and bags of food into the car. Give us a hand, will you? he said.

Robbie! This is important! That's the car key, the house keys – and the one to my desk at work. There's not a spare of that, even!

You lock your desk?

I've got to get them back. Where can they be?

Calm down, said Rob. Calm down and think.

Well, we came out of the house. . .

But I was last out.

Aye, so you must've had yours then.

I've still got mine.

I ken you have, Rob. I'm just thinking aloud.

Jesus. He put a six-pack of tall brown beer bottles in the last space on the floor of the boot, and closed it.

I had the keys last night, she said. And I definitely had the card last night, cause I took money out of the wall afore we went to see the blues band, mind?

Aye. But who opened the door when we got home?

Eh. . .

I'll just stick this away, he said, and strolled off with the empty trolley.

When he came back she was sitting in the driver's seat with the motor going.

It's obvious, she said as he got into the car. They must've fallen out of my pocket when I took my coat off and we were rolling around on it.

Christ, of course! That'll be it, right enough.

She eased the car out through the shoppers and onto the road. We'll have to go and look for them, she said.

Aye, we'll easy find them. The memory of the spot's imprinted on the skin of my knees. Let's go there right now – afore the rain comes on.

Except – shite! – there's all that frozen stuff in the back. A chicken, and prawns, and your pizzas. . .

Karen, he said. Drop me off by the school and I'll nip out there myself. I'll find them no bother. You take this stuff home and stash it away. I'll be back in time for tea, okay?

Are you sure?

For you? Sure I'm sure!

Five minutes later he was walking through the woods to the north of the town. On his right the land fell away in ten-metre cliffs and mud-banks to the sea, which was grey and cold-looking. The air was cold too; there were sharp blaffs of wind coming in off the

18

water. He walked a bit quicker, nodded and smiled as he passed a tottering old woman with a rat-sized dog tucked under her arm, then paused, looked around, and cut off into a thick clump of tall gorse bushes.

They were closer together than he'd remembered, and he put both hands up in front of his face to stop thorns whipping into his eyes. He shoved in between two big bushes, then suddenly was standing on a heugh-head over the sea. One more step and he'd've been over the edge. It wasn't a very high cliff, but the black rocks at the bottom of it looked pretty fucking hard and jaggy.

A huge wave came rolling in. He watched it toppling and toppling, never falling, continually toppling forwards – till it smashed on the rocks below. Shards of water flew up and spirked all over him, stinging his eyes. He took a step back and rubbed his palms across his face.

So where was the fucking spit of land with the keys and the spunk stains? He gazed back towards the town, but there was nothing that looked right there. As soon as he turned to the north, though, he spotted it. It was impossible to miss, it had a big lump of a concrete building sticking out the end of it like a wart at the tip of a finger. There was still about half a mile to go; the urge to fuck must fairly've been speeding them on the night before.

Rob pushed his way back through the gorse bushes to the path, paused to catch his breath, then walked quickly on, glancing up at the sky as he went. The cloud was getting thicker, the wind fiercer. He'd only his denim jacket on; he didn't want to be stuck out in the country if it started pissing down.

After a few minutes he came to another big outcrop of gorse

bushes by the path. These weren't so densely packed as the last lot. He cut off the trail and into the whins.

The grassy taing opened out in front of him, and rain began to spatter on his shoulders. He walked halfway up the spit and began to look around. It didn't take long to find where they'd been lying: the grass was flattened and crushed, and there was a sodden lump of tissue that he'd seen Karen wiping herself with.

He went down on one knee and started running his hands over the patch of squashed grass. The rain was falling heavier now, and the earth was clagging onto his fingers. He stood up again, scanning the area around their bed, and spotted something glistening. He dived forwards and picked it up. It was a ten pence bit. The rain was coming down like a urinal flush. It was hopeless. He turned his collar up, took one last glance about, then started running, running up towards the ruin at the far end of the taing, which seemed to still have a roof, over part of it at least.

The grass was getting skitey in the downpour, and he almost slipped as he came running up to the big concrete walls of the ruin. He put a hand out to steady himself, then stepped round towards the rectangular entrance way. It didn't go straight into the building; it led off rightwards between two concrete walls, then there was a sharp turn to the left. He hurried along. There was no roof here, and the rain was belting his face and neck. There was another sharp turn, to the right, and he turned it and his foot squelched on the rotted body of a sheep. Fuck! There wasn't much left of it, just some rags of filthy wool, a rickle of mottled bones and some clods of rotten flesh, one of which he'd pleitered into. The eyes had been pecked out long ago.

Why the fuck was he standing staring at a sheep's corpse?

He jumped over it, took the last few steps into the building, and was plunged into darkness. After five seconds his eyes were getting used to the lack of light, and he could make out where he was.

It was some kind of wartime gun emplacement, the gun long gone. It must've been a big bastard of a thing though. Now there was just an almost circular room, with a narrow slot cut out of the side that faced the sea. A big circle of rusted metal was set into the concrete floor, a kind of rail for a wheel or something to move around on. And there were other lumps of flaking rotten iron studded into the walls and framing the slit window. Gusts of wind blew straight in off the sea. They were stirring up a strong smell of old pish. Probably he should be grateful for the pish. Probably it was covering up the stink of festering sheep.

On the floor in front of him, under a small hole in the roof, was a puddle of cleanish water. He stood in it and flexed his trainers up and down a few times, hoping that any bits of sheep gut or shite would rinse off.

Apart from the puddles, the floor was half-covered in rubbish: crushed and rusty beer cans, an old Sweetheart Stout bottle, the lassie's face scabbed with mould; fangs of broken glass, shreds of newspaper; crisp packets, fag packets, a carrier bag with something lumpy and dark inside. In one corner was a pile of decomposing clothes; it looked to be mostly thick, old-fashioned nylon bras in various neony colours. In another corner he could see a shrivelled-up condom. Even that seemed bulky and old-fashioned, the rubber thick and opaque, more like the finger of a dishwashing glove than a featherweight modern doob. Though probably there'd be a few of those dripping about the place too if he fucking searched them out.

It was obvious that the place was used as a shagging shed. It had

21

all the usual signs, all the incriminating evidence; even the ashes and charred stones showing where they lit fires to heat themselves up before getting down to business. Christ, they could've had a sheepskin rug for the side of the fire if they'd dragged it in from the entrance!

The idea made him feel a bit sick. He looked round the walls of the place. BOB and AFC were in drippling red paint. Who'd go to the bother of carting a tin and a brush away out here? Bob would. Mental. There was sprayed stuff too. SMOKE YOU DOPE! and a leaf, and a big sun with a smiley face. Somebody else had splashed a load of black stuff – oil maybe, or tar – over the face of the sun. There was a lot of marker stuff. I FUCKED LINDA HERE. SO DID I. KICK A POLICE TODAY. IF YOU WANT A SHAG PHONE 343, ASK FOR FREIDA. IF YOU NOTICE THIS NOTICE YOU'LL NOTICE THIS NOTICE IS NOT WORTH FUCKING NOTICING. KARIN SUCKED MY COCK. MINE TOO. E'S ARE GOOD. MAD IVAN RULES. MHAIRI SCOTT IS A SLAG, SHE IS SLACK. I'LL KILL YOU SMITHY, I KEN YOU WROTE IT. STILL BREATHING, STILL WAITING.

There were a lot of things that couldn't be read because there were cracks in the ceiling, and parts of the walls were black with running damp. There were also patches of moss crawling about, and sooty scrapes and blotches. It was easy to make out at least three classic rampant cocks, though, with bulging balls, wee slits in the end of the knob, and drops of spunk shooting out of the tip in a curve. If the guy who first drew that had copyrighted it, he'd be a fucking millionaire by this time.

Rob was a connoisseur of these rampant cocks – he worked in school toilets for fuck's sake – and these ones were pretty good, pretty high quality. One of them was particularly arty. He walked over to take a closer look. It had crinkly hairs coming out of the balls, veins going down the side of the shaft, and the spunk gobbed out the end of it, arced across the wall, and ended up squirting into an alcove that was cut into the concrete just to the side of the gun-slot. It really looked like the cock was firing off into a big square fud.

Rob laughed.

Then he realised that the alcove wasn't empty. There was something lying inside it, something metal catching the light. He peered into the cubby-hole.

Fuck! It was Karen's keys! And underneath the keys was her wee plastic wallet, with a small stack of coins piled up beside that. And balanced on top of the coins like a scales was a tortoiseshell comb. He had one just like. . . His hand went round to the back right pocket of his jeans, and the comb wasn't there. He grabbed the one from the alcove and examined it in the light from the window slot. This had to be his; it must've fallen out of his pocket while they were riding. Of course he hadn't noticed: his mind was on other things at the time! All this money was probably his as well. He pocketed it. He also lifted Karen's keys and, after flicking through to check all the cards were still there, buttoned up her wallet in his breast pocket.

There was nothing else in the alcove, just bare concrete. That was quite strange, actually. Everywhere else was covered in dirt and shite; surely there should've been at least a fag butt or a sweetie wrapper blown in there? There wasn't even any dust. It looked like somebody had washed the thing out before putting the keys and stuff inside.

Rob froze, then jumped round. There was nobody behind

23

him. There was no sound of footsteps. Just the wind whooming through the slot in the wall and the zigzag entranceway. Still, he had what he'd come for. Why fuck about? He looked out over the sea for a second. It was moving, but not going anywhere. And the rain was pouring down into it. If the rain came down heavy enough, would it fill up all the gaps between the waves so the whole sea was flat and still? Fuck that: there was enough of a deluge already. But so fucking what, he wasn't going to hang around this dump any longer than absolutely necessary.

Rob jogged to work. He went down the High Street where nothing was open except the fishmonger's and the newsagent, then turned into the Front Road and ran along the Promenade. The sea was rattling on the pebbly beach over the railings, but apart from that it was quiet.

Running was a good way to start the day. If he fell out of bed and drove to work and was just waking up as he got there, it always felt like the whole day belonged to work, that the work was in control. But if he got up slightly earlier and had his breakfast and a good jog before getting to the school, then he had time to come right awake, to make the day his. Okay, he would spend a chunk of hours in the middle of the day working, but it was him making that choice, he was in control: the day started and finished with Robert Catto and his thoughts.

Actually he didn't have many big thoughts in his head. Folk always assumed that he was working out arguments, or making up stories, or planning the rest of the day or the rest of his life as he went running about. Karen used to, when they were first living together. He'd take a long way round on his way home from work in the afternoon, spend an hour going up and down the quiet backstreets of Ferrybrae, sometimes getting home after Karen, even, though she never finished at the office till half-five at least. Then she'd ask him, Bad day at work was it? Running out your aggression are you? No, Rob would say, Work was fine. What were you thinking about all that time then? she'd say. You! he'd answer, and go to kiss her. No, but really? Eh, I don't know. I wasn't thinking about anything. I was running, not thinking.

What tended to happen was that a thought came into his head, and he'd start to follow it, but before very long there'd be a big thump and the thought would get knocked clean away. The thump was his foot hitting the ground. A couple seconds later the same thought might appear again, or a new one crop up, but no matter what they were they only ever stuck in his skull for half a moment till his trainer hit the tarmac and they got jolted out. The only thinking he could do while jogging was in bursts an instant long.

But that didn't bother Rob. He didn't ken how it happened – he just kent it wasn't by thinking it through – but by the time he was in the bothy getting changed out of his shorts into his work clothes, he found that he felt like Robert Catto. He'd become Robert or Rob during the run, that was how it felt – all Rob's thoughts and beliefs and feelings and memories joined together and sitting snod exactly where they should be. It was like shaking up a jigsaw puzzle in its box, then opening the lid and finding that all the pieces had fallen into their correct places and the picture was complete.

He turned in the school gates, went past the main doors and sprinted to the far end of the car park, where there was a door leading into the corridor next to the bothy. It was known as the Tradesman's Entrance, because it was used by the cleaners and

25

janitors but not the teachers or the pupils – unless they wanted to sneak out of the building for some reason.

There was a light on in the bothy window. Rob frowned and looked at his watch. It was only quarter to; somebody else was early too – earlier! He went through the door, that school smell hitting him as it did sometimes after a weekend away, and into the bothy.

A jacket was hanging on Donald's peg, but he wasn't to be seen. Rob slung off his backpack, took out his breeks and shirt and got them on, then reached up for his dust-coat and hung the pack on the peg there instead. But he was still warm from the run, so didn't put his coat on yet, just stood with it in his hand, looking out the window at the car park and the woods beyond.

Somebody came into the room. Aye aye Donald, he said, without turning round.

Aye Rob. Fine morning.

You're sharp.

Donald came over to the bench, hovered his hand over the side of the kettle, then, finding it cold, lifted it over without unplugging it so the spout was under the tap. He filled it up.

Against safety regs this, you ken, he said.

I ken, said Rob.

The flex shouldn't reach as far as the sink.

I ken.

We should do something about it.

I dare say.

Coffee?

Rob finally turned to face him, and nodded. So, what's with the early start? Trying to impress me with your lack of laziness or something?

26

Hah! No, you wouldn't believe it! Clocks went forward yesterday, right, so I changed the alarm on Saturday night. What does Bernie do yesterday morning but wake up, mind it was clocks-forwards day, and move it on again! Course, I was out of the house by then, I didn't ken she'd done it. So this morning the alarm got me up and I was having a cup of tea thinking, That's funny, where's breakfast TV theday?

It hadn't started?

It hadn't started. So I reckoned once I was up I might as well come in. I thought I'd do all the clocks in the classrooms; don't trust some of those dopey bastards of teachers to remember!

Rob laughed. Did you do the boiler timer?

Eh, not yet.

Not yet?

Nah.

Speak about dopey bastards! You should've done it first, the place'll never heat up in time.

Donald shrugged. I'll do it now.

Nah, I'll do it, said Rob.

I'll make the coffee then.

No, you come and make sure I do it right. He got into his dustcoat. That's how I came in so early, he said. So I'd have plenty time to get the boiler set. Seeing as you're here, you can check me.

Rob got the boiler-room key out of the key-box, and they headed off down the corridor, past the cleaners' cupboard, the chair store, the fuse room. Rob stopped and looked at his watch. Two minutes to, he said.

Then thish plashe goesh shky high, said Donald in a Sean Connery voice.

Rob unlocked the door and they went in. Where's the light switch? he said.

There's an emergency torch hanging somewhere, said Donald. The switch's outside – for fear of sparks, ken. I'll get it. He stepped outside, the tube light flichtered on, and he reappeared.

Rob was standing in the middle of the room, sniffing. Christ, that smell of gas always gets to me, he said.

I can't smell anything.

Can you not?

Donald wrinkled his nose, shrugged. Dust?

It's just a taint, like. It won't be anything serious. I was the same at my last place in Aberdeen. Kept thinking I could smell gas in the boilerhouse, thought the whole place was going to blow up. So I shut off the plant, got this emergency guy from the gasboard out. He had a computer with a funnel on the side of it – counts the atoms of gas in the air or something. And he gave it the thumbs up! Three parts in a million, he said. What's that I can smell then? I say. Your head's full of gas, goes Chapman – he was the head jannie there – Your head's full of gas, laddie; good job you don't smoke or you'd be in danger of exploding every time you lit up. Then the rector comes in. Shut your yacking! he goes, And get the fucking heaters on pronto, or the staff'll be walking out, the cunts!

Did he say that?

Well, not exactly.

I didn't think it.

I don't ken what he said, cause he was about ten miles away at the time, running, just in case there was an explosion!

There's the control panel there, said Donald.

Rob nodded, got down on his hunkers, and gazed in past the

big burner-unit to the back wall where a small box with a digital display sat amongst a mass of wiring.

I've looked at it before, he said, But I still don't get it: what the fuck was the point of hiding it away at the back there, where no cunt can get to it?

Fuck knows. Probably the panel was put in by the sparks a week before the gas board came to do the boiler. Probably they never talked to each other, that was all.

Jesus Christ. Rob knelt on the concrete floor and crawled forward underneath the big square flue that carried the hot air out of the burner and away through pipes and ducts to heating vents all over the school. It does smell of gas down here, he said.

The pilot light's on your left.

Rob paused to look in at the small blue flame burning steadily behind a grille at his elbow. He breathed out heavily, and the flame flickered, then steadied itself again. He crawled a bit further forward. Right, he said. What time have you got?

Eh. . . three minutes past now.

Okay. Let's see. The screen in front of him said 0702 in red lines, with a small 2 on the left of that, and a small 0 on the right. Beneath the display were buttons marked 0 to 9, plus others saying I, O, D and + and −. Do I need to switch it to standby while I reset the time? said Rob.

Nah. Only if you're going across a whole lot of instructions and you don't want it bumping on and off. So no.

Rob nodded, and the back of his head hit the metal flue above him. Fuck! His voice echoed around with the clang of the flue.

Okay?

Aye. He paused, then slowly raised his head again. And I take it I can just plus it forward, don't need to actually use the set buttons?

29

Aye, you're as well to just do that with the time display. But. . . here, do you smell anything right now?

Rob sniffed. Eh, no, I don't think so. . .

Well you should do. I just farted! Donald laughed.

I'm plussing it now, said Rob. He pressed the + button and the digits on the screen blurred. He lifted his finger and the figures stopped at 0757. Fast this thing!

Aye. You can always reverse though.

What time do you make it. Five past?

Dead on.

Rob didn't hold the button down this time, just jabbed at it with the tip of his finger. As soon as he'd jabbed it three times there was a faint hissing noise then a sudden burst of ignition in the burner-box by his elbow. He pressed the + button five more times, but somehow ended up on 0807, so moved his finger to jab at − till the display went to 0805. The he looked at the screen for a second.

You have Monday as Day 2? he said.

Aye. So it never actually comes on on Day 1.

Right. Keeping his head low, Rob started crawling out backwards. As he passed the grille he glanced in at the hundreds of blue flames now burning behind the pilot light. Then he was out and standing up.

You're red in the face, said Donald.

Rob rubbed the back of his head, then brought his fingers round, looking for blood. Gave my brain a real dunt there, he said.

Donald grinned and said something, but his words were drowned out by a roar from the boiler as the big fan that drove the hot air out of the burner-unit and away through the flue switched itself on.

Donald shouted, but Rob still couldn't make it out. He pointed to his ears, shrugged, then nodded towards the door.

Outside, Donald said, Good job you got your head out from under that flue in time; you'd've been deafened!

Like sticking your head up Concorde's arse, said Rob, locking the door.

Still, said Donald. Better than having to shovel coal into a furnace all day.

They walked along the corridor, Rob bending over to brush dirt from the knees of his breeks.

I reckon we should go back to the good old days, he said. When every classroom had its own fireplace, and the kids all had to bring a brick of peat in every day to keep the bastard going. Christ, imagine the fine smell of peat drifting about instead of this godawful gas all the time!

They both laughed, and kept on past the bothy to open up all the doors in the school.

Rob was out in the car park with a brush, a binbag, and a long-handled scoop. From inside the bothy it'd looked to be a still afternoon, but now that he was out he found a fair old breeze coming in off the sea. The bits of rubbish kept blowing away just as he went to sweep them up. For a while he'd let it get to him, and he'd frowned and fucked as he chased after scurrying crispbags and rolling Coke cans. But after a few minutes of this it suddenly came to him that the rubbish really was trying to run away from him, that all the bits of litter were little creatures of various sorts, all desperate not to be swept up. He imagined them shouting to each other.

Here comes the bastard with the brush again!

I'm not going in his bloody black bag, and that's an end to it!

Aye, me neither, it's a good life being a chip poke wandering about the car park – I'm *never* going in the black bag!

Rob laughed to himself as he collected the rubbish. He went to sweep up an empty fag packet, but at the last second it darted away from in front of the scoop and hid under a Mini. He laughed again. Okay, you made it this time, he said under his breath. But you can't run for ever. . . He tiptoed round the back of the car, got his scoop down in position, then, when the next gust of wind came, caught the fag packet as it tumbled out, and scooped it into his binbag. Ah-ha! he cried, and laughed to himself some more.

Ahem.

He looked up. It was the rector. He must've been creeping up while Rob was engaged in mortal combat with the Silk Cut packet.

Mr Moran. Hullo.

Good afternoon, Mr Catto.

Aye, it's fine. A bit blowy though. Rob looked around the sky, then back at the car park. The rubbish gets everywhere in this wind, he said. But Moran wasn't really paying attention, he was peering off into the woods. Rob turned to follow his gaze. Aye, I did do a bit out there too, he said. But it's just such a big area, it would've taken me for ever. So I thought I'd better do the immediate surroundings first.

About the woods, Mr Catto. . .

If you really want them cleared out, you'd need to get a big squad of folk working through them.

Yes, but. . .

One or two janitors could never do it.

I'm sure.

Maybe you could do a kind of sponsored rubbish collection or something? Get the first years involved – they like that kind of thing. Get them forms made out with so many pence per sack of rubbish collected. It'd be good for funds too!

Mr Catto! The woods!

Aye, I was just saying. . .

Have you seen anyone lurking about?

What?

Any lurkers? Anyone hanging about at all?

What, like kids skiving off?

No, no. He frowned. Maybe it's nothing, but Mrs Ellis came to me after lunch reporting that she'd seen a lurker. A man in a parka, hanging about the woods here.

Mr Jackson wears a parka, said Rob.

No, it wasn't one of the staff. It was a stranger. Mrs Ellis was quite clear about that. A burly figure. She'd never seen him before, but there he was hanging about in the trees, just as the children were coming in after lunch.

Rob looked out into the trees. There was no sign of anybody going about. Quite right too; the woods didn't lead anywhere, they just separated the school from the farmland to the north, there was no reason for anyone to pass through them. But no one had been passing through them.

I haven't seen anybody, he said.

Hmm.

And I've been out for a good half hour.

Have you been looking?

Well, I didn't know to look in particular. But I've been keeping my eyes open – I always do.

And nothing?

33

No, there definitely hasn't been anyone loitering since I've been out. Except for me. I mean I was wandering about in the woods there, picking up litter. It could've been me Mrs Ellis saw.

Moran looked him up and down through narrowed eyes. But you're not wearing a parka.

That's true. Was he definitely wearing a parka?

That's what Mrs Ellis said. With the hood up.

It hasn't been raining!

With the hood right up. Moran wrinkled his brow, and nodded down his nose at Rob.

Rob frowned. Do you think he was lurking on purpose?

Well, we can't be too careful these days.

No, sure. Maybe we should get the police in?

No, no, no. That would start up all sorts of rumours. Moran sighed. And it's probably all quite innocent. Somebody out walking the dog happens to glance over at the old alma mater, pleasant memories make him pause a moment – and Mrs Ellis catches his eye. The last thing we need is the police quartering the grounds: before we knew it there'd be panic, the press would be involved, parents would be keeping their children away from school. . . Disaster.

Aye, it's probably nothing.

Almost certainly. But!

But?

But I'll just continue my walk around the environs. And if you could detail your men to come out and have a good look around this area every so often – just to show themselves as much as anything – then we'll be covered. But it almost certainly is nothing at all.

Best to be on the safe side, eh?

In this day and age, absolutely. If even a single child got interfered with, and the press got hold of the story, we'd never hear the last of it. Terrible. So: keep it quiet, but keep an eye open.

Right-oh, Mr Moran.

Good man, Mr Catto.

The head strolled off round the far end of the school, hands behind his back, chest stuck out, the wings of his black gown fluttering in the wind about his legs. Rob turned back and began sweeping up rubbish again, but he couldn't settle to it. He kept getting the feeling that he was being watched, and it made him uneasy. There was nothing to the feeling, that was obvious; he hadn't had it at all till Mr Moran had put the idea in his head, and there was certainly nobody to be seen out amongst the trees. But now the feeling was in his brain, and he couldn't shake it out.

After a few more minutes sweeping, he went back to the bothy and sat staring into space till Billy came in with a problem in the exit light system.

They were out at the Indian restaurant with folk from Karen's work. It was the 30th birthday of one of the guys in the same office, and this was the party. Just folk he worked with at the meal, then afterwards they were supposed to go on to one of the hotels, where there was going to be a disco, with more family and friends turning up. Rob liked Indian food, but he didn't really want to eat it with a bunch of folk he didn't ken. But Karen had said he never would get to know anyone if he didn't get out and meet them in the first place.

You're the only person I want to know, he'd said, putting his arms around her waist.

She pushed him away, laughing, and carried on dressing.

They'd had their starters, but the main courses were slow in coming. Everyone was drinking a lot to fill in the time. The guy whose birthday it was had been to India, and he was saying how where he'd been staying they never used plates, all the grub was served on leaves.

On leaves! one of the other guys cried. Small portions, was it? He mimed forking something up from the palm of his hand, then looking again and – the food was finished! Everybody laughed.

Nah, said Grant, the one with the birthday, These weren't leaves like you get off trees in this part of the world. Not like birch leaves or anything. These were like palm tree leaves, big and thick, bigger than the plates you get here even!

If we ever get any plates, said Andrea, who was going out with Grant. The whole table laughed again, and a couple folk looked around for the waiters.

Should we get more drink, said an older guy called Alec. Or do you think that'd slow them up even more?

Maybe they're waiting for the plates to come out of the dishwasher, said Andrea. Tell them we'll go out and get some leaves off the trees.

There was laughter, and Karen called out, More drink! as a waiter passed, heading for another long table of drunk folk at the far side of the restaurant. Rob looked across at Karen. A red spot had appeared on each of her cheeks. She smiled and winked at him when she saw him watching her. Then she turned to the rest of the table.

I always wondered how they managed it, she said.

Who? said Alec.

Adam and Eve, how they managed to cover themselves up with leaves.

Folk laughed.

I mean, you take your average leaf, she went on. It's not very big, is it? And Adam especially, how did he cover himself with a leaf? What's the Bible saying here – that Adam had a titchy you-know-what?

There was loud laughter again, and a woman called Susan raised her eyebrows and said, A pine needle would be quite sufficient for some men I could mention.

Karen reached for Rob's hand during the uproar, and broke in as it died down, But you know what I mean, eh? I reckon they must've been using one of these giant Indian leaves that Granny's talking about. That would do the job, eh Robbie?

Whooh! everybody went, and Rob could feel himself flushing red in the face.

Some folk have all the luck, said Susan, amongst the laughter.

Rob laughed too, but took his hand away from Karen's and started playing with the paper serviette in front of him. He felt something touch his leg, and looked across to see Karen winking at him again.

So Grant, were you in India for a holiday? he said.

Changing the subject! said Susan. Modest too!

No, said Grant, grinning. It was work. I was taking care of telecommunications on the beach while one of our semisubs was test drilling out towards Sri Lanka. Pretty boring, actually.

Rob nodded.

What is it you work at yourself? asked Andrea.

I work up at the high school.

That's right, I mind Karen saying. What is it you teach again? Don't tell me. . .

No, said Rob.

37

Don't tell me, said Andrea.

I'm not a teacher, I'm a janitor.

Oh. Andrea pulled a funny face of embarrassment. That must be interesting, she said. Alec snorted, trying to keep in a laugh. No, but seriously, she went on, I think it must be. . . She paused for a second, thinking, then cried, At last! The grub!

Three waiters were rushing to the table with armfuls of plates and bowls. They started calling out the names of what they had, but folk weren't listening, or had drunk too much and forgotten what they'd ordered. Rob hadn't forgotten though; he always had the same thing.

Chicken dopiaza please! he called, but the waiter didn't hear him.

Bugsy, the young guy who was sitting on the other side of Karen from Grant, started shouting, Chicken dopiaza here! Chicken dopiaza here!

The waiter slid a plate in front of him. Dopiaza. . .

What's this? said Bugsy.

Chicken dopiaza. The waiter was sweating. Now who wants king prawn karahi?

Me! said Bugsy.

I thought you wanted. . .

The dopiaza's mine, said Rob. The waiter sighed, picked up the plate from in front of Bugsy, and moved it across the table.

Ann, sitting opposite Bugsy, said, Cheek! loudly, then turned to Rob. I don't know why folk get jobs in restaurants if they can't even be polite, she said.

Rob shrugged, and avoided the waiter's eye.

Soon everybody had their food, and the rice and naans were spread out along the table. Bugsy and Ann were slagging off the staff of the place, but Rob was trying not to be dragged in; he was looking up the far end of the table, where one of the waiters had come over and was bending to speak in Susan's ear. She frowned, said something, and the waiter pointed out into the lobby of the restaurant. Susan got up and followed him away from the table.

Look at that, said Rob.

Karen looked up from dipping a chunk of naan bread in her bright red sauce. Maybe the babysitter's phoned, she said. I hope there's nothing wrong with Tara.

Tara?

Shh!

There was a commotion out in the lobby, several waiters talking loudly, Susan shouting No! and then a couple of thumps and the restaurant door being banged open. Somebody shouted something about calling the police, and the next thing was a loud DUNT on the main window of the dining room. Everyone looked up, and a figure moved away into the shadows beyond where the restaurant lights fell. A second later Susan came back in and sat down. She picked up her knife and fork, and went to start eating, but then saw that everyone was looking at her.

Some nutcase, she said.

Your ex? said Andrea, and laughed. Nobody joined in.

Never seen the guy before, said Susan. But he claimed he knew me, apparently. That's what he told the paki boy, anyway. He never said a thing to me though, just kind of glumshed in my face. She gave a big shiver of her shoulder. Gyaads!

Terrible, said Alec. He reached out and patted Susan's hand.

I asked him what he wanted, but he just kind of laughed. That's when I told them to chuck him out. He looked like he'd escaped from the nuthouse or something, he kept the bloody hood of his coat up the whole time!

You do attract some funny guys, said Ann.

Rob had lain down his fork. Hold on, he said. What kind of coat was he wearing?

Och, a real scummy old thing. A parka, with fur around the snorkel bit, ken.

Rob stood up. Excuse me a minute, he said.

What's the matter? said Karen.

I'm just going to the, eh. . .

Rob edged along between the seats and the wall, and stepped through into the lobby. Then he pushed open the front door and went out onto the pavement. There was nobody about. Twenty metres away was the High Street, and there were noises of singing and shouting coming from the pubs and the chip shop there. But there was no sign of life on this street at all. Rob took a deep breath, then turned to go back in. Through the slats of the window blinds, he could see his table eating and talking; he couldn't hear anything, he just saw their lips moving. As he watched, Grant reached his fork over to the plate of dopiaza in front of Rob's empty chair, speared a piece of chicken, and lifted it up to his mouth. Rob saw Grant laughing, and Karen grabbing hold of his wrist, trying to stop him putting the meat in his mouth. But Grant took a grip on Karen's arm with his free hand, then forced the fork up and closed his lips over the food. Then he let go of Karen, and she punched him on the shoulder. He laughed, opening his mouth so Rob could see the half-chewed chicken lying on his tongue.

At one o'clock, Rob got out of bed, put on his shorts and top, and

40

went for a jog. But it had come on rain, so he only stayed out half an hour. It wasn't that he minded getting wet – he just put up the hood of his sweatshirt and carried on – but after a while the pavements started getting greasy, and he didn't want to slip going round a corner and fuck his ankle.

Karen still hadn't come back. Of course it wasn't really late. The disco at the hotel was licensed till one, so by the time everybody had drunk up and said their goodnights, it would likely be two by the time she got home.

At one forty-eight he heard the door opening. She was in the bathroom for what seemed like ages before coming up the stairs. A couple of times she stumbled and thumped. Then she tiptoed into the bedroom, being quiet.

Hullo, he said.

She came over and sat on his side of the bed. Hullo. Did I wake you?

Yeah, but it's okay.

She leant over and kissed him. Her mouth smelled sweet of drink, and her hair had night air in it. A few drops of rain fell onto his face as she bent over him.

Was it good? he said.

It was okay. The disco was pretty crap, but it was a laugh, ken. She got up and went down the end of the bed. Are you feeling okay now?

What? Oh aye. I think I just ate too much, ken. That rice fairly. . .

Did you see what Alec was eating? she came in. Vindaloo with extra chillies! I think he was trying to impress Susan. I've never seen anyone so red in the face!

He rolled over, intending to turn his face away from her and go

41

to sleep, but as he moved he caught sight of her standing at the bottom of the bed getting undressed. She'd taken off her tights and her skirt and pants, but hadn't begun to unbutton her waistcoat or her blouse. Seeing her standing there like that gave him an immediate erection.

Here, he said.

What?

Come here.

She came round to his side of the bed again. He threw the downie back as she approached, grabbed her by the waist, and pulled her on top of him. They kissed. The buttons of her waistcoat scraped his skin. He moved his hands over her thighs and buttocks, and a few seconds later she fitted herself over him and started rocking back and forth.

Jesus. . .

What?

I'm going to come, he said.

Not yet!

She started to undo the waistcoat. He closed his eyes so he wouldn't see. He could feel himself away to come. He tried to think of something else, but couldn't think of anything to think of. Karen opened her blouse, then rested her hands on his chest as she changed the angle she was moving at. Rob tried to cut himself off. He imagined his cock drifting away from his body. It was still going in and out of Karen, but it wasn't anything to do with him any more. The cock was having a great time, but it was nothing to with Rob, he was just a body lying there, while a cock fucked his wife, somebody else's cock fucked his wife.

He came, a scream bursting out of his mouth at the same moment. Karen fell forward, her chest banging down onto his

42

chin, and she speeded up her movements against him, holding on tight with her arms round the back of his head.

Not yet, not yet, she said.

Rob just lay there.

All three jannies were going around emptying bins. Rob was covering the playground, Billy was on bogs, and Donald was doing the ones in the corridors and the canteen. After the first big brown binbag was full they'd tie the top and start another one. After they had four full ones they'd take them out to the skip-sized eurobin in the shelter at the end of the car park. The second time he made the trip to the eurobin, Rob found the others standing there already. Donald was heaving in the last of his bags, while Billy held the lid open.

Billy shook his head as Rob approached, the binbags jostling his shins. Sorry boss, he said. We're full up here. You'll have to put it all back where you got it.

Rob dumped his bags down at the side of the bin. The amount of rubbish the bastards produce is incredible, he said. And this is just what gets in the bins!

Donald laughed. Aye, what about all the shite they drop on the road here and in the woods?

Rob frowned. Listen, he said. That reminds me. . .

Aye, never mind jannie stroke police, said Billy. Jannie stroke scaffies, that's what we are!

Listen lads. . .

Sorry boss! Donald grabbed the lid of the bin and flung it wide open. Be my guest! A shimmy of black flies buzzed up off the pile of rubbish.

Rob tossed the first of his bags into the middle of the swarm,

then said, Listen, I was out on litter patrol the other afternoon –
Tuesday – and something came up.

If you found a fiver it was mine, said Donald.

And if it's a tenner it's mine!

Donald and Billy laughed.

No, it's nothing like that. It's Moran. He was wandering about
looking worried, so I asked him why, and he told me. Rob tossed
another bag into the bin.

His Batman cloak'd flown off without him.

No Don, it wasn't that. It was, well, I thought it was a load of
shite at the time, but now I'm not so sure.

Rob chucked in his last two bags, nodded for the lid of the bin
to be closed, and wiped his hands on the sides of his dustcoat. No
matter how careful you were, Coke or some other sticky stuff
always seemed to come seeping out of the bags and onto your
fingers.

Well? said Billy after a few seconds. What was the head on
about?

Rob frowned again, shrugged. He said Mrs Ellis had seen some
strange character lurking about in the woods there. A guy with the
hood of his coat up even in the sun.

Mad bastard! cried Donald, and smacked his fist into his open
palm.

No, but seriously, said Rob. Moran was worried this was some
kind of pervert hanging about.

Haven't had one of those for a long time, said Billy.

He'll be imagining it, said Donald, shaking his head. He's
paranoid, he'd jump at his own shadow.

That's what I thought. I mean, I was out and about that day, and
I never saw anybody lurking. Rob took a step away from the bin,

and scanned the car park and the trees beyond. He could feel the others following his gaze. Now I'm not so sure.

Have you seen someone, like? said Billy, quietly.

Rob nodded. Worse than that: I've seen the bastard in action.

In action? said Donald.

I was out last night with the wife and some of her pals – at the Bengal Bay. And this guy in a coat with the hood up started giving us hassle.

Threatening you with promises of rain, was he? said Donald, and laughed.

This is serious! One lassie, Susan, he tried to. . . to show her his cock, or something.

Dear oh dear. Billy shook his head.

Aye: exactly. I chased the cunt, but he got away. Ducked down an alley or something. Everybody was pretty upset, ken. But I calmed them down after a while.

Did you call the police?

No, Billy. Some of the females wanted to, but I said we were already keeping an eye on the bastard up here. For operational reasons it would be better to trap him interfering with a child than just flashing at a grown woman – a very well grown woman, if you know what I mean.

How's that? said Donald.

Well, you ken what judges are likes these days – that feart of clogging up the jails you can get away with murder just about!

But no one gets away with doing stuff to kids?

Aye. And we could put the boot in a fair bit and no one would think any the worse of us.

I wouldn't advise that, said Billy.

We could kick the bastard's head in, said Rob. In fact, we could

45

rip off his balls and it would be alright cause we'd just be protecting the kids, see?

Billy was standing right beside him now, looking out into the woods, arms folded, forehead creased into seriousness. I can see your point Rob, he said. The police would discourage such actions, but I see what you're getting at.

Aye, said Rob. It's up to us. *We* have to deal with the bastard.

Maybe, said Donald. But before anything else we have to catch him in the act. If he does act.

He'll act, said Rob. Believe you me, he will act. And when he does, we'll get the cunt, I'll make sure of that.

Rob got hold of his memo pad, flicked through it to the first blank page, and picked up a pen. But Billy was footering about behind him, testing smoke alarm batteries with a meter or something, and for some reason this was putting Rob off. So he went out of the bothy and did a circuit of the corridors.

When he got back to the bothy, Billy was gone. Rob sat down at the desk, thought for a few seconds, then wrote:

FAO Mr Moran, Rector

Rubbish has been on my mind recently. We recycle more than ever before, of course, and I am all for that: I just wish more of the kids would put their cans and bottles in the receptacles we provide. But not all litter can be recycled. While filling binbags this morning, I was reminded of a TV documentary I saw a few weeks ago. It was about cars driven by rubbish-fuelled engines. I believe only certain types of rubbish are usable (potato peelings were one, I think) and that it has to be broken down and treated before it produces energy; I seem to remember a kind of fermentation takes place.

I propose we kill two birds with one stone, by installing a rubbish-powered central-heating system for the school. Pupils could then dump their litter into chutes leading down to the fermentation tanks, meaning less binbag-filling for the janitorial staff, and cheaper heating for the school.

It's true that most pupils don't go around dropping large quantities of potato peelings, but I'm sure the system could work with other sorts of rubbish as well. Crisps, for instance, must contain virtually the same chemicals.

If you want to discuss this scheme further with me, please do not hesitate to get in touch.

Yours, R. Catto (Head Janitor)

Rob read the memo over, tore the top copy out along the perforated line, and put it into an internal mail envelope. Then he wrote the dominie's name on the next empty square on front, and chucked it onto the out tray.

Rob ran straight home, something nagging him. It wasn't till he was opening the front door that he remembered. And what he remembered made him carry on running, up the stairs and into the bedroom.

It was Karen's waistcoat, the smell of it. When she'd bent over him in bed last night, there had been a strange smell on her waistcoat. Not strange as in funny, but strange as in unusual. It didn't smell like Karen's clothes usually did: it had the scent of something else on it, *somebody* else. Some other man.

Rob slid open the wardrobe door and started rifling through

the row of clothes hanging there. Hers took up at least three quarters of the rail. Apart from his wedding suit, a couple shirts, and his good leather jacket, it was all dresses, blouses, jackets, smart suits for work, belts and beads, and waistcoats. She had four or five of those; they were one of her favourite things. In fact, when Rob first met her she was wearing one. He minded how that particular waistcoat had quite big arm holes, and, because it was summer and she wasn't wearing a shirt underneath, he kept getting glimpses of the curved side of her breast as she leant forwards. He was sitting in the sun outside a pub, having a pint on his way home from work. She was at the next table over with a bunch of her pals from college. It ended up with him buying about four pints, just so he could sit there and look at her tit through the armhole of her waistcoat. And by that time he was drunk enough to get over his shyness and go and talk to her.

Christ, just the memory of the way she looked that day was enough to give him an erection. He rested his shoulder against the door of the wardrobe and took deep breaths. Then he leant forwards and thrust his face into the middle of the row of clothes, taking another deep breath. The taste of her filled his mouth and throat.

After half a minute he leant back again, fingered through the waistcoat section, and pulled out the one she'd been wearing the previous night. It was a kind of gypsy affair, with swirls of threads and woollen flowers all over it. He sniffed the fabric. Nothing. He unbuttoned the front of it, and smelt the cloth on the inside. Again, nothing, just a faint smell of Karen.

Fuck. He was sure there had been something else last night. Maybe it was something faint, just a whiff, so faint that half a day hanging in the wardrobe was enough for it to be wiped out and replaced by the usual Karen smell seeping in from the clothes hanging alongside.

He put the waistcoat back in its place, slid the door shut, and sat down on the end of the bed. He was sure that he hadn't just been imagining it. There had definitely been something unusual tainting her. Not another man's spunk, it was daft to think about stuff like that. But his aftershave, maybe, that was possible: it could've got to that stage. Or his breath, the smell of the other man's breath as he moved his mouth over her skin, down from her lips, along the line of her neck, curving down over the soft breasts and the hard nipples.

Rob's cock was hard. He put a hand down the front of his shorts and started chugging it up and down, picturing that mouth moving over her, over Karen, over his fucking wife.

The fucking dirty bastard! If Rob ever found out who it was he'd kill the cunt, he'd smash his head in! Aye, and be proud of it: that kind of cheating dirty cunt deserved everything he got! As for Karen, well, she would deserve everything she got too.

But first he had to get some proof. If he hadn't smelled something strange off her waistcoat, where could it have been from? Her blouse. That would now be in the laundry basket by the wardrobe.

He reached over, lifted the lid of the basket, and peered inside. The blouse was lying on top. He reached in and pulled it out, the bra she'd been wearing coming along with it, the strap tangled up in a sleeve. He pushed all the air out of his lungs, right down to the bottom corners, then pressed the blouse against his face and breathed in slowly, shifting his nose about to smell different places. There was sweat and deodorant under the arms, faint Karen scent everywhere, stale smoke layered on top of that. Then a sudden burst of intense sweet sourness: aftershave, breath, spunk!

He opened his eyes. On the sleeve of the blouse was an orange stain the size of a fifty pence bit, a couple more reddish fatty spirks round about it. Karen had spilt some curry, and the smell of the spices had been with her all through the rest of the meal, the dancing, the taxi home, and her riding Rob as he lay there, distracted.

Shite: he'd been defeated. She could've been drenched in another man's sperm, and he couldn't't've told: the reek of the curry camouflaged everything.

He stuffed the blouse into the laundry basket, and fell back on the bed.

There was a shuffling and giggling outside the bothy door, then Billy's voice saying, Shut up you lot! Get inside!

The door opened. Three second-year boys came in, tripping over their feet, Billy following behind them with a frown on his face and his arms spread out as if the kids were likely to make a break for it any moment.

What's going on? said Rob.

Billy closed the door behind him, then reached his arm out over the boys' heads. He was holding a rolled-up magazine.

Take a look at this, Mr Catto, he said.

Rob took the magazine, unrolled it, and glanced at the cover. It was a copy of *Razzle*. He flicked through a few pages, catching glimpses of bits of skin and hair and underwear, then looked up.

What's the story?

I caught these young perverts in Room 15, said Billy. If they'd just been sitting reading quietly I'd never've noticed, but they were making a hell of a racket – shouting, laughing their heads off. . .

Rob looked at the woman on the magazine cover, then back at Billy again. Can I have a word Mr Copeland? he said, and pushed away the timesheets he'd been working on.

The boys started to shift their feet, and one of them muttered something.

Billy paused in opening the bothy door. Don't touch anything! he shouted. Don't breathe!

Outside in the corridor, Rob took a step away from the door then turned to face Billy. What's going on? he said.

What do you mean?

I don't want to see this stuff.

Well, I certainly don't want to see it, said Billy. But I found them mucking about with it, so what could I do?

You could've bawled them out and chucked it in the bin, for God's sake!

But they'd just've picked it out again.

Billy. . .

Anyway, you ken what Moran was saying about standards and that. This is the kind of thing he was talking about. It's filth, this! It's got to be stamped out! Especially with this weirdo lurking about the woods, eh? I mean, where did they get it from? Did some guy in the woods give it to them maybe? In exchange for what? Once you start thinking about it. . .

Rob looked away down the corridor for a second. A teacher passed the end of it and waved when she saw Rob gazing in her direction. He didn't wave back, just sighed.

That's fair enough, he said. But can I just get one thing straight?

Billy shrugged.

I don't want you and Donald coming to me every time you catch somebody with ten B&H or a *Playboy*. I've got better things to do. Come to me if you find them selling crack in the snack bar or gang-banging Mrs Ellis. Otherwise, just deal with it yourself, eh? Just take the magazine and tell them to fuck off, okay?

It was just with Moran saying that you should be. . .

In the first instance blah blah blah. I ken, Billy, I ken. So this has been the first instance, okay, and all I'm saying is, from now on could you sort out this kind of wee thing yourself? I've got bigger things to worry about. Like this fucking lurker for one.

Aye, got you, said Billy, and shrugged again. Just thought I'd play safe this time, ken?

Fine. Fine.

So I'll tell them to fuck off now then?

No, it's alright Billy. You get on. Rob checked his watch. It's nearly rammy time. I'll do it. Give us the mag, eh?

Billy frowned. I gave it to you.

Oh fuck! Rob half-laughed, raised his eyes to the roof of the corridor, and paused outside the door of the bothy for a second as Billy lurched away. Then he burst in. Get your hands off! he cried. You'll burn your fingers!

The boys leapt back from around the table and stood with their hands by their sides. They'd been leaning over the magazine, which was lying open at a picture of a woman standing by a cactus wearing nothing but a stetson and a holster-belt.

One of the boys sniggled as Rob flipped the magazine shut. He turned to face the three of them. It's not funny, he said. He looked at each of them in turn, let out a sigh. Okay, I know you're thirteen. . .

I'm fourteen, said the tallest boy.

52

So am I, said one with a baseball cap on.

I don't care, said Rob. Shut up. What matters is, you're that age when all you can think about is sex. Every minute of the day. Even when there's starving Africans on the news, all you can look at is the women's tits. I ken what you're like.

All the boys were looking down, the middle one going red in the face.

But that's not good enough. All we're asking is for six and a half hours, nine till half-three, just a quarter of the day, that you prise your dirty wee minds off of sex and onto algebra or whatever.

Why should we? said the tallest boy. I'm never going to use that when I leave.

Rob laughed. And you think some woman's going to shag you when you leave? Ha!

The other boys giggled, and the tall one dropped his gaze again.

Listen, said Rob, I'm not going to make a big thing about this right now. I've got better things to do. But if I see any of you three with this kind of muck again, you're going straight to Mr Moran. And he, I'm sure, will go straight to your mothers.

The boys looked worried.

Rob opened his mouth to say something else, he wasn't sure what, but at that second the electric bell in the corridor started to belt out, and he shut his mouth till it had stopped.

The tallest boy took a step towards the door.

Hold your horses! said Rob.

Sir, you can't make us late for maths, said the tall boy.

Aye, Stott'll go mental, said the one in the middle.

Just one more thing.

What, sir?

DON'T CALL ME SIR!

Is that it?

No. What I want to know is, where did you get this from? Did you buy it? Did someone give it to you?

Nobody spoke.

You, said Rob, pointing at the smallest boy, the one with the baseball cap. What's your name?

Michael Shelley.

Well Mr Shelley, where did you get it?

The boy sneaked a look at his friends.

It's no use looking at them, said Rob. It's you I'm asking.

The boy pressed his lips together, looked past Rob's shoulder, out the window.

The second bell went, signalling the start of classes. They were all jumping about from foot to foot, as if they were about to pish themselves.

Well?

It was Sandra Burnett gave it to us, came in the tall boy. Can we go now?

Sandra Burnett?

Aye, said the middle boy. In third year. She's a right slag.

They all laughed.

Shut up, said Rob. You shouldn't say that about a girl.

But it's true, said the tall boy.

I don't care what's true, said Rob. All I'm saying is you shouldn't say it.

Rob chucked the *Razzle* into the bin and headed out of the bothy. He walked along the service corridor till it joined the main corridor opposite the school office. Mrs Ellis was sitting inside, typing. She was wearing a set of headphones like a stethoscope and

54

typing away at a great speed. Rob stared at her fingers as they twitched. If you filmed her hands and slowed it down, you could work out what she was typing even without seeing the computer screen. Dear *Razzle*, I thought I'd tell you about an interesting experience I had at my work the other day. The caretaker came in to lag some leaking pipes, and. . .

Mrs Ellis looked up and gazed in Rob's direction, her prune-lips pursing, her fingers flying on. He laughed to himself. No chance! he said out loud, and gave her a wave. She wrinkled her nose in return and swivelled her eyes back to the screen in front of her.

Sunlight coming through the office window lit up her crusty grey hair so Rob could see the dark shape of her skull against the light. He looked at the curve at the back of it for a second, then, blinking the brightness out of his eyes, turned right along the main corridor.

English classrooms led off on each side. Some of them were silent, others had kids' voices arguing and calling out. It all depended on the teachers. Usually there was nothing to worry about no matter how loud the classes were, as long as furniture wasn't being moved about. If you went past and desks were being grated over the floor, or chairs were being banged against the desklids or the walls, that was usually a sign the teacher had lost it. Then Rob would glower through the wee window in the door till one of the kids saw him. That bastard would quieten down, then the folk sitting next to him would notice and look and see him at the door and they'd quieten too. And gradually they would all sneck up and sit down and get their hands off each other. Bursting in bawling was nowhere near as good. It always scared them better if you just stood and stared in silently, especially if it was a lassie's attention you caught first.

After English came secretarial and then social studies. Social studies was basically politics, except kids weren't supposed to know about politics, so they had to give it a different name. Same as the rest of the world: you could give them as much propaganda shite as you liked, as long as you never mentioned the word propaganda, kept calling it education or entertainment.

Rob turned into the corridor of sweat. The gym changing rooms were on the right, with the games-hall in the back of them. As he passed he could hear jimmies squeaking and voices echoing in the hall:

My ball! My ball! Leave it! Yes! Stung! Bastard!

A whistle blew.

At the next corner, a long corridor headed off into the technical department and then the art rooms – as far away from the real school as possible. But he turned in the opposite direction and started climbing the stairs there. A smell of mince and burnt cheese appeared about step three, and got stronger as he went higher. By the top of the stairs he was just about cowking. Cutlery was being rattled in the canteen, plates were being scraped, women's voices were shouting out to each other as they cleared away the slops of the dinners from the plastic tables. He didn't go in, turned down another long corridor instead.

Rob was in favour of kids getting a pork pie and a packet of nuts each for dinner. Much more hygienic than clarty big trays of sticky chips and gluey stew. Each item would be individually wrapped in plastic, sealed in from all germs and contamination, kept fresh in a fridge-lorry right to the door of the school, then doled out to the kids every day. Some kind of vending machine could be invented.

No need for sweaty cooks or steaming stinking kitchens or giant dishwashers that always broke down.

Best of all would be a Mars bar each for dessert. There you got the good sealed plastic wrapper, of course, but inside you also found another tight wrapping – chocolate, casing the layers of stuff in the middle. If you cut one in half you could see the tight unbroken sheath of chocolate round the brown and grey inside – completely clean and untouched. Some folk bit off the chocolate first, got their teeth round the thick bit on top and nipped it off, let it melt across their tongue before they started on the chewy bit. But even better would be getting the Mars bar out of its plastic wrapper, then getting a knife or razor blade and slicing off all the chocolate. Skin the bastard. With a bit of practice you could probably get it so there wasn't a single fleck of chocolate remaining on the flesh of the thing.

Only problem then would be the innards of the Mars'd look so good you wouldn't want to eat them. Definitely you wouldn't want to get fingerprints all over it, chocolate and sweat spoiling the perfect cleanness. Contamination. The only way would be not to touch it with your hands, not pick it up at all. Just have it on the plate there in front of you and get your head down, get your mouth around the end of it and suck it in. Suck and chew, suck and chew, suck and chew.

Rob had passed all the maths classrooms without even noticing. He'd had half an idea to peer in the window in Leonard Stott's door and spook the boys who'd been wasting his time earlier. But now he was past maths and near the end of modern languages. Ahead was the door to the fire escape. Beside it a big window of wired glass looked over the car park, through the trees on the far side and out towards the open sea beyond. If you pressed your face sideways on the glass at the far end of the window, you could see the road leading out of the car park and away into the houses at the edge of the town. Bought houses. A quiet estate. Till the bastarding council built a big fucker of a school on your doorstep. Hordes of screaming maniacs disturbing your peace every day – chucking rubbish in your garden, kicking footballs through your picture windows, telling you to fuck off if you looked at them wrong. And that was only the teachers. Ha ha.

Who could blame you if you felt like creeping out of your place and hanging around the school in a dirty fucking raincoat? Anyone in their right mind would want to spit on the place. Spit on the place and piss on the kids. Spit on the school, piss on the kids, shit on the dominie's desk. Anyone in their right mind would want to do that.

But the folk in the bought houses weren't in their right minds any more, they'd been driven crazy by the school. So they wouldn't do anything constructive, they'd just lurk a bit then go off and walk along the cliff path, kicking a chuckie into the sea every now and then, hoping that erosion would hurry up and wear away the cliff and half a mile of land behind it, till one fine day of gales the whole damn school went sliding into the sea, and everyone inside with it.

Rob looked out the window. There was nobody in the car park, nobody in the woods. Probably there was nobody on the cliff path either. Useless cunts!

A movement caught his eye. Down amongst the trees. Down near the ground. In the depths of the wood. Something had moved. Or somebody. He stared at the spot. He kept staring. He stared till his eyes watered.

Rob lifted the *Razzle* out of the bin. He looked at the front cover, and at the back, then brushed the side of his hand across the glossy paper. The bell in the corridor started ringing. He glanced up at the clock: three thirty. Tucking the magazine under his arm, he stepped over to the filing cabinet, pulled open a drawer, and fingered through the dividers. They were mostly empty; nobody used the filing cabinet except for him, and he hardly needed to, apart from sticking away timesheets and memos from the head.

He flicked back to C, held open the dividers, and dropped in the magazine. Filed under Cocks and Cunts. But if anyone was snooping and came across it he could say it was C for Confiscated Material. He slammed the file drawer shut and left the bothy.

Outside in the turning circle, Donald was watching the kids piling onto the buses that took them home to the country places. The drivers leant their elbows on their steering wheels and stared ahead as the kids shouted and kicked at each other, swung their bags about, shoved to get in the door and down the aisle to the back seat.

Two girls came rushing past Rob, barging him to one side. Take your time! he shouted.

Donald turned and raised his chin in greeting. Some of them'll be under the wheels one of these days, eh?

Rob stopped beside him. Or under the driver, he said.

Still, you can't blame them for running, said Donald. Lowsing time on a Friday afternoon – what more could you ask?

Who's on tomorrow?

Hih! Aye, I suppose so.

No, but who is on?

You're asking me? You're paid to ken that.

59

Rob looked at him, then laughed. It's me actually, I kent it was. But I was hoping you'd volunteer, like, give me the day off.

Donald laughed too. I could do it if you like, he said. If you've something on. I reckon it's my turn next weekend, so I could just swap with you.

Ach. . .

Have you something on, like?

The bus in front of them fired up its engine, sending out billows of black diesel exhaust. Then it eased away out of the turning circle, the kids rattling about inside, jumping up and down, banging on the windows. As the back seats went past, Rob could see someone bending to get a fag lit from their neighbour.

He cleared his throat. No, it doesn't matter, he said. I've nothing planned. I just got a bit of a feeling, ken. I just suddenly felt I couldn't be bothered coming in.

I ken that feeling. But I've got an excuse – I've been here eight year!

Aye. Four *weeks* – I shouldn't be moaning, eh? I'll do it no bother. . . Here, Donald, look at that for fuck's sake.

Rob had half turned away and was gazing into the woods between the turning circle and the road. A skinny girl with shoulder-length black hair was leaning against a tree, smoking.

It's her cheek that gets me, said Donald. She can't wait till she's off of the grounds, she has to show us all her brass neck and light up the minute she's out the door. Typical!

Do you ken her?

The girl looked in the direction of the two jannies, exhaled a cloud of smoke, and turned away again.

Oh aye, everybody kens her. That's Sandra Burnett.

Rob looked at him. What do you mean, everybody kens her?

60

A lot of problems there, boss. Nothing but problems.

Rob looked back at the girl, nodding to himself. I was wanting a word with her actually. He sniffed. Could you start locking up, Don, and I'll add to her problems for her.

Sure thing. . .

Donald went off whistling, and Rob gave his shoulders a shake, cleared his throat, and walked down towards the girl at the edge of the woods.

As he approached her she turned to face him, watched him come stepping off the turning circle and into the trees. She kept on smoking, and looked him up and down as he stopped in front of her.

Are you Sandra Burnett? he said.

She held his gaze. Who wants to know?

Rob sighed. I do.

She put the cigarette to her lips and took a long draw. Well, I suppose I am Sandra Burnett, she said, then breathed out a jet of smoke.

Rob shifted his feet. Listen, he said. If you have to smoke, could you at least do it somewhere else than here?

It's after school hours, she came back. I can do what I like.

He paused. He could feel anger stirring in his gut, and he didn't want it to rise up. It's maybe after hours, he said, But you're still on school grounds, so you don't do what you like at all. You do what I like.

Is that right?

Aye, that's right.

She held the cigarette away from her in loose, thin fingers, and dropped it. It landed on some dead leaves and twigs, still glowing. He looked at her.

Happy now? she said.

No. He took a sideways step, planted his foot on the fag, and ground it into the earth. Now I'm happy, he said.

She bent to pick up the bag at her feet, then started to move past him. Good, she said, I'll be off then.

Wait, he said, and put an arm out in front of her to stop her passing. His hand touched her neck, and he dropped it immediately.

What now?

I have to ask you something.

She shrugged. Go on then.

I took a piece of property off some second-year boys today.

So?

So they said it belonged to you.

She looked away. What was it?

I don't want to say.

How can I tell if it was mine then, for god's sake?

Rob looked away too. It was. . . a magazine, he said. If what they said was true, you'll know what I'm talking about.

Now she did look at him, her face set. It was an old *Razzle*. Okay? Is that what you wanted from me?

So you did give it to them?

No! They nicked it out of my bag at break – wee bastards.

She started to walk off. Rob went after her.

Listen, he said, I don't ken where you got it from, but you shouldn't be reading stuff like that.

Why not? Reading's good for you. In English they're never stopped telling you to read this and that shitey book.

Aye, but. . .

62

So I should get gold stars for reading in my own time, that's what I reckon.

Sandra, listen. . .

She turned on him. Can I go to my house now?

No, hold on a minute.

You're stopping me going home?

No! Rob held his hands up. I can't stop you. But I can ask. . .

Ask away. She waited, but he didn't say anything, and eventually she turned and walked off through the woods towards the road.

Rob watched her go, threading in and out amongst the tree trunks, sunlight and shadows moving across her back and the backs of her legs as she went.

The blues band wasn't so good. They did Sweet Hame Auchenblae again, but this time Rob didn't enjoy it. It wasn't funny, it was just a stupid thing to do to a great song. He drank faster than usual, downing four beers quickly after the slow first one, and he made Karen drink quickly too. Every time he went for a drink for himself he got her one; whenever she set her glass down he stuck his elbow in her ribs and glowered at her till she picked it up and started drinking. The last couple of rums he bought her were doubles. She seemed not to notice, just slung them down when he nudged her, kept on bumping her legs in time to the music. Another thing she didn't notice was that the band was shite.

He leaned over. Let's go, he said.

What?

I want to go.

I'm enjoying this.

I said, let's go.

Och, Robbie, why?

Sex.

She gave a half-laugh. Can we not wait till they finish?

No, let's go now.

What are you like? Rampant or what!

He grinned, grabbed her hand. Got it in one, he said, and stood up, tugging her after him.

Let me get my coat on at least! She felt beside her on the seat for her jacket, but Rob reached over her and grabbed it, held it out in front of him as he moved away from the table, pulling her behind.

Outside, they walked quickly along the High Street. Then Rob led the way away from the estate, and out the road to the edge of town.

Karen laughed as she tried to keep up with him. Did somebody put something in your drink? Mr One Eye been taking aphrodisiacs, has he?

Your cunt's the only aphrodisiac I need. If Mr One Eye gets to dip his head in there and sook he'll be quite happy.

Robbie Catto!

Karen Catto. You're fucking hot stuff.

No I'm not.

You just about roast my cock, that's how fucking hot.

Nuh. She shook her head. I'm freezing.

I'm telling you.

And I'm asking you – can I have my coat back?

He was still clutching it in his hand, the ends of it swinging about as he strode on. No point, he said. No point in putting it on. You'd just be taking it off again in a minute.

Is that right?

They were passing the entrance to the school car park. Rob glanced in. All was as it should be, security lights blasting down around the door, elsewhere in darkness. No cars in the car park. No loiterers lurking. He gripped Karen's hand tighter.

That's right, he said.

But it's cold, she came back. Come on Rob, it's miles to the bunker.

He stopped walking. She bumped into his side. He jerked her away from him for a second, then back against him. He put his arms around her shoulders and pressed her in tight against his chest.

What are you saying, fuckbird? he whispered into her hair. Are you saying you can't wait, eh?

Well. . .

You're the fucking rampant one, Karrie, you're the one that can't wait, little hot-cunt. He started bending her over backwards, pressing his mouth against her cheekbone, then the side of her face. She arced away from him, and thin bones stood out under the skin of her neck. He closed his teeth around one of them.

Robbie. . .

Let's do it.

We're in the middle of the street!

There's nobody about.

It's not even right dark!

Fuck's sake. He leant off her, looked away for a second.

She put a hand on his chest. It's not that I don't want to. . .

He turned to her again, grabbed her by the elbow, and yanked her along a couple of steps. Then he put a foot up on the low dyke that separated the pavement from the woods.

Come on, in over.

In here?

My cock's about to burst, fuckbird. I can't make it out to the cliffs.

He raised her elbow and put his other arm round her backside and lifted. She laughed and stepped up onto the dyke, looked around for somewhere to jump down on the far side. He put his hands on the outsides of her legs and slid them up over her tights till they were under the stretchy material of her skirt, his thumbs snugging into the angle between the curve of her arse and the tops of her thighs.

I can't see where I'm going, she whispered.

He gave her a shove, she shrieked, fell forwards, and crashed onto the undergrowth below. There was the sound of her rolling over a couple times, then her voice coming up: You bastard!

Rob glanced each way along the street, then vaulted over the dyke after her. He landed on his feet, but on a steep slope, and pitched forward onto his knees, then flat on his face into some crackly leaves. He lay there for a few seconds, till breath started to come back into his bashed lungs and his eyes started making out shapes and outlines and patches of lighter colours in the darkness. A couple metres to his left a big patch of lighter stuff shifted. You're a bastard Rob, it said. Are you alright?

He didn't reply, but got up on his hands and knees and crawled over towards her.

Rob?

He caught hold of her ankles, she gasped, and he gave them a jerk, pulling her flat out on the ground, away from the tree she'd been leaning against.

Rob, I'm not comfy.

He ran his hands up the side of her legs again, pushed the skirt

66

up high, hooked his fingers over the tops of her tights and pants, and pulled them all the way down.

These leaves are prickly! she said.

He knelt up for a moment, undid his belt and shoved his breeks down below his knees, then his boxers. My prick's prickly, he said, and lowered himself down over her, pausing for a moment with elbows locked, and gazing into her face. He could see she was smiling. Nobody fucks you like your husband, eh?

Rob. . . nobody else fucks me at all, she said quietly.

Keep it that way.

He stretched his neck down to press his mouth to hers, then let his body lower further, supporting himself with one arm. With the other arm he reached down and fiddled with the lips of her cunt for a few seconds, parting them and rubbing at the wet flesh behind them a few times. Then he felt for his stiff cock and steered it down till the end of it was resting at the gape of her cunt. He took his hand away, lifted it to beside her head, paused a moment to look into the shadows around her eyes, then leant his weight forward and plunged his cock inside her.

Oh, she said.

He pulled it out to the gape again, paused, then pushed it in. Pause, then out, a shorter pause, then in. Her fingers gripped his backside, he could feel her nails digging into the soft skin there. Out, pause, in, pause, out, pause, in. . .

Oh. . .

He imagined her arse pressing down on the ground as he thumped into her. Leaves crackled against it, sharp twigs snapped, a stone dug into her flesh, a holly leaf jabbed her skin, jabbed with each of its jaggy points.

Out, in, out, in. . .

Every time he thrust he imagined a different point of the holly leaf piercing her skin. Pricked from above and below at the same time. It was a crazy picture, it was driving him crazy. The spunk was reaching boiling point in the cauldrons of his balls, just about ready to. . .

Cunt, somebody said.

He stopped.

Keep going Rob, come on.

He looked up, raised himself on his elbows, scanned the woods around them.

What's the matter Robbie?

Bastard, he said.

Eh? Who is?

There was the sound of smothered laughter closeby, then somebody tiptoeing away over the twigs and leaves.

Rob jumped to his feet, Karen yelped, and Rob staggered away to the side as his breeks twisted round his ankles.

Fuck, he said, and dived down and grabbed them up and started running.

Where are you going? said Karen.

After the bastard, shouted Rob, one hand clutching the breeks to his belly, the other reached out in front of his face, feeling for tree trunks in the dark, warding off whippy branches.

Karen shouted after him, but he couldn't make out what she was saying for the crashing of his feet over the woodfloor and the thumping of the blood in his brain. Up ahead somewhere were the bastard's running footsteps, and maybe the sound of laughter again. Rob strained to hear and tripped over a sticking-up root, went flying, stumbled into a tree trunk, giving his shoulder a terrible smash.

The breath was knocked out of him. By the time he got it back and was upright again, all was silent.

Fuck. He'd lost the bastard. The fucking pervy cunt had got away. He leant his back against the tree while he fastened his belt and started to do up the buttons on his fly.

Then he heard it, footsteps echoing across tarmac, and he knew immediately where the bastard was.

Rob plunged forwards again in between the trees, and in only a dozen metres was out of them and into the moonlight, standing at the edge of the school car park, the big black shape of the school buildings looming dead ahead. Away to his right, almost at the far end, a large hooded figure was sauntering along, shoulders bouncing as he walked.

Bastard! shouted Rob. Come back here!

The figure whipped round, and for an instant Rob glimpsed a broad face, pale in the moonlight, under the shadow of the hood. Then he started running fast, very fast, and Rob set off after him.

Rob should've caught him. He was pretty fit, and used to running. But the bastard had a good head start, plus with every step a barrel of beer slushed about in Rob's belly. It was slowing him down and it was giving him a stitch, like somebody was sticking a knife in his guts.

The bastard turned the corner round the art department, and Rob nashed on as fast as he could, sweat spurting out of him from the exertion and from the pain in his side. He ran till he reached the corner by the art rooms then stopped, gasping, and propped himself against the wall there for a second, scanning the grounds in front of him.

Away to one side was the open expanse of the playing fields. The bastard couldn't've gone that way, he'd never've got to the cover at the far side by this time. On the other side the buildings zigzagged down to the main front door with the bus turning circle nearby and the trees round about that. He'd be in there. He'd've seen the trees as he came round the corner here and made straight for them. He could be sitting just inside the nearest bit of woods, watching Rob looking for him. Or he could be away in the depths of them heading for the fields beyond. Or he could even be down by the turning circle, coming out onto the road and walking down it like any normal man, not like a cunting pervy bastard fresh from wanking in the woods by the playground. Cunt of sickness.

Rob sighed and turned back into the car park. Somebody was halfway across it, hurrying towards him. His heart started for a second till he saw it was only Karen. He sighed again, then walked towards her.

What happened? she said as they got closer. I got a fright. Were you chasing somebody?

He looked at her. Did you not hear him?

All I heard was you grunting. Are you saying there was somebody watching us doing it?

Fucking pervert!

She shivered, and put her arms around him, shivering more.

I'll get the bastard, he said. Alright, he's slipped me thenight, but I'm going to get the cunt. That's one thing for sure.

He pulled away from her a little, and gazed out into the dark woods, his fists clenching and relaxing and clenching again.

Rob, she said.

What?

Your fly's open.

On Saturdays the school was used by sports groups and a youth club. Most of the building didn't have to be opened up, so only one janitor was required. There was a two weeks off, one week on rota, and this weekend it was Rob's turn to work.

In the morning there was a junior youth club in the drama studio and at one end of the games hall; at the other end of the hall thin people with muscles were climbing on the rock wall. Rob watched the climbers for a minute.

A guy with a ponytail was running up and down the wall on a rope. Next over, a woman with cropped hair and no rope was inching upwards, her legs stretched out incredibly wide to let her toes grip on two protruding half-bricks. Her neck arched into space as she scanned the pattern of smooth and rough stone, zigzagging fissures and scattered cubbyholes above her. She fixed her gaze on a point above and to her right, then slowly lifted her hand from its hold, strained upwards, paused with the arm outstretched, relaxed again, and thrust it into a narrow crosswise crack. Rob could see the muscles in her arm knot as she jammed her fist into the depths of the crack and started to heave herself upwards. He turned and left the games hall.

First thing in the morning, still in his jogging gear, Rob had gone out into the woods between the car park and the road, looking for signs of the previous night. He'd found nothing. He wasn't even sure he'd got the bit of ground where him and Karen had tried to fuck: he'd thought he'd maybe find broken twigs and crushed glass where they'd been lying, or maybe a fagbutt or a dropped wallet or a spunky snotrag behind a nearby tree, where the bastard had been standing. But in fact the whole floor of the wood was trampled and mashed, there were fagbutts and bits of litter everywhere, scraps of paper that could've been hankies or spunkrags or pages from jotters were snagged on brambles and

71

dissolving in puddles all over the place. The kids ran through the woods and hung about there every day of the week. It was hopeless.

So he didn't go back to the woods, but walked instead round by the art department, past the corner where he'd rested after losing the bastard, and on down the far side of the school. As he walked, he peered out into the trees, trying to spot likely places where he would've run if he'd been the one making an escape. But the trees were densely packed together, there were no obvious gaps between the trunks where Rob could've dived in and hidden.

Soon he was on one of the paths leading to the bus turning circle. The trees were much more widely spaced out here, and there were decorative bushes and boulders scattered about. If Rob had been escaping, this is where he'd've headed for. There was plenty cover, but still enough open space to duck from one hiding place to another, enough gaps to get a good look at whoever was chasing.

Suddenly Rob jumped off the path and rolled down behind a big lump of granite. After lying still for a few seconds, his face pressed into the long grass, he got up on all fours, crawled forward, and poked his head round the side of the boulder. He scanned the playground he'd just crossed. All clear. He snapped his head back, surveyed the trees between him and the turning circle, then leapt up and ran, crouched almost double, threading in and out of the trees. Twenty metres ahead was a thick clump of rhododendron. He sprinted over and flung himself down behind it, quickly dragging his feet in after him, so nothing at all would be visible to anyone coming across the playground.

He laughed to himself, then said under his breath, Can't catch me, you bastards.

After setting up the big straw targets for the archery club, Rob headed back to the bothy. As he turned into the corridor opposite the school office, he lifted his head and sniffed the air. Amongst the disinfectant and floor polish smells were wisps of something sweet.

He sniffed again, and reached in his pocket to get out the key to the bothy. Something moved at the dark end of the corridor. He looked up. A figure was standing, silent, in the doorway of the boiler-room. Rob's heart was beating. He stood up straight, gripping his hands into fists, and faced square-on to the guy.

Who's there? he said.

There was no reply, only the sound of feet moving slightly on the ribbed carpet. And breathing. The bastard was breathing.

Come on, said Rob loudly. I can see you, cunt. Come and get me then, come on.

Mr Catto? It was a girl's voice.

Rob opened his mouth, then shut it again. He frowned and gave his shoulders a shake to loosen the tensed muscles. Then he said, Aye, but come out of there, you shouldn't be along this way.

There was movement in the shadows, and a girl walked out of the doorway and towards him. It was Sandra Burnett. She walked right up to him, not smiling, but not looking worried either.

He made himself frown again. You shouldn't be hanging around here, he said. Especially when it's not a school day.

You told me to come, she said.

What?

You wanted me to come and see you. She shrugged. Well, here I am.

He turned to the bothy door and tried to unlock it. He had a bit of trouble getting the key into the latch, but then it slipped home

73

and he shoved the door open. Come in, he said, and held an arm out till she'd stepped by him. He glanced along towards the main corridor, then followed her in, closing the door behind him.

She was standing with her back to the sink, her head bent over as she picked at a thread hanging from the hem of her short black skirt. Rob moved past her and she drew her head back, that sweet smell coming waving out from inside the folds of her hair. He laid down his paper on the worktop, lifted the kettle to check its weight, then switched it on.

He went and sat down in his usual chair, and looked at her. She had straightened up again, and he found that his gaze was on a level with her hips; he was staring straight at her legs where they came out of her skirt. A risky place to be looking. But if he looked up she would see where he'd been staring and it would be worse. He closed his eyes.

Sit down, he said, and waved an arm towards the other seats. He heard the nylon of her inner thighs rubbing together as she stepped over, dropped her bag to the floor, and sat in Donald's chair. He blinked his eyes open again. I don't think I told you to come, he said. But now you're here, what do you want?

She sighed. Is that not obvious?

Rob frowned, thinking. No, it's not.

She looked away from him, and around the room. I want my property back.

What property? Rob watched her face.

My magazine. You took it off those boys yesterday, but it was mine, and I want it back.

Ah. Now I get you. Rob sat back in his chair.

Well?

I'm not giving it back.

74

She flinched. You have to.

No, I've confiscated it. It's not the kind of thing you should be reading, it's completely unsuitable. You're not getting it.

That's not confiscating, that's thieving!

I could already've burnt it for all you know. That's all it's fit for.

She leant forward in her seat, looking worried now. You can't burn it. Please. Say you haven't done that.

She actually looked terrified. He kept staring at her, smiled.

Oh god, she said, and brought a hand up to cover her eyes.

He waited a while, then said, As it happens, I haven't burnt it yet. She dropped the hand from her face, but her eyes were still closed. But part of my duties is upholding the moral standards of this place, so I don't see why I shouldn't burn it.

Because it's not mine! It's my dad's! I took it from under his bed. If he finds I took it he'll kill me, he will, and if you burn it he'll see it's gone, he'll ken it was me took it, and he'll kill me!

Rob stood up and walked round behind the girl, looked down on her. She didn't seem to be actually greeting, but she was pretty close.

Please give it back. He's been away, but he's coming home thenight, he'll kill me.

I doubt it.

Please.

Rob turned to the filing cabinet and pulled open the drawer. It roared on its bearings. What were you looking for under your father's bed, he said, flicking slowly through the empty dividers. Dirty socks?

Sandra let out a choked noise. I was looking for a magazine.

What, has he got the *Jackie* under there as well, has he? That would seem more like your reading age. He pulled out the magazine and leafed through a few pages as he waited for her to speak.

He's got *Razzles*, she said at last. And *Penthouses*. And some other ones: *Escorts*, and some in foreign languages. She squared her shoulders, looked straight ahead. I read them. They're interesting.

Interesting!

A hell of a lot more interesting than that shite we get in English.

Dear oh dear. He threw the magazine over her shoulder and onto the table in front of her. It fanned open on a spread of two women having a water-pistol fight in the nude. So this is how you get your kicks is it, Miss Burnett? Looking at pictures of naked women in dirty magazines?

I'm not a lessie, if that's what you mean.

Oh no?

It's the stories I like. I don't really look at the pictures.

Sandra. He put his hands on her shoulders and squeezed. She tried to turn so she could see him behind her, but he was holding too tight. Sandra, he said again. I don't want you to read the stories *or* look at the pictures. I want you to take this home, put it under your father's bed, and leave it there. Leave them all there. Okay?

She struggled against his grip, but he held her firm.

I said, okay?

I'm not saying anything till you let go of me.

He pressed his fingers into her shoulders. He couldn't feel any bra straps. He had a sudden urge to slip his hands off her shoulders and down the front of her loose T-shirt, searching for her breasts, grabbing them, squeezing them instead.

He stepped back. It's a deal, he said.

She stood up, snatched the magazine off the table, and stuffed it into her bag. She turned on him, and he saw that she didn't look scared now, she looked angry. She was breathing heavily, and her lips were parted over clenched teeth.

I'll tell you the deal, she said. If you *ever* touch me again, if you ever give me hassle, I'm going to say you attacked me. You took me in your office and you raped me. Cause I've done it Mr Catto, I've done it all, loads of times, but nobody kens. So if I say you fucked me and they look up my hole they'll see I'm no virgin. Then *you'll* be fucked.

Rob looked at the way she was standing, the shape of her body. She looked older than fourteen. He looked her in the eye. She was young there. You wouldn't do that, he said. I don't believe you.

Are you going to take the risk? You'd be a dead man.

He looked at her chest. Her nipples had hardened and were poking against the material of her T-shirt. He reached out towards her.

What are you doing?

His hand hesitated, then shot out, grabbed her hair, ripped her head back. She took hold of his arm in both hands, but he was stronger, he held on, then leaned above her, lowering his face over hers till they were all but touching. He felt her breath on his cheek. He spoke very quietly:

Don't push me, he said. You've a reputation, Sandra Burnett. Me, I've got a flawless record, twelve years' worth at two schools. Nobody would believe your lies. So don't fucking push me.

She said something behind tight-closed teeth. Her eyes were so blue they looked like gas flames.

Don't speak, he said. Just get away from me. But he didn't release her. For a second he pulled down even harder on her hair. Water started to gather in her eyes. He waited till it spilled over in tears, one down each cheek. Then he let her go, shoved her away

77

from him, towards the door. She looked back at him for a second then yanked the door open so hard it smashed into the wall. And she banged out.

He stood there, taking great gulps of air into his lungs, then slowly knelt down on the floor by her chair. He laid his head on the fabric at the back of it, and breathed in the sweetness that had been pouring out of her.

On the Sunday morning they painted the hallway and the stairs, but the sun was blazing down outside, so they chucked it in just before one and drove out of town. They had a bar lunch in a village that used to have a railway running through it. After that, Karen insisted on driving.

Why? said Rob, getting into the passenger seat anyway.

I want to show you something.

Show us your tits.

Karen drove away from the hotel, past an overgrown embankment. I want to show you something you haven't seen before.

Show me your secret diary then.

My secret diary?

Aye, the one where you write down all your secrets, all your dirty thoughts, all your dreams and fantasies. The Secret Life of Karen Catto, that one.

She laughed. I don't have a diary at all Robbie. When would I get the time to write it up? Her eyes flicked over at him. Come to that, when would I find time to have a secret life?

You must have some secrets.

Not from you.

You must have.

Not really.

The car reached the main road. Karen peered down the long straight to her right and said to Rob, How is it on your side?

All clear here, he said, adding, as she eased across the road, if you're quick.

She put her foot down and the car louped forward across the main road and onto the single-track beyond, just as a massive tour-bus blundered by, horn blaring.

God's sake Rob!

He laughed. Anyway, he said, You must have secrets, otherwise why do you need a lock on your desk at work? Eh? You only lock up what you don't want folk to see, and you don't want folk to see secrets. It's proved! So what are you hiding from me girl?

She was crawling down the narrow twisty road, slowing even more at all the blind corners. It was beginning to be annoying, but he wasn't going to let it distract him.

Robbie, she said at last, Everybody's desk has a lock these days. To stop folk walking off with their pens and their Tippex. Nothing more secret than that.

But what do the pens write? What does the Tippex cover up? Eh? You're paranoid theday.

He looked out the side window. There was a ditch, then a dyke, then a field of shaven sheep. If he threw himself out of the car he could roll over into the ditch and just lie there. Cars would go past and no one would see him. Leaves would fall and grass grow over the top of him and he'd never be found, just be left in peace for as long as he wanted, for ever.

He looked to the front again. Where the fuck are we going, anyway?

To the beach!

You're joking.

No, it's brilliant, it's miles long. We used to come here when we were young.

There's a beach at home, down by the prom.

Wait till you see this place though. The sand's just white! And it's enormous. It was always a great treat coming here in summertime. Me and Morag used to love it.

Did you build sandcastles?

My dad did. Me and Mo drew faces in the sand, put stones on for the eyes, shells for the teeth. We used to run along the edge of the surf, pretending we were horses.

The road curved round the back of some farm buildings, then ran alongside a stretch of trees. Ahead, it looped away across the fields again, but Karen slowed down and stopped the car in a layby underneath the trees.

Is this it?

This is it.

I don't see any beach.

It's through the woods, daftie. She opened her door, turned her head towards him slowly, grinning. I'll race you, she said, then leapt out of her car, slamming the door behind her, and tore off into the trees.

Rob went for his door, yarked against his seat belt, sat back, released it, then jumped out and dashed after her. The trees were big and old and spaced out. It was easy running, and she'd got a good start, and was out of sight and earshot. He punched the air, running faster.

Yo hoo! This way!

He looked up. She was ahead and away to the left, on top of a small hillock amongst the trees. He changed course towards her and put his head down as he started up the slope. He could hear her laughing as she crashed through the dried leaves on the other side of the hill. He was breathing hard, but didn't slow, kept on up the slope and over the top, leaping the trunk of a fallen pine, then down the steep far side, leaning back to avoid tumbling forwards, then head down again and full speed after her, a straight chase, as she neared the edge of the woods and the bright open space beyond.

She broke through into the sunshine a second before him, and whooped, then he passed from the last shadows too, down a low rocky bank, and onto a huge expanse of smooth white sand that stretched away miles to both sides and hundreds of yards ahead to the flat blue sea.

Karen had thrown herself down on the sand, and was lying on her back, laughing, red in the cheeks.

Beat you! she cried. So much for the super-fit jogger!

He laughed too, and started skliffing in a circle about her, looking down at the way her hair fanned out against the white sand.

Alright, you're quick over a sprint, he said. But what about a real run? What about to the end of the beach and back?

Away you go! Come and lie beside me a minute.

No, I'm going to show you, get up.

She laughed. Give me a minute to get my strength back then — or an hour maybe.

Ha! Useless woman. Watch this.

He started running away from her, his feet skittering at first, sending sprays of sand out behind him, but soon getting a grip and moving quickly over the beach.

He raised his head and looked ahead: it stretched out clear in front of him almost for ever. That was something great about jogging along here as opposed to a pavement or a street: there you had to be constantly sidestepping and swerving to avoid dustbins and cars and lampposts, tree-roots sticking through paving slabs, mounds of dogshit, kids on bikes. Here you could just run in a straight line for miles, nothing to stop you. You could probably be blind here and go for a run no problem. Of course, if you were blind you wouldn't be able to see that the beach *was* all clear, you'd have to get someone to give you the okay before you set off. And that would have to be somebody you could trust, somebody you could be sure wouldn't lie about the clearness, who wouldn't forget to tell you about that dead sheep halfway along you were going to trip over and go headfirst into. That kind of person could be hard to find.

But Rob wasn't blind, he could see ahead quite clearly, and the funny thing was, of course, that being able to see made it possible for him to make on he was blind in more safety than a real blinder could.

He closed his eyes, forced himself to keep them shut, and ran on.

Two steps later he went flying, his footing fucked, and landed with thuds, his palms getting grated but his face safe except for a few spirks of dry sand flying up over it and into his hair. He lay there for half a minute before opening his eyes, rolling over onto his back and elbows, and looking to see what the hell he'd tripped over. Nothing. He could see where his footmarks stopped and where the scuffed-up sand started where he'd landed. But there was nothing in between them, no rock, no ribbon of slippery seaweed, no gnarl of driftwood. He'd fallen over his own feet.

Okay, so being a blinder was fucking difficult, even when you had the use of your eyes.

He stayed sitting and looked back along the beach towards Karen. She wasn't lying down any more, she was up on her feet, running around in little circles and lines, stopping every now and then to consider, then setting off again, footering about at some daft game like a young kid dancing through the playground in a world of its own. Rob snorted to himself, and looked out to sea.

There was something about the sea. It was still blue, but it was bigger somehow. No, it wasn't bigger, it was getting closer, that was all. Too slow to see if you watched it, but steadily all the same, the tide was moving up the beach.

He looked landward, wondering how high up the sloping sand the waves would reach, but stopped thinking about that immediately he saw the ruin. Right on the verge of the beach, right where the sand humped up into a grassy bank stuck with trees, was a small rocky mound. On top of it was a tall thin building put together with massive red stones. It had only a few small windows, and even they were more like slits than anything you would see a view out of. A castle.

Rob got up and walked towards it, and as he got closer could make out more details: a small arch of yellow stones in one wall would be the door, a jagged lump of masonry sticking out of a top corner would be the remains of a tower, the jabby-nettles and docks that swarmed around its base were growing in cracks and nooks in piles of blocks tumbled down over the years from the top of the walls.

He scrambled up the mound, held his hands high, clear of the nettles, and paused at the doorgap. Inside was more rubble, a birch tree, a stone staircase climbing halfway up a wall then breaking off, and a ring of holes in the stonework ten feet up where timbers for the first floor must've been socketed.

Rob went inside.

Someone was shouting his name. It would be Karen. He stooped out from his shelter under the broken staircase, and threaded across the floor of the castle in between the piles of rubble and clumps of thistles.

Robbie!

He stood on a block and looked out through a slit in the wall.

Robbie!

Karen was walking along the beach, every few steps cupping a hand round her mouth and calling his name.

Robbie! Where are you?

He watched her. She didn't sound worried, she was just strolling along. As he watched, she came across the patch of ruffled sand where he'd fallen. She looked at it for a second, then glanced further along the beach, then back at the disturbed area. She turned a right angle, and started following his footsteps up towards the castle. She looked up, and was grinning now.

Ah-ha. Robbie Catto. I can see you.

He was pretty sure she couldn't. The slit gave a broad outlook, but from her point of view he'd be invisible. He didn't say anything, just stood there watching her approach.

Come on out, Robbie. I've something to show you.

She was starting to come up the castle mound. It would be at this point you'd fire your gun. Or maybe, if the castle was old enough, it would be now you'd draw back your bow and shoot the arrow right into the heart of the enemy, killing her dead.

I ken you're in there, Robbie.

From the way her eyes were searching, he could tell she still hadn't spotted him. The castle builders had really known what they were doing: the defences of the place were excellent.

And now that had been proven, it was okay to leave. He stepped down from the block, away from the slit window, and guldered out, Hullo-oo! His shout echoed round the ruined walls.

Hullo! came her reply.

He crossed to the door with its arch of weathered yellow stone, and waited for her to come round the corner. As she appeared he yelled, Halt! Who goes there? Friend or foe?

Friend! she cried.

Advance and be recognised.

She marched up towards him. Do you ken me now? she said when she was about two feet away.

He slung down a rifle from his shoulder and thrust it out in front of him, looked her up and down. Never seen you before in my life, he said. I'm afraid I'll have to bayonet you to death. He lunged forward with his gun, and she skraiked and jumped aside, then ran off round the castle.

He gave chase, following close behind her all the way, till she careered down the rocky mound and jumped off the edge of the bank onto a dune of sand below. He hesitated, then jumped after her, the gun flying away and forgotten.

She was walking off along the beach, back to where she'd come from. He followed.

You found the Red Castle then, she said, as he came alongside her.

Aye, it's great. Dead old, but those big thick walls are excellent: just the job.

We used to call it the Red Castle when we were kids, she said.

But I don't ken if that's its real name. Ask my dad, he'll know. He knows all the history around here.

She reached out and took Rob's hand, then swung their arms in rhythm as they walked along the beach.

There was a famous murder there once, she said. I can't mind what it was all about, you'd have to check with the expert: the old man. Something about the laird of the place being away out hunting, and his rival riding in and killing his wife and children. And the place has been known as the Red Castle ever since. Not cause of the red stone, you see, but because of all the blood.

Rob nodded. I love it. Amazing atmosphere. It's a wonder more folk don't know about it.

Ach, everybody round here knows about it, she said. It's been there for ever. But it's meant to be a bittie dangerous, ken, you're meant to be at risk of a tower falling in and landing on your head. So I think parents aren't so keen to take their bairns playing there any more.

It seemed sound enough to me, said Rob. I'd say it was more likely to be washed away by the sea than to fall down.

Oh! She slowed momentarily, then started walking quicker, pulling him along at her side. That reminds me, she said, there's something I want to show you afore the tide swallows it.

They hurried along the beach to the spot just below where they'd first come out from the woods. It was here that Karen had been trotting about earlier on, and as they got nearer, Rob could see what she'd been doing.

A giant heart had been stamped out in the sand, with an arrow going in at the top right side and looking as if to come out on the left side near the pointy end. But now waves were coming foaming up the beach, and the tip of the heart and the point of the arrow were covered in water.

Oh no! cried Karen, and broke away from Rob and ran up to the side of the heart. Quick, she shouted over her shoulder. It's being washed away, come and see before it's too late.

Rob daunered over and stood beside her. Inside the heart she had walked out letters. They must've said:

KAREN

L

ROB

But the waves were eating away the writing from the bottom end up, so now it looked like:

KAREN

L

ᴅ ᴏᴅ

Och! said Karen.

Aye, said Rob. And what I want to ken is, who's this guy ᴅ ᴏᴅ that you love?

It's you I love. She turned to him and put her arms round his waist. I got it just right as well, she said, And now it's all being wrecked.

What you should've done, he said, Was put IDT beside it.

IDT?

If Destroyed True. Then you would've been alright no matter what happened.

I never thought this would happen, she said.

He looked over his shoulder and watched the last of his name getting washed away.

Rob let Karen drive home. He didn't speak as they drove through the country, just looked out the window. It hadn't rained all week, apart from that greasy shower on Wednesday night, and the ground was pretty dry. Now there was a strong wind coming in off the sea, and the dusty red topsoil of the fields was being lifted and whirled up into the air. The car drove along a single-track road between two ploughed parks, and on both sides a great drift of red dust rose into the air. Rob scrunched down into his seat and pressed his face against the window to look as directly upwards as possible. Still he couldn't see how high the soil was being blown. It just kept rising.

If the wind kept up the whole surface of the earth would be blown away, lifted up from under everybody's feet and carried into the air. What then? You'd be standing on your doorstep and all the soil from your garden would have gone. You wouldn't be able to walk over to the street. Your wife would come trotting up the road, she'd be alright there cause the tarmac would never lift up, too heavy, but when she got to the garden gate she'd have to stop. There'd be a big gulf between the two of you – the house standing high on its foundations and the rocks below, like the Red Castle on its mound, then a great gap where the garden used to be, a big hole away down into the black depths of nothingness – and then Karen standing on the pavement, unreachable.

She put her hand on his knee. He jumped upright in his seat.

A penny for them, Robbie.

He looked at her.

She moved her hand to the gear stick and changed down to

fourth. What's on your mind, honey? I can tell you're worried about something.

Rob looked straight ahead. They were driving down the hill that led into the town from the south side. Below and to the right was the harbour, then beyond that the prom and the pebbly beach, with the shopping streets and the houses spreading landward from there.

What? he said.

You've something on your mind. You should tell me. You ken it always feels better if you tell me your problems.

The estate with their house was away to the left, partly hidden by the old flax mill and warehouse at the side of the river. And the school was hidden too, in amongst the trees that sprouted at the northern edge of the town and covered the slopes that started to climb there.

Rob shifted his gaze away from the horizon and towards Karen in the seat next to him. A strange feeling came over him, that she was further away than the woods around the school, and the cliffpath beyond that. He felt water coming into his eyes, and turned to look out the side window at the big granite villas passing by on his side.

I've no problems, he said. Nothing I can't deal with. It's a work thing, that's all. It could be serious but it's probably not. Whatever, it's up to me to sort it. That's what I'm paid for, that's what they expect of me, that's my responsibility. And I can handle it. Don't you worry.

But I do worry.

You shouldn't. It doesn't concern you.

You concern me, Robbie.

He closed his eyes. I don't need looking after, he said after a few seconds. I can take care of myself.

I ken, she said. But I also ken there's something on your mind. You should tell me.

I don't know about my mind, he muttered. But there's something getting on my nerves all right.

She was silent for half a minute, then she said, I was only trying to help, Rob. I love you.

Stop the car! he said loudly.

What?

It's no use, let me out!

She checked the mirror, started to slow down.

Pull over! he shouted.

Alright, alright!

Before the car had stopped he was unfastening his seatbelt and opening the door. I'll get myself home, he said, stepping out onto the pavement.

She leant over the passenger seat and looked up at him. When, do you think?

He shrugged. I don't ken.

What are you going to do?

He looked back at her. I'm going to stop you driving me crazy, he said, and swung the door of the car shut. Immediately, he started walking back the way they'd come, getting well away from the car. But it didn't matter – Karen didn't get out or roll down the window to talk to him, she just put the Fiesta into gear and continued down the last bit of the hill towards the busy streets of the town.

Rob stopped walking and turned to watch her go. What the fuck was he supposed to do now?

He'd had enough of her nagging and prodding for the day, that was for sure, but where else could he go, who else could he fucking talk to? Whoever it was, he wasn't likely to find them in this part of town. He started walking down the hill.

The good thing about the women in the Burnett lassie's *Razzle* was that they never had any notions of their own. They never had stupid ideas about visiting childhood picnic spots or discussing problems from work. All these women ever wanted to do was whatever the men suggested. And all the men ever suggested was fucking. It was simple. It was easy to ken where you were with that kind of woman. Karen could just be a bit too difficult at times: she had things on her mind he didn't know about, he couldn't control.

Rob had reached the bottom of the hill. There were people davering about here instead of cars just zipping past. He walked slower. He was passing shops now too. One was a newsagent. He stopped and peered through the window, past the posters and small-ad cards cluttering it up. There'd be a top shelf in there crammed with the kind of woman who'd cause him no trouble at all. His cock started to harden at the thought of it. He squinted up the back of the shop to see who was serving, a man or a woman. Fuck! It was neither, it was a young girl. He recognised her from the school. Second year, he thought. Fuck. Maybe her folks owned the shop, or maybe it was just a weekend job – a little extra money, and the chance to pinch a packet or two of fags.

Whatever, he was fucked. He couldn't buy stuff like that from a pupil, he had a reputation to keep up. It'd be all over school by Monday break if he was seen buying a wank mag. School jannies weren't meant to do the like of that, they were meant to protect the kids from stuff like it – porn and perverts. Fuck. What Rob really had to do was forget the fantasy women and start hunting down the bastard in the parka, the fucking lurker, the perverted fucking psychopath in the woods. But where to start the hunt? Rob stared into the newsagent's, his focus gradually blurring till he wasn't seeing piles of papers and racks of greeting cards inside any more, but just his own dark reflection in the plate glass window.

The first job Rob set himself in the morning was writing a memo to the head.

FAO Mr Moran, Rector

Since you first alerted me to the possible presence of a lurker in the vicinity of the school, my staff and I have been keeping a close watch on the woods, pitches, playgrounds etc. There was one possible sighting about a week ago (this took place well after school hours, and in the town centre, so I didn't feel justified in bringing it to your attention at the time) but apart from that, nothing. Until last Friday.

Late that evening I intercepted a man, exactly fitting Mrs Ellis's description, in the wooded area to the east of the school. My general impression was of a desperate and probably dangerous character. No one was on hand to help me apprehend the suspect, and I didn't want to risk tackling him myself, as it's well known that these people often possess almost superhuman strength.

It is now beyond doubt, however, that a strange man is hanging around the school, and I think it would certainly be worthwhile increasing security. Perhaps a task force of police could be billeted in one of the rooms overlooking the woods.

I'm sure they would effect the capture of this pervert very quickly. I would be more than happy to assist with the arrest if required.

Yours, R. Catto (Head Janitor)

After signing the memo, Rob read through it, sighed, then crumpled it up and tossed it towards the bin. It bounced off the edge, and rolled across the floor towards the filing cabinet. Rob looked at it lying there. Then he got off his seat and crawled over towards the balled-up memo. After watching for half a minute more, he pounced on it, held it under his cupped hands for a few seconds, then started uncrumpling it, flattening it out on the greasy bothy carpet.

Rob was on canteen duty. He was meant to stop the kids chucking food at each other and having water fights. He'd just seen one boy sabotage a salt cellar under the table, screwing the lid off then balancing it back on top. Rob kept watching, and a minute later the boy in the seat opposite picked up the cellar, went to sprinkle some salt into his soup, and ended up with the entire contents, a small mountain of white stuff, sticking out of the orange cream of tomato. His friends creased up with laughter, and Rob grinned too. The victim gaped about, outraged, as if hoping to find someone who'd whisk away his plate and give him a fresh one. No chance.

Rob laughed to himself. He remembered canteen dinners as being about the best time in all his years at school. You could have a laugh and stoke the boilers at the same time. Everybody just concentrated on shovelling the stuff down them, then taking a rise out of whoever was last to finish. It was great. And the funny thing was, it was the big bastards with the big mouths that could get through their platefuls quickest, and the wee runts who were slower and got picked on and their pudding nicked. So the big bastards got bigger and the skinny cunts got even skinnier.

Rob had seen a documentary on telly recently about chicks in a nest, and how the weakest one was likely to get fed less than its brothers when ma-bird came back with the worms. It needed the grub more than them, but it couldn't put up a good enough fight for it. It was a fucking shame, but the way of the world and always had been: as was proved by the kids in front of him. Rob was probably meant to try and stop that kind of thing going on, but who was he to go against the forces of nature?

The kids were drifting away now. Some of the sixth years tended to hang around for ages blethering, but all the younger ones just ate as fast as they could then dashed off to the playground or the pitches. Or the woods. Half the bastards were probably nashing off to hide in the trees – smoking, sniffing lighter fuel and feeling each other up. It was atrocious. Out of the nest and straight into the fucking dens of vice.

Speaking of which, the crowds had thinned out in front of Rob and he could see, sitting by herself at a table against the end wall of the canteen, Sandra Burnett, teenage porn queen. He took a step back behind the water machine and watched her as she forked chips one at a time into her mouth. She was eating slowly, reading as she chewed, often leaving several seconds between swallowing and lifting the next chip. She had a magazine spread out on the table in front of her, the salt and pepper and her glass pushed away so it could be opened at a double spread across the table. The cheek of the girl! To read that kind of stuff in the middle of the canteen, with staff and other pupils streaming past!

The thought of her being so blatant really got to Rob. He felt his heart beating faster in fury.

Brian Jackson the gym teacher stood up from the long staff table in the corner of the room. Rob had thought a few times of having his dinner in the canteen – the grub looked pretty good and filling, and it cost next to nothing – but the idea of having to sit with a bunch of arseholes like Jackson always put him off. They'd be the type to tell him to stop playing with his food, without a doubt.

Now Jackson was heading for the exit. He zigzagged through the tables, nodding at a couple of the footballing boys as he passed them. Then he made a detour away from the door, and stopped in front of Sandra Burnett. Rob frowned. Jackson was talking to Sandra, but Rob couldn't see how she was reacting, cause the teacher was in the way. He put his hands behind his back and strolled away from the water machine, looking in the opposite direction, where a couple of the cooking ladies were beginning to wipe down the empty tables.

He looked back towards Jackson and Sandra. From this new viewpoint, he could see the teacher was speaking to the girl, apparently asking her a string of questions. To which she only replied with shrugs and shakes of the head. Then Jackson leant over the table, looking down at the magazine, or maybe down the front of her blouse, Rob couldn't be sure. He reached out a hand and flicked over a few pages of her *Razzle*.

Jesus Christ. Rob waited for fireworks.

Nothing.

Sandra said a few words, and Jackson nodded and took a step away from the table. He said something else, smiled, then walked away from her, heading for the exit again.

Rob turned to look in the opposite direction till Jackson was gone. It was incredible, absolutely fucking incredible, that a fourteen-year-old lassie could be sitting reading a dirty magazine during school hours and a teacher would just thumb through it and walk away, leave it with the girl! It was a sign of how atrociously bad morals were getting in the school.

Unless of course it wasn't a porn mag Sandra was reading. That hadn't occurred to Rob.

He looked towards her again, and she had put the magazine away. Now she was sitting back in her chair, watching him, and smiling.

One of the strip lights in the games hall had gone. The rule was that when one wore out, the whole lot had to be replaced. This was because a special mobile scaff tower had to be ordered from the education office to get up to the high ceiling, and it cost money. So all the old lamps had to be chucked out, even though only one of them was dead. If you waited till each of them went, you could be requisitioning the platform every couple of weeks for the next six months, and your budget would be fucked.

Rob and Donald were on top of the platform and Billy was down below, checking the brakes didn't slip on the wheels or something.

Rob unscrewed the mesh protector from around the tenth lamp and Donald caught it as it came away. Rob put the screws in his pocket, then reached up and eased the old tube out of the holder. The top of it was covered in dust, and Rob sneezed as he brought the tube down and the dust floated about. Donald passed him a new tube with one hand, taking the old one in the other and sliding it into the corrugated paper carton the new one had just come out of. Rob had meanwhile clipped the new lamp into the holder. He took out the old starter motor, fitted a new one from the bag by his feet into the socket and pressed it home, then picked up the mesh again and started to screw it into place.

Sore on the fucking arm muscles all this reaching up, he said.

Pain in the neck, said Donald.

That too. And my fucking wrist's sore with all this screwing.

Donald laughed. I thought it was wanking that gave you a sore wrist, not screwing.

You would know, said Rob, working on the third screw.

Bernie was in a right roose with me last night, said Donald. No chance of the other there! I stayed out late at the blues pub, came home blootered. Thought I might see you there, actually.

Rob shook his head; a couple spirks of sweat flew off his brow. Nah, I've gone off it, they play the same songs every week.

Still, it was jumping last night, I tell you. A few of the sixth years were there – looking at their old maths teacher on bass I suppose.

Rob tightened the last screw. Oh aye, what's his name, Frizzell?

Graham Frizzell. I had a couple of jars with him after the gig. Me and him got to ken each other quite well back when he was being carpeted.

Rob sat down, leaned over the edge of the platform, and called out, Okay Billy, on to the next one. Not many to go now.

There was a clang down below as the brake was let off, then the tower started to shudder and shake as Billy shoved against it and started to inch it across the floor.

Donald held tight onto the guardrail. Put your back into it, he cried, and laughed. Whipcrackaway!

Bugger off! shouted back Billy, but by this time he'd got up a bit of momentum and the tower moved on smoothly till he halted it under the next lamp. He put the brake on and the two on the platform set to work.

I never kent Frizzell got carpeted, said Rob. I thought he got promoted or something. He's teaching up at Stonehive now, eh?

Aye. He had to get out of here, that was for sure, but they couldn't actually give him the boot. So they shifted him north.

Rob got the last screw out and gave his hand a shake to untwist the wrist muscles as Donald removed the mesh. I never heard that. What did he do, like?

Broke a loon's leg.

You're kidding!

No, a big fourth year it was. He turned mental at Frizzell for some reason, just went for him. Threw a calculator past his head, then jumped on him. Frizzell panicked, lashed out, kicked at the boy's shin. Next thing he kens the boy's on the floor screaming, and the police are interviewing him on an assault charge.

The fourth year?

No! Frizzell!

Jesus.

Aye, the union had to fight like billy-oh on that one. Not me, the teachers' rep, EIS – it was the head of physics at the time, eh, MacIntosh. He retired not long after. Anyway, it was a right stooshie. In the papers and everything.

Moran wouldn't've been pleased.

No, he was raging. Him only in the job half a term as well. I reckon he would've given Frizzell his cards if he could've, but the union was great, got him off completely on grounds of self defence.

Must've taken some doing.

You should've seen the kid: a big six footer, broader than me.

He used to lift the wee first years with one hand and hold them up against the wall.

Christ, if I'd been him coming I reckon I'd've lashed out too!

Oi! There was a shout from down below.

Rob leaned over the edge. What is it Billy?

Are you working up there still, or have you knocked off for a fly and not tellt me?

Christ, give us a break, we're sweating up here.

Aye, said Donald, I reckon the heating's on too high in this hall.

Hot air rises, said Billy.

If that's right, Rob said, How come it gets colder the further up a mountain you go?

Eh . . . Billy stood with his mouth open.

On to the next lamp! cried Rob. Onwards and upwards! He laughed, and so did Donald.

Billy released the brake and threw his weight against the tower, grunting. What are you blabbing about anyway? he said after he'd got the thing moving. I can't hear you down here.

We're talking about Graham Frizzell, replied Donald. Mind, he got shifted to Stonehive for kicking a fourth year.

Oh aye, said Billy, He should've got sacked, but he was a funny handshaker. . .

What! cried Donald.

. . . and so was the chairman of the education committee, so he kept his job. A bloody scandal, that was.

Rubbish!

Rob laughed. God, and here's you giving me the party line. I'm glad Billy's handy with the unbiased version.

Unbiased? Him and his conspiracy theories? I wouldn't've thought you'd've much time for those.

Billy brought the tower to a stop and the brake clanked on. Donald lowered his voice:

You ken he thinks that's why you got the job and he didn't?

Why?

He reckons you're a mason and that got you in above him.

Rubbish. I'm not a mason.

Tell him that. He'll probably prove you joined at the age of five without even knowing it or something. He's got a bee in his bunnet about it.

He's barking up the wrong tree: I'm not the joining type. I can barely join my fucking writing.

He's got a thing about it, said Donald. Same when he was in the police. He reckons the reason he never got to be a sergeant or whatever was cause he wouldn't join the brotherhood. All the rest of them were in, he says.

I bet they were. Rob quickly took the screws out from around the mesh. I like Billy fine, he said quietly, And I wouldn't say this to his face, but the reason he never got promoted in the pigs was probably the same reason he never got my job. He tapped the side of his forehead. He just hasn't got it up here.

Donald nodded.

What are you talking about lads? shouted up Billy.

Rob winked at Donald. We were wondering if you wanted to come down the lodge thenight, he said. There's a knobbly knees competition, and the winner gets to be next town provost.

There was a pause, then, Are you serious? said Billy.

Rob told Donald and Billy to take down the scaff tower, and left the games hall. He checked his watch and walked quickly along the corridor of sweat, then down the main corridor and outside.

By the time the bell went at half-three, he was strolling round the turning circle, past the line of parked buses. Streams of kids ran past him along the curved pavement, and rammies of them gathered, yelling, round the bus doors. A few of them calmed down a bit as he passed, but most took no notice. The ones that calmed down were the ones making least racket in the first place, and that was the problem with kids: it was the easy ones, the ones who never stepped out of line, that took most notice of you and tried to act grown-up. It was the bastards who fought and thieved and started riots in empty rooms who took the least notice of anything anyone said to them.

Like Sandra Burnett. Trying to persuade her not to bring the porn mags to school had been useless, it seemed. If that was what she'd been reading in the canteen, she was obviously even more depraved and shameless than he'd thought. His heart was beating fast, he noticed: just the thought of her was getting him in a rage. He had to see her, to talk to her again, to get her to see sense about the porn. She needed a good talking to, that was for sure. And he would be happy to give her one.

But Sandra wasn't to be seen. He'd reached the junction with the road and looked up and down it for half a minute; there was no skinny tall girl with a fag in her hand in either direction. And she definitely hadn't been lurking about the edges of the wood either, he'd had a good look all along there.

It was a bit much really. It fucking pissed him off. It was a bit much she couldn't turn up where she was supposed to and let him get a look at her. It was typical of the type of problem that sort of child would give you.

He turned away from the road – and just about collided with Billy, who was hirpling down the pavement at a fair old speed.

Jesus Billy!

Sorry boss!

What's your rush?

I don't ken. I just seen you standing here like you were about to sprint after somebody, all bunched up to leap off, like, and I goes, Aye aye, trouble here surely. So I thought I'd come down and help deal with the bugger.

Rob stared at him. With who? he said at last.

Billy shifted his feet, looked around. I don't ken: you were the one looking ready for a fight.

A fight! Rob laughed, and relaxed. A fight, that'll be right. Come on.

He gave Billy a clap on the shoulder and walked back up towards the school. The pavement was empty; all the kids were on the buses, and all the buses were away. He'd never even noticed them leaving.

I was looking for somebody, he said, as they headed round to the Tradesman's Entrance. But it wasn't for a fight.

It looked like you wanted a fight.

No, I just wanted. . . I don't ken. I just wanted a word with that Sandra Burnett. I had a bit of unfinished business with her, and I wanted to sort it out thenow.

Billy chuckled. If you start sorting out the Burnetts you're likely to end up like your maths pal!

Eh, who?

Frizzell, Graham Frizzell. The one that broke the loon's leg and got the boot.

What's he got to do with Sandra?

Nothing, but the loon that got kicked was her big brother. Did

102

you not ken that? David Burnett, that was him, the one with the cracked shin, the one that chucked the desk at Frizzell.

A desk! I heard it was a calculator!

He was a big lad, could easy've chucked a desk. Billy shook his head. If I mind right he threw a lot of stuff about at various times: desks, chairs, smaller kids. It was a habit of his.

Jesus.

He had a lot of problems, that boy. Same as his sister, she's got a lot of problems too. Hers are different, mind you.

Rob held open the door and they walked inside and along towards the bothy. Seems to me she doesn't have too many problems, he said. Seems to me she just causes problems for other folk.

Billy unlocked the bothy door and let the key chain fall back into his pocket. Then he paused, leaning on the door handle, and said, That reminds me: ken what David Burnett's doing now?

The big brother?

Aye.

No.

He's in prison. Billy pushed open the door and they went into the bothy.

What did he do, brain somebody with a desk?

Billy chuckled. No, he's not banged up, he works there.

You what?

Aye, he's a warder, a screw. Promoted as well. Big Davey Burnett, locker-upper at Peterhead jail.

Rob opened the key box, got the ground-floor keys down and gave them to Billy, then put the first-floor ones in his own pocket. Funny how folk turn out, eh? I bet nobody here would've guessed he'd end up doing that.

Billy tossed his bundle of keys up and caught them as they fell. Except for me! he said, and grinned.

Rob led the way out of the bothy and along the service corridor.

I could've told them, said Billy. Course, nobody asked me. But I could tell: Davey had worked out something about the school, something that 99 per cent of the kids don't, and a lot of the teachers neither. That it's all a game. And it only keeps going cause both sides stick to the rules.

They turned into the main corridor and headed for the main door. Billy swept his arms wide in front of him to separate the two sides.

Most kids don't realise the power they've got, he said. They think the teachers are the bosses, and the dominie is the boss of bosses. They think the teachers have the knowledge and the power and that the bairns have no choice but to go along with what the teachers say. Shite! What do you get in a classroom? Thirty kids and one teacher; the kids could just walk out, the poor bugger with the degree couldn't stop them. Thirty kids could hold a teacher down and batter him!

Even easier if it was a woman teacher, said Rob.

Aye, they could do what the hell they liked, and no one could stop them! But they don't: they do what they're tellt, they stick to the rules and let the game go on. Why? Cause they don't realise it *is* a game!

They'd reached the main door, but Billy didn't lock it. He turned to Rob and kept on blabbing, slicing the air with his hands.

And that's just the same as in the jail, he was saying. I don't ken if you've ever been in a jail, Rob, but I've been to a load of them, and I tell you this: they're just the same as the school. Okay, the

104

staff there have batons and liquid cosh and riot gear if they want it, but still, the whole system depends on the prisoners coming out of their cells when they're told to, eating what's given to them, walking on the set side of the corridor, doing their rec at the set time, going back to their cells when they're told to. . .

How about locking the door? said Rob.

Billy looked blank for a second, then laughed. Oh aye! He pulled the school door to, turned the big key, then gave the brass knob a rattle to check it. See, he said, Locking and unlocking doors all day long, just like in the jail. And god, it's not so long ago the teachers could belt the kids, give them a slap if they wanted – just the same as in the jail.

But nowadays the wee bastards attack the teachers and they can't fucking defend themselves. Which brings us round to David Burnett.

They headed back towards the corridor of sweat.

David Burnett worked it out, Billy said, locking the door that led onto the path to the pitches. He saw that the only reason the work of the school went on was cause him and his pals and all the bairns played the teachers' game. And every so often he'd decide, for his own reasons, not to play any more. He'd just stand up and say, Fuck it! and the whole thing would grind to a halt around him.

But what would he gain from that?

Billy shrugged. I don't ken. Power, maybe, or the feeling of power: the feeling that he was in control of the whole wee world of the school, cause he could bring it to a stop any time he liked. It must've felt good to him that, cause by all accounts he wasn't in control of much else in his life – at home I mean.

They had passed through the technical department and Billy was locking the door that led to the wood and metal store outside.

Billy, said Rob, Why am I following you around down here? I should be upstairs doing the firescapes and the canteen.

Cause you're listening to my explanation, said Billy. You're young. I was in the police twenty-four years – I ken how these things work.

No, said Rob. Not at all.

I do, said Billy.

No, but that's not why I'm down here. I'm here cause I keep thinking, just one more door, one more lock, and Billy'll surely get to the point of his story, he'll surely start making sense. But you keep blethering on, and I'm still none the wiser!

Billy laughed. Well it's over late now, he said. I've done all my doors!

Jesus!

I'm away home. He laughed again.

But what about Davey Burnett, you never finished telling me about him?

Billy shrugged. I suppose he liked that feeling of power, and he wanted a job where he could get it again – over folk who wouldn't fight back too much. So the prison service was ideal. He could've been a teacher, I suppose, but he wasn't thick enough to want that for a life: so into jail he went. And on with the game.

Karen was going to be working late all week. Rob didn't want to be sitting in the house by himself for hours, so planned to do a decent run after school every day.

He locked the Tradesman's Entrance, then sprinted across the empty car park into the woods on the far side, and settled to a steady jog along a path that curved through the trees. His feet thumped on the packed earth of the path, jarring his bones and his brain, stopping him from thinking. He was glad of that. Lately his head had been full of thoughts, and he didn't like the feeling; it was good to get out running and smash them up a bit..

The path forked. One route turned back towards the school, the other kept straight on, deeper into the woods. Rob wasn't sure where it ended up, but he started down it anyway. The way was narrow, and little used by the look of it; a couple of times he just about skited on patches of long grass, another time he had to stop and untangle a bramble that had come coiling over the pathway at ankle height and jagged into his sock.

But soon the narrow path jouked round a rocky outcrop and joined a much wider one, and Rob found himself jogging along parallel to the sea. He didn't look out at it much, just kept his eyes on where his feet were going, but he was aware of its presence anyway. The air felt fresher and cleaner here than it had on the other side of the woods. There was a bit of a breeze blowing in off the water, but it wasn't just that, the air actually tasted different: nippier, tangier, more refreshing. He took a string of deep breaths. He could really feel the air prinkling down into the depths of his lungs. It was like the kind of cold clear water he used to drink from burns in the hills west of Aberdeen, when his mum and dad took him hiking there, years ago. Twenty years ago. Amazing how tastes from that long back could flood into your mind as soon as you thought of them. It saved having to climb the fucking steep bastarding hills again. He had a lot of really clear memories of his folks from around then too; maybe that was why he didn't feel he had to visit them either. No, that wasn't it at all. It was just that they lived four hundred miles away: a long way to jog.

He lifted his head and opened his eyes wide as he could, so the cold air would wash over his eyeballs and seep in round the back. It stung, but it felt good. He blinked the tears out of his eyes, saw where he was running, and stopped.

Immediately to his left stood a barrier of gorse bushes. Beyond that was the grassy spit of land with the concrete pillbox on the end. Rob walked forwards till he came to the place where the bushes thinned out, where he'd twice pushed through before. Now he went into the bushes again, and in a few seconds was out onto the short grass of the taing. The sea was blue on each side, and it made the grass on the taing look incredibly green, brighter green than grass usually was, like somebody had crawled about and sprayed every blade with metallic green paint. And the sun, still high in the clear sky, but almost directly behind him, lit up the angular walls of the bunker, making the grey concrete glow almost pink.

He strolled along towards the point, slowing at the dip where him and Karen had screwed. It felt quite exposed out here in the open, but actually that had been a much better screw than the one in the privacy of the dark woods the other night. Maybe it was something to do with the fresh air again, the way it prickled all over the skin like cold electricity, waking up every atom in the body. Maybe doing it on top of a mountain in a gale would be best of all. Or on the roof of a car as it drove along. Though you'd have to have some special kind of roof-rack fitted for that. And the guy driving the car might get a bit worked up by the banging coming through the roof above his head, and he'd want a go too. That could lead to fights: jealousy coming into it. If the guy driving got jealous he might take it out on you by changing direction. Instead of taking you along quiet romantic country lanes, he'd head the car for the centre of town, and drive all around there, stopping at traffic lights, slowing as he passed crowds of shoppers in the High Street. Imagine looking up just as you were about to come and finding you were shagging in the supermarket car park! Terrible! Especially if it was with some dog! I mean, okay if it was Karen, cause she was a ride. And she was his wife. So he wouldn't mind being found fucking her on either count. But what if you got drunk and picked up some old slag – Susan from Karen's work, maybe – you'd be double damned then: being a laughing stock for shagging some old hag, and getting frowned upon for doing it with somebody illicit. Terrible, terrible. And all because you let somebody else do the driving.

Rob stepped over some stones lying in the grass and walked the last few metres to the bunker. He laid his hand flat against it. The concrete felt warm and smooth, almost like skin. He went round towards the entrance passage, trailing his hand along the wall as he went. He glanced along the passageway, which was less cluttered with rubbish than he'd remembered. Then he grued, as he pictured the rotting sheep lying just past the corner. God's sake, he said to himself, then passed round to the front of the pillbox.

You must like this place.

Rob jumped, looked over his shoulder, then back to the front again. He was alone.

More enjoyable with someone else, of course. Unless you're me. If you're me you actually prefer it with nobody else which is fine for it's rare there's anyone ever here.

Rob looked up and to the left and saw something moving away from the window in the front of the pillbox. He took a step backwards, watching the slot.

One eye and half a face peeked round the edge, the eye hidden behind some kind of thick-lensed glasses. And you're the only person to come more than once, it said, and started laughing.

How do you know. . . said Rob, and his voice cracked. He cleared his throat and started again: How do you know I've been here before?

Wouldn't you know if someone had been in your house? said the half face.

Aye.

Well. The half face frowned. I don't like people coming into my place, it said.

Rob didn't speak, just stared. The face slid slowly sideways, and disappeared. Rob waited for it to reappear, but before it did, somebody tapped him on the shoulder, and he spun round and backwards.

A thickset man with ginger hair and a donkey jacket was standing at the corner of the pillbox, a long bleached stick in his hand. The stick was poised in the air, pointing towards Rob's chest.

Shake, said the man, and wobbled the stick up and down.

Rob looked at him, then at the stick.

I can't shake your hand, said the man. It's my own strength, I don't know it. Well, I know it roughly, but I don't know the details of it yet. And I don't want to crush your hand. So if you shake your end and I shake my end, we'll be being friendly and no bones broken.

Watching the guy, Rob took hold of the end of the stick, and let him move it up and down a few times.

It's good to be friendly, said the guy, taking the stick back and shouldering it like a rifle. It greases the palms. I try and always be friendly, though some folk react against it. I say it's their loss. In the long run. You see, you were friendly in coming out here, and then I was friendly despite you trespassing on my land. We both were friendly.

I just came out for a run, to be honest. . .

The guy frowned. You mean you weren't being friendly after all? He lowered the stick so he was holding it out in front of him like a spear.

It's not like that. I just never expected to see anybody here.

The guy nodded, let the stick slide through his hands so the bottom end of it rested on the ground.

Rob was finding his stare a bit hard to take. He looked at his watch.

What's that? said the guy.

What?

That thing on your arm.

My watch?

Your watch, I thought that's what it was.

Rob stared at the guy.

So why were you looking at it when you were talking to me?

Rob shrugged. I just wanted to know the time. I don't want to be late for my tea.

Ah-ha. It's tea you're needing, is it?

Well, eh. . . Rob looked at his watch again.

Will you stop doing that while you're talking to me!

Sorry, I. . . here! Who're you to tell me what to do?

When in Rome, do as the Romans, said the guy.

What's that supposed to mean for fuck's sake?

For fuck's sake you come walking into my fucking house, right over the fucking garden wall you fucking come and then you fucking stand there and fucking ask why you should do what I fucking say!

Calm down, said Rob.

If you hadn't fucking come I wouldn't've fucking told you fuck all but you did fucking come so you must've fucking wanted to hear it.

Let's get one thing straight, said Rob. Get this in your head: I came through the woods for a run, I didn't ken there was anybody here, let alone somebody living here which seems to be what you're telling me, though it's a bit hard to fucking believe seeing as the last time I looked this place was a pisshole, not fit for a dead sheep to bide in, and if you're telling me you live here you've got some fucking explaining to do.

The guy looked at him, then, Fair enough, he said, turning on his heel, and strode away round the corner of the bunker.

Oi! called Rob. Where are you going? Come back!

I'm here, said a voice from above Rob's head. He looked up and it was the ginger-haired guy leaning out of the window slot, a pair of swimming goggles covering his eyes.

You had those on before, said Rob.

It's very smoky in here, said the guy. It's the way the wind's blowing. If it's off the sea I wear these to protect my eyes. He ducked back inside the bunker.

Rob stepped back and took a jump up, but the window was too high for him to see in. What are you doing? he called.

Making tea. The echo in the pillbox made the guy's voice sound loud and booming.

Can I come in? said Rob.

No.

Oh. Why not?

112

I wasn't expecting guests. I haven't tidied. I'd be black affronted to let you in now, the state of the place.

Rob nodded, though the guy wasn't looking at him. He glanced up to check he wasn't being spied on, then sneaked a look at his watch. He hadn't really taken in the time when he'd looked at it a couple minutes before. But now he saw it was nearly five o'clock.

Bastard!

Rob jumped. What?

Burn you bastard! came the booming voice from inside the pillbox.

What's the matter? said Rob.

The bastard fire won't burn, said the guy. How's the water going to boil if all the fire'll do is smoulder?

Listen, said Rob. I think I'll. . .

Fuel! cried the voice, then the guy leaned out of the window. Give us up that fuel, will you? he said.

What?

There. He nodded to where he'd been standing.

The big stick?

Aye. Break a couple lengths off, will you?

Rob shrugged, then picked up the stick, held it firm in both hands, and whacked it down on his knee. Aiya bastard! His knee hurt, but the stick was unbroken: it was a tough old bit of dried-out driftwood. He got a stronger grip, down at the thin end this time, and tried again. But it bounced off without even cracking. He looked up at the guy and said, It's too thick.

Give it to me.

Rob handed him the stick, the guy disappeared into the

bunker, and a second later there was a grunt, then a sharp crack and a splintering sound. Got you now, you bastard! said the guy.

Listen, called Rob. I think I better give the tea a skip this time. My wife'll be home soon and I wouldn't want her to worry.

The guy appeared round the corner, goggles pushed up on his forehead. She won't even notice, he said.

How do you know?

The guy grinned. You know what she's like.

Aye, I do – you don't.

Sure. I'm just guessing.

Rob nodded towards the bunker. So do you really live in here?

The guy turned away. Well, wouldn't like to make you late for meeting your wife, he said. A beautiful woman like that, thin ankles, better not keep her waiting.

How do you know. . .

He walked away round the corner, and Rob followed him. He was crouched down a few yards up the taing, pushing some beach stones out of a line that stretched, one stone wide and one stone high, right across the breadth of the point. He turned around and grinned up at Rob. Just opening the gate for you, he said.

Rob nodded. Thanks, he said, and walked through the gap. I just stepped over this earlier, he said. I never even noticed it.

You'll know next time, said the guy.

Rob was home in time to change and think before Karen got back from work. He ran down from the bedroom to meet her.

Honey! she cried, smiling as he came towards her.

I've worked it out, he said, stopping on the bottom step. Billy was wrong. Well, he wasn't wrong, he was right, but he just didn't take it far enough. So he might as well have been wrong. I'm right, though, *and* I've taken it far enough. I've taken it all the way through and worked it out, so whereas he was wrong with the right idea, and doubted, I'm right with the right idea, and certain.

Karen dropped her bag by the electricity box and started taking off her coat. Billy from work? she said, still looking at him.

From work? From prison more like! That's what he thinks, he thinks the school's a big prison, that's what it acts like, and it's all a game between the teachers and the kids. I'm not sure where we fit in. In the middle probably, in between the two sides, that's usually where the jannie is: right in the fucking middle of the trouble.

Karen hung up her coat and stayed standing with her arm leaning up by the hook. She bowed her head. I'm knackered, she said. I'm going to have a seat.

Listen! shouted Rob. This is important! This is the secret of how the whole world works! Christ, you're lucky to hear it, you're privileged to be here: the first person to hear the secret of the world since I worked it out!

Great, she said. I'm going to go and have a seat, and you come and tell me all about it. She crossed the hallway and went into the living room.

Rob hesitated for a second, then leapt off the step and after her.

Billy just didn't take it far enough, he said. It's not just the school that's a prison, do you see what I mean?

Karen had taken off her shoes and was lying along the settee. I'm tired, she said.

Aye, they've been working you too hard.

So what's new?

Exactly! They've been telling you what to do, ordering you about – just like jail warders, and you the prisoner!

But I get paid for being told what to do, she said, and yawned.

So do the folk in jail! Did you ken that? They get paid wages for the bits of work they do! Not as much as you, probably, but then nobody gets as much as you, let's not get into that right now for fuck's sake. The point is: they get ordered around, then they get paid, then they go back to their cells. And you get ordered about, you get paid, then you go back to your house.

Well, where else would I go?

Anywhere, anywhere in the world!

Robbie, wise up.

You could. You could just wander off anywhere in the world. Wander off away from here and never come back.

She opened one eye and looked at him. You get your holidays soon, she said. We could go somewhere then.

Ach. . . no! He crossed to the fireplace and leant with his hands on the mantlepiece, his head hanging down. His head felt heavy with the weight of his ideas, and him not being able to get them out. Holidays, he said. Holidays are just like. . . what do you call it? Parole! Parole for good behaviour! If you're good they let you out for a few weeks a year. But you still have to go back. Do you see what I mean? Billy was right, but he just didn't go far enough, so he was wrong. I'm going further, I'm getting it right. I'm going all the way till I'm right.

Honey, she said, I've had a hard day. Can I tell you about my hard day at work? Sit down and stop pacing about and I'll tell you about it. Come on.

I can't sit down, he said. I haven't finished yet. I've got to get to the end. And your day doesn't matter, the details of it are just small things. . .

What? To you maybe, but to me. . .

No, listen, listen: this isn't a personal thing, fuck personal things. I haven't been talking about my day at work, I haven't started on that even. What I'm telling you about is a law, a rule of the world, a new one I've just discovered: work's just another kind of prison, and we all go along with it, we all chuck ourselves into jail at the age of sixteen, and we won't get out till we're sixty-five! Prison, that's what it is, prison!

You get weekends off too, she said.

It's no use, he said, shaking his head. You're just not understanding, are you? You're like Billy, you just don't go far enough. Nobody'll go fucking far enough, that's the problem, that's how they're all still in the fucking jail! Cause it's not just work that's like prison, it's the whole world! Think about it! Every second of your waking life you're following some rule or other: if it's not work it's what your parents tell you, or your wife, or the laws of the fucking land. And the telly! The politicians and the ads on the telly're telling you what to do the whole time! He wiped his mouth with the back of his hand. And the joke is, we all do what we're told! Even when we go on holiday all we're getting is a longer length of chain on our shackles. It's a disgrace. We're all in fucking prison, and we don't even admit it, we don't even see it half the time! And that's how they get away with keeping us here!

Rob, said Karen, raising a hand to cover her eyes, I'm feeling really knackered here. How about if I can just lie for five minutes, then I'll put something on for tea?

I've a good mind to break out, to run away, to go and live in the bunker by the cliffs!

Karen sat up, rubbed the heels of her hands into her eyesockets, then said, I'm going to put some food on, Rob. You don't get microwaves in bunkers, that's the problem with them. Otherwise

I'd be down there straight away, believe me. Cause Rob, I ken what you're talking about. Prison. I ken the feeling.

She looked at him, then stood up and walked away.

The bell had gone, and Rob was chasing the last kids out of the canteen and towards the classrooms. At the top of the stairs he stopped, his attention drawn by a ruckus going on outside the first maths room. A scrum of third years was crowding round the door, laughing and falling about, the boys making most noise, but some of the girls joining in too. Action was required. Rob strode towards them, getting his face set stern for telling them to shut up and get in lines till their teacher arrived.

That's enough of that, he started to say as he passed the first few folk, girls hanging back from the crowd. Then he heard a woman's voice going, Get back, get back! and he realised the teacher was there after all. No bigger than the boys crushed around her, the newest maths teacher, Ellen Petrie, was squashed up against the door, trying to make herself heard over the yells and laughter.

Shut your mouths! shouted Rob and, hauling a couple of boys away by their shoulders, pushed into the steer. The kids started to quieten and backed off an inch or two, but still the teacher was elbowing for room when he reached her.

Get off! she cried, as a big loon behind her shoved his bag into her back.

Somebody pushed me! he answered. It wasn't my fault!

Well push them, Gary, not me!

I never shoved him miss!

Did sut! Gary stepped backwards.

My fucking toes! shouted somebody.

Language! said the teacher, but she wasn't concentrating on the kids really. Her head was down, the back of her neck flushed, and she was fumbling with the keys on her keyring, clutching a briefcase under one oxter and a pile of jotters under the other. As Rob won through to her, the jotters started to slip, and he leant forward and caught them just before they fell out of her elbow's grip. He shoved them back into her armpit, and she looked up, surprised.

Trouble, Miss Petrie?

Eh, oh. . . She straightened up. Her cheeks were flushed too, and her eyes looked filmed. It's just. . . She fumbled with her keys again and inclined her head towards the shut door of the classroom.

Rob looked. A photo-spread ripped from a magazine had been stuck across the door. It showed a woman in stockings reclining along a settee, one hand behind her head, the other down between her legs, fingers splayed, pulling apart the lips of her cunt. The page had been positioned so the gape of her cunt was right over the keyhole.

I tried to pick it off, said Miss Petrie, But they've used rather a lot of Sellotape. . .

A big guffaw of laughter went up from the boys crowding round about.

Shut up! shouted Rob, turning towards them. You lot are in serious trouble. Then he turned back to the teacher. Can I have the keys Miss Petrie? Thanks. He selected the right key, leant forward, and pressed it against the woman's cunt. It wouldn't go through, and Rob could feel himself starting to get heated.

Maybe if you. . . the teacher started.

Wheesht, said Rob, I'll manage. He wiggled the key about a

119

little, felt the glossy paper starting to give, then pushed it through the picture, right up the dame's arsehole. He turned the key, took a step forward, and shoved the door open.

There was cheering and a few whistles from the pupils.

Right, get in and shut up, he said loudly. The kids started jostling through the door, barging him and the teacher as they passed.

Nice picture of you, Miss, said one wee boy as he passed. Rob flicked out his arm and caught the boy across the back of the head with his hand.

Jesus! cried the wee boy, but other folk swept in after him and carried him away.

The teacher turned to him. Thanks for that, Mr eh. . .

Rob.

Thanks Mr Robb. I'm sure I would've got in any minute, but. . . but. . .

No problem, he said, over the shoulders of the last few pupils. I've done it before.

She blinked at him.

Opened stuck locks, he said.

She jutted out her jaw. I'll find out who did this, she said. He'll pay, I promise. Straight to Mr Moran! His parents will. . .

Stop!

Rob raised an arm and blocked the doorway to the last pupil. It was Sandra Burnett. She looked at him, curling her top lip.

What's the matter, Mr Robb?

Rob chuckled. I think we may have found the culprit already, Miss Petrie.

You're joking! cried the girl.

Surely not? said the teacher.

120

I have good reason to suspect her, said Rob, dropping his arm and taking hold of Sandra's elbow instead.

I never did nothing!

Come on, you're guilty through and through. I'm sure the head will agree. Let's go.

Do you want me to come? said the teacher.

That won't be necessary, said Rob. I'll explain the situation to Mr Moran. But I will take the evidence.

He pulled the key out of the lock, handed it to the teacher, then got his fingernail under the edge of the Sellotape and started to peel it off.

Don't rip her, jannie! somebody called from the classroom, but Rob ignored it. He pulled the sticky tape off all round the picture, taking off flakes of paint in a couple of places, then turned, the picture in one hand, the other pressing into the small of Sandra's back.

Let's go, he said.

Are you sure. . . said the teacher.

Leave this to me, he said over his shoulder, pushing the girl away down the corridor.

At the top of the stairs, Rob stopped. I've changed my mind, he said. Come back.

Quite right, said Sandra, turning towards him.

Aye, I'm going to sort this out myself, he went on. Moran's soft, but I never am. He reached in the pocket of his dust coat and pulled out his big chain of keys.

I don't believe this, said Sandra.

You'd better, said Rob. I've had enough of your provocations.

Beside the double doors to the canteen was a small store room. Rob unlocked it, stepped inside, and flicked the light on.

Come on, he said.

Sandra slouched in, letting her bag slip off her shoulder and onto the floor.

Rob pulled the door shut, and went past her and some stacks of plastic chairs to the far end of the room. A couple extra canteen tables were collecting dust there. He laid the picture of the naked woman on the nearest table, and flattened it out with the palms of his hands. He examined it. The woman had curly blonde hair but black pubes. Her mouth was open and her head thrown back, as if flashing her gash to the cameraman was giving her multiple orgasms. A shuffle behind Rob reminded him he wasn't alone.

Come and look at this, he said.

Sandra sighed. It wasn't me, she said. Do you think I'm thick?

I know this is your kind of thing, he said. Come and look at it.

She came up beside him and glanced at the woman, then away.

Do you think this is funny? he said. Eh? Do you?

No.

So why did you do it?

I didn't.

Do you think it's funny to try and shock your teacher?

She shrugged.

Look at it! Would you like to find this stuck over your front door?

I told you. I don't like to look at the pictures. I like to read the stories.

Stories? Jesus, don't give me stories!

I'm not! It's nothing to do with me! My dad would kill me if I started tearing pictures out of his magazines. . .

She said more, but Rob didn't listen. He was concentrating on turning the picture over, peeling it off carefully in a couple of places where the remains of the Sellotape had stuck to the tabletop. On one side of the back was a series of small photos showing the model stripping off, on the other side was a few paragraphs where the girl told about her sex life, and about her greatest sex fantasy. Rob read it.

The model said the fantasy that turned her on most was being the girl at a boxing match that holds up the board between rounds with the round number on it. She said she dreamed of noticing that one of the boxers had a big hard-on under his shorts as she paraded past, and within seconds him and her were having wild sex in the middle of the ring, with all the bright lights shining, the crowd cheering them on. And when the first boxer came, the second one was waiting to take over, sweat glistening on his chest muscles as he flung himself on top of her. At the end the referee held her hands in the air and the crowd went wild: she was the champion. The model said, What really gets my pussy wet is the idea of those guys touching me with their boxing gloves. I love the feel of leather on my skin, and the thought of them stroking me all over with their big gloved fists is enough to make me come right here and now!

Somebody was breathing loudly. It was Sandra. She was leaning over the table at Rob's side, reading the same bit he'd just read. He watched her face. Her lips were moving slightly, her eyes darting back and forth along the lines of print. Heavy breaths were making her body tremble.

He went to say something, to tell her to get away from the porn and wise the fuck up, but didn't. He kept watching her, watched till her eyes reached the bottom of the page. For a second she let them rest there, as if hoping more print would appear from somewhere, then she straightened up and turned to face him, looked him in the eye, lips parted over her small white teeth.

What do you think of that then? Rob said quietly, staring into her eyes. Is that the kind of story you like?

The lassie's daft, said Sandra.

How?

For wanting the men to be wearing gloves. Feeling hands holding you, sliding all over you, that's the best bit about it.

They looked at each other, Rob staring at her eyes, her staring back.

Then he seized her, leapt forward and wrapped his arms round her shoulders, pushed his face against hers, his mouth searching for her mouth and finding it, and kissing. And immediately she kissed back, opening her lips and sticking her tongue between his. She started to wriggle, so he tightened the grip of his arms, but she moved her mouth to one side and said, I want to. . . so he slackened his hold for a moment and her arms went out around him. They kissed. Their top teeth banged together. Rob pulled away for a second, then plunged in again, kissing as hard as he could, and now his arms were beneath her denim jacket and T-shirt. Her skin was cold, he moved his hands over it, and behind his back he felt her rugging out his shirt-tails and sliding her hands down to cup his arse. Suddenly he fell to his knees in front of her, jammed his face against her T-shirt, and felt for a nipple with his teeth. Her breasts were small, but the nipples stood out through the cotton, and he took one between his front teeth and rolled it around with his tongue.

Her hands squeezed his shoulders, she made a noise, and he grunted back. Fingers, she said, I love fingers. . .

He let his hands fall to the ground, then found and gripped her ankles. He slid his hands up her legs, up over the knees, up under the black skirt, up to the bottom of her pants. He tried to pull them down, but couldn't get a decent grip under the tight skirt, so instead used one hand to pull the crotch down slightly, and eased the other hand inside. It was hot in there, and there was some frizzy hair.

Fingers, she said, but he was working his hand over her mound, up and down, cross and across. . . then he paused and pushed his hand up and back, his first finger shoving inside her warm wet cunt.

She made a noise and he twisted his finger. The elastic of her pants was cutting into the back of his wrist, but he kept working his finger in and out, round and round. And a sweet smell poured out of her now, his face was at her waist looking down at his arms disappearing up her skirt, and his mouth was full of a sweet smell of pure sex as her hips pushed forwards against his face.

Fuck, fuck, fuck, she was saying to herself in time with the rhythm of her hips, and with the same rhythm she was mashing his head against her, kneading his shoulders, tugging his hair.

Oh fuck, oh fuck, said Rob, and started to stand up. His cock was bursting inside his work breeks as he got to his feet. I'm going to come, he said, Jesus fuck. . .

Immediately she pushed his hands away from her, reached forward, undid his spaver.

Boxer shorts! said Sandra, and opened the fly on them. His cock stood out, almost vertical. It's red! she said, then spat on the palm of her right hand and started to smooth the spit in over the head of his cock.

Jesus, Jesus, I'm coming, I'm. . .

125

Sandra jerked her hand back, a spurt of spunk shot out of his cock and arced onto the tabletop. Then came another smaller blurt, then some drips, which fell to the floor. He closed his eyes and raised his face to the ceiling, leaning back on the edge of the table for support.

Jesus, said somebody. You are a hard man. It was Sandra.

He looked at her. She was pulling her skirt straight, looking from the trickle of spunk on the table to his cock, still standing, aching now.

Fuck, said Rob. Jesus fuck.

Sandra was smiling, pushing hair away from her forehead where it was sticky with sweat.

Fuck, said Rob.

I better get back to maths, said Sandra.

Rob closed his eyes. Fuck fucking fuck.

He heard her walking away across the room, and turned as if to speak. He couldn't think of anything to say, but just looked at her as she bent to pick up her bag. Her nipples were still standing out through her T-shirt: it would be obvious to the whole school what she'd been doing. Fuck fuck fuck. . .

Like I said, Mr Catto, that picture has nothing to do with me. So don't hassle me about it. She opened the door. And I won't hassle you.

She stepped out and walked away down the corridor towards the classrooms, leaving the door wide open. Rob pulled his dustcoat over his softening cock and sprang forward to close the door. Before he did he stuck his head out and watched her go. She seemed to be rolling her arse in an exaggerated sexy fashion, almost like she knew he'd be watching. But at the classroom door she didn't check to see if he was, just knocked and went in.

He pulled back inside the store, shut the door behind him, and breathed in the thick sweet and vinegary smells of the sex. He looked down the far end to the trails of spunk on the floor and tabletop.

Jesus Christ, he said to himself. What a fucking mess.

Probably he was just imagining it, but as he passed the buses he couldn't help feeling that the drivers were all sitting looking down on him and thinking he was shit. It was to do with the way they were high up on their seats behind their big steering wheels, and he was just daunering along the pavement. But also the way so many of the smug bastards were making a big point of showing how macho you had to be to drive a fucking bus. The one in the third coach along, for instance, a young guy wearing a cut-off T-shirt, seemed to be arranging the way he leant on the steering wheel in order to show off his bunched-up muscles most impressively. And what would he get out of it? A few giggles from the young girls as they got on board. It was pathetic. A couple buses further down was an enormous guy with a black bushy beard, who Rob'd heard was a top man in the heavy events on the Highland Games circuit. Not that Rob was impressed by that, but it just went to show you the type of cunt that went in for bus driving. The guy in the last bus was a brother of the heavy eventer. He didn't have a beard, just a big walrus moustache, but poking out from under it was a cigar about six inches long. The driver looked to Rob like he had a big cock sticking out of his face. Probably that was the effect the guy fucking wanted. What a gang of wankers! As if he and all the others thought there was some connection between driving a big bus and having a big prick. It was obvious that was what the drivers all thought, and Rob had to

127

stop himself bursting out laughing as he went by them, seeing right through to their stupidity. Rob had always been a believer in the theory that what you did with your cock was more important than the size of it. Not that his was small or anything, no fucking way, it probably was bigger than average, you could ask anyone. Well, not anyone, but anyone who'd seen it, and they'd say he had a big cock *and* knew what to do with it. And he didn't need a caber or a Cuban cigar to prove the point.

Except maybe this afternoon what he'd done hadn't been the best thing to do with it. He'd definitely let himself get led off the straight and narrow by that girl. She was even more depraved than he'd thought, he could see that now, and it was essential that he take control of the situation before she got him into serious trouble, public trouble.

Rob stepped back off the pavement and looked over the heads of the crowds of kids as they jostled along and onto the buses. Billy would've got round to the head of the turning circle by this time and would be watching over the steer there, but Rob didn't want to go and ask him if he'd seen Sandra. He didn't want the old bastard getting funny ideas in his head. More funny ideas. As if that masonic shite wasn't bad enough. . . But the first few buses had pulled away, and most of the folk who walked into town had already passed him, and he was beginning to think he'd missed her, or that she'd maybe gone off by some different route. The thought of missing her made his stomach turn over and his heart start racing: he was that wound up about talking to her and telling her she mustn't come near him again.

Then someone coughed behind him. He turned and gazed into the woods, and at first didn't see anyone. Then Sandra Burnett stepped out from behind a rhododendron for a second, looked at him while she took a drag on her fag, and moved back out of sight.

Rob glanced around the turning circle. None of the few folk left were paying him any attention, and the last coach of kids was just pulling away, hiding him from Billy for a couple seconds. He walked quickly into the trees, pushing his hands into his dustcoat pockets, and went round the bush Sandra had emerged from behind. She was sitting on a big granite boulder, smoking, but when she saw him coming she stubbed the fag on the stone and let it fall to the ground. Rob stopped in front of her.

For a second he just looked at her, then he said, Why are you sitting here?

She nodded towards the turning circle behind the tangled branches of the rhododendron. I'm waiting for everybody to go, she said.

Eh?

Then I can go home.

Rob frowned. Why do you have to wait till they're all gone?

I hate them. I'm not going near them, not even to walk down the road.

Rob made a face. You must have some friends.

They all hate me. She laughed, and looked up at Rob. He didn't laugh.

I'm sure that's not right, he said. But anyway, that's not what I wanted to talk to you about. . .

Melissa Gowan was my best friend, she broke in. But she's in the hospital now for not eating. Ken what I said to her? I said, If you're going to kill yourself, Mel, why not do it right out and get it over with? Don't fuck your friends about with this slow starvation routine. Hih. They wouldn't let me visit her after that.

129

She reached into the bag at her feet, took out a packet of Silk Cut, flipped the lid open, then hesitated as if carefully selecting before taking out a cigarette and putting it between her lips. She fished out a lighter from the pocket of her denim jacket and lit up.

Listen, said Rob. I wanted to sort a few things out.

I'll tell you, Sandra went on, as if she hadn't heard him, I could show her a thing or two about suicide. And I might yet. I don't see why I shouldn't. Everybody hates me and I hate everybody so what's the point of living? One of these days I'm going to jump off a cliff and be done with it.

Here! Sandra! Sandra, Sandra, Sandra! Don't talk like that!

She looked at him, her lips pouting. Why shouldn't I? Give me one good reason.

Well. . . for a start, not everybody hates you.

Oh yeah? Name one.

Your mother and father.

Ha! It's well seen you've never met them.

What do you mean? Having fights with them are you? Sandra, that's just the age you're at.

It's an age I've been at for fourteen and a half years then. She shook her head, blowing out smoke. They hate each other and they hate me, full stop.

Well, what about. . .

Don't mention teachers, please. I'm not one of the clever ones the teachers dote on. And I'm not one of the thick ones they're paid to like. I'm just in the middle. They don't even notice me except for when they're giving me a row for something.

That's not true, he said.

Well, she said. Why did you come seeking me out? Was it not

to give me a row? Was it not to go on again about my reading matter? Or blame me for things I didn't do? She looked him in the eye. Or call me a slag for things I did do. Come on Mr Catto, spit it out, why were you looking for me? I know why: cause you hate me, and you can't bear to let me forget it.

Rob gazed at her. I don't hate you, he said.

She didn't reply, just stared off into the depths of the wood, smoking.

Sandra. She ignored him. Slowly he put his hand out, reached towards her, and let it rest on her shoulder. She looked round and up into his face. Sandra, he said, I don't hate you. She turned her head to look at his hand on her shoulder, then tilted her face. And she kissed the back of his hand.

Spelks of electricity shot up his arm, his chestbones contracted round his insides, his head buzzed, his cock kicked.

Thank you, she said.

He took his hand from her shoulder and slowly drew it back towards him, but she grabbed it before he could put it back in his pocket. Gazing at the hand, seeming to examine it from the nails to the hairs at his wrist, she said, I don't hate you either. I'm sorry if I've been giving you a hard time. It's just. . . the rest of the world hates me, so why shouldn't you?

He moved his free hand and placed it on her other shoulder. I care for you Sandra, I do. He stroked her hair, one long slow stroke, and moved his hand under it to touch the soft skin at the back of her neck. Her head bowed forward and she kissed the hand she was holding again.

I care for you, he said. And I'd like to help you. That's why I think. . . me and you. . . well, what happened this afternoon was a

131

mistake. We mustn't ever let on about that, and we mustn't ever do it again.

She kissed the tip of each of his fingers in turn. In school? she said.

He shifted his stance to ease the pressure on his hardened cock. Aye, he said. We must never do that kind of stuff in school again.

In the bedroom he stripped off and chucked his dirty clothes into the laundry basket next to the wardrobe. Then he wrapped a towel round his waist and nipped downstairs into the bathroom and turned on the shower. When the water came steaming he stepped in, drew the plastic curtain round him, and started washing: hair, then oxters, then groin. He bent over under the spray of the water. There were globs of gummy spunk stuck on the barbs of his pubic hair and under his foreskin. He put shampoo on his pubes and scrubbed it into a lather, and he held his cock under the force of the shower to wash it clean. Then he quickly did his feet, let the hot water rinse him all down for a few seconds, and turned it off.

He went up the stairs, dried himself, and started getting dressed. He paused after pulling on his fresh boxer shorts and listened. No, it hadn't been Karen coming in. It hadn't been anything. But it set him thinking.

He stepped over to the laundry basket, picked his old boxers off the top, and brought them up towards his face. He sniffed. They reeked of sweat, and of spunk-drops leaked from his unwashed cock all afternoon. He crumpled them up and thrust them down into the depths of the laundry basket, mixing them with the dirty clothes near the bottom, which dated back to the last time him and Karen had fucked, a week or so before.

Rob was getting changed into his shorts and T-shirt when Billy walked into the bothy.

Christ, you're getting keen!

Aye, said Rob. I just felt like a bit of a stretch over the break. I mean, you're on canteen duty, I'm off, so I thought I'd get a bit of fresh air in my lungs for half an hour or so.

Quite right, said Billy, going over to the sink and starting to wash his hands.

I mean, what would I do otherwise? Sit here and read my paper, put my feet up: nothing useful.

Good to get a rest though, surely?

No, makes more sense to go out and stretch myself a bit. I mean in our job you have to be prepared for anything, don't you? Battle fitness should be essential at all times.

Aye, said Billy, using the towel hanging by the sink.

There's nothing strange about it at all, said Rob. It's a good thing to do. Fighting fucking fit.

Billy laughed. Christ, Rob. Am I slagging you for it?

No, no, it's just. . .

Go on yourself! said Billy. I used to be all for fitness. When I was in the police, ken. I did those Canadian Airforce routines every day. Till I got injured. That was when I had to stop.

It's good to be fit, said Rob. Healthy body, healthy mind.

Billy sighed. I haven't had much choice since I got kicked by that fucking horse!

Rob started jumping up and down on the spot. That how you got your gammy leg, is it?

What? No, that's arthritis! The horse kicked me in the bloody head!

Rob laughed. So that's your excuse!

Here, said Billy. It's not funny, loon. It was in the course of duty, as well. During the miners' strike.

Rob stretched out, then up, pressed his hands against the ceiling. Ancient history, he said.

A load of us were sent down from here to Fife, you see, to boost the numbers at the picket lines. And one morning these mounted boys were called in as well – god knows why. Anyway, one of the miners. . .

Rob went over and opened the door of the bothy. Listen, he said, I'd like to sit and hear all this, but I reckon I should get going, ken, otherwise I won't get any exercise at all.

It's quickly told, said Billy.

Not quickly enough, said Rob. You lived didn't you? So why make a big thing out of it?

Oh. Billy shrugged. Some other time then: I could tell you over a pint, some night.

Aye, said Rob. Some Sunday through the week.

He stepped out into the corridor, walked down to the Tradesman's Entrance, and ran away across the car park. He didn't head for the woods, but kept straight on and out the main gates of the school, past several bunches of kids. He turned left, jogged up the road and started to run towards the town centre. Then he stopped, as if changing his mind, and doubled back, heading out the path that led towards the cliffs.

They met where the clifftop path joined the narrow one through the woods. They didn't speak at first. When Rob saw her coming hurrying through the trees, he turned, glanced up and down the cliff path, then walked off it towards the sea, down a slope covered in gorse and bracken. When he got to a clear patch of grass he

134

stopped and waited. There was another couple yards of grass, and then the ground fell away in a low but sheer cliff. He could hear the waves battering away at the base of it. And now there was the sound of her pushing through the whins. He turned, and she emerged, breathless, and dropped her bag to the ground. For a second they just looked. Then she took a step towards him, he reached out to her, and they went for each other.

The kissing was very brief, and then she had her hands in his shorts, one gripping a buttock, the other writhing amongst his cock and balls. He tugged her blouse out of her skirt and ran his hands up the sides of her body, ribs corrugating against his fingertips. She wasn't wearing a bra, and his thumbs met the upslopes of her breasts and glided up and onto her nipples, pressing them in against her bony chest, rolling them in circles.

She pulled away, and he opened his mouth to speak, but shut it again as he saw her taking off her denim jacket, then unzipping the side of her skirt and letting it fall to the grass.

Don't look, she said, but he'd already seen she was wearing small white pants, and he didn't need to look any more anyway, his hands went down the sides of them, rested on the flanks of her thighs for a second, then eased the pants down. He moved one hand to cup the whole of her arse, and the other to aim between the front of her legs, rubbing at the curved mound under the soft crinkly hair there, rubbing and slipping in further as she moved her legs slightly apart. His middle finger grooved in between the lips of her cunt and he bent it from the second knuckle and pushed it up inside her, and she let out a yelp and clasped her arms tight about his neck. He started to push her down towards the ground, and she immediately hung all her weight around his neck and tucked her feet around his calves, so when her back hit the grass he was placed perfectly on top of her, and the top of his cock, poking above the waistband of his shorts, snugged in against the mouth of her cunt. He started to push it in further, then made himself stop. He looked her in the eyes.

Should we be doing this? he said.

I need you, she said.

Good, he said. Eh, are you on the pill?

She didn't answer, but reached out and felt in the pocket of her jacket that lay to one side. She took out a packet of three and handed it to him.

Right, he said, and ripped open the wee box. He held one of the condoms in his teeth till he'd torn the end off its wrapping and got it out. He fitted the thing onto the top of his knob, then rolled it on. The stuff they greased the rubber with was cold, and for half a second he thought he felt his erection starting to fade, but then he looked down at the girl lying beneath him, her blouse raised up over her small breasts, plastic pearl studs in her ears, and he forgot to worry and lowered himself into her, moved her legs further apart with his knees, then put a hand down to her cunt, rubbed it a little with his fingers.

All this time she'd been lying still, but the instant he moved his fingers out of the way and eased his cock forward and into her cunt, tight as the neck of a bottle, she started bucking her hips like crazy. He put his hands down under her buttocks to help him stay inside, and she thrust up against him as he drove his cock into her, wrapped her legs round his again, her heels digging into the soft bends behind his knees. Her arms hugged him tightly.

He could feel her nails jagging into his flesh just below each shoulder blade, he could feel her hips banging into his as she flung herself against him again and again, and he could feel the spunk

136

working up a head of steam at the base of his cock. He brought one hand round to check the doob was still pulled up to the hilt, then lifted the hand to lie on her breast, trapping a nipple between thumb and first finger. He squeezed it hard, and she gasped.

I'm going to come, he said,

Say you love me, she said.

Ah Christ, Christ, I'm fucking, fucking . . .

His back arched, his head rearing up away from hers, and he held there for a couple seconds, his face twisting, lips pulling back from his teeth, eyes screwed shut, and she held him even tighter. Then he relaxed down onto her.

Quarter of a minute later he said, Let us go will you Sandra? I'm feart of this thing falling off.

No! She tightened her arms and legs about him.

Sandra! Let me go!

No!

Right. He forced his arms out the way, using most of his strength, and broke her hold, then knelt up, pressing her feet in between his thighs and the backs of his calves.

She gave a cry, and let him go.

Finger and thumb holding the condom onto his softening cock, he stood up, hobbled a couple of steps away, shorts around his ankles, and looked down at her. She was just lying there, not even starting to tidy her clothes, breasts and sparse haired cunt still on show.

Fuck's sake girl, he said. Cover yourself a bit.

She hesitated, then started pulling up her pants.

He turned away, eased the doob off his shrivelled prick, held it up for a second to look at the gob of glue inside, then tossed the thing high into the air, away towards the sea. It didn't fall immediately, but was tumbled by the breeze whisking up off the cliff. Droplets of sperm scattered out of it and blew back inland, spattering down on Rob as he stood there, arm still raised from chucking the thing away.

Fuck's sake! He danced about, but it was no use, blobs of stuff landed on his bare arms, his T-shirt, his face.

Behind him Sandra laughed. It's raining spunk! she cried, and started giggling like crazy.

It's not funny, he said, wiping at his face, trying to get the spots of still warm sperm off his cheeks and lips.

It is! she said, laughing and gasping for breath. It's like God's having a wank.

What?

She gulped for air, paused, then laughed some more. I've worked it out, she said at last. The world's just a big *Razzle* for God, a big porn mag. Whenever he's a bittie bored sitting up there, he looks down and somewhere, somewhere in the world, somebody's having a shag. And God gets out his giant cock, and he looks down at us lying here doing it, and he's. . . uh. . . uh. . . uh! She wanked an enormous cock, two-handed, in front of her. I'm coming. . . oh. . . oh. . . Ahh! She flung her arms aside, opened her eyes, and looked up at Rob. And down it all comes, buckets of spunk all over us!

Her face was split with a grin, and there were tears in her eyes with all the laughing.

You're sick, said Rob.

I am, eh?

He nodded. I like it, he said. He tucked his T-shirt inside his shorts. Do you think we really were being watched? he said, and started looking around.

I reckon that's why God made the world in the first place, so he'd have a 3-D blue movie twenty-four hours a day.

Rob turned to her, scanned the whins behind her for movement, then shrugged. I saw a guy out near here, he said. A funny guy. Don't ken what to make of him. . .

Forget him, said Sandra. Come and sit down.

He frowned. Better get back, I think.

What! I want to have a fag!

Well, you do that. I'll just get going.

No, she said, I want to talk.

He sighed. Why do women always want to talk after sex?

She looked at her watch. It had a cartoon character on the face of it. It's only ten to one, she said. You don't have to leave till ten past.

Five past.

Okay, but that still leaves us fifteen minutes. She shifted to one side a little, and patted her hand on the ground beside her.

Rob gathered some phlegm into his mouth and gobbed it out, with the wind, into the bushes. Then he sat down. Sandra laid a hand on his thigh, just where his shorts stopped, but he didn't react. She took her hand away, reached for her bag and got her cigarettes out. She held the packet out to him, he gave his head a shake. She took one for herself, lit up, then put the gear away again. For half a minute she concentrated on the fag, and he stared ahead. She looked at him.

Say something, she said.

He shrugged.

Go on.

I can't think of anything, he said.

Oh. She took a big draw on her Silk Cut, and blew the smoke into his face. He blinked. Did you never smoke? she said.

When I was young, he said. About sixteen.

Sixteen? Call that young?

Well. . . I smoked a fair bit when I was at school and when I first started working. But then I stopped.

Just like that?

Just like that. I decided I wanted to be fit, not a wheezing old wreck, so I stopped smoking and started running. Running, squash, a bit of five a side.

My mum's always giving up, but I always encourage her to start again. That way I can scrounge fags off her when I'm skint.

Rob cleared his throat. Giving up's easy. You just ask yourself, who's the boss, me or this fag? And if you decide it's you, which I did, you've got the wee bastards beat.

She looked at the half-smoked cigarette in her fingers. Who's the boss? she said to it. The fag didn't reply.

Rob sniffed. I'm the boss, he said.

She nodded, raising the fag to her lips again. They sat in silence.

Getting chilly, said Rob after a while. It's the wind off the sea. And these shorts.

You were hot enough earlier on, she said.

So were you. Fucking wild, you were girl.

She smiled. Is that not good?

Fuck's sake. Where did you learn to behave like that?

Oh. . . here and there.

You're not a virgin, then?

I told you I wasn't.

He nodded, frowned. Have you done it with a lot of folk?

140

Och no more than two or three. . . She looked at him out of the corners of her eyes. At any one time.

What?

Ihm-hm.

I don't believe you!

Believe what you like. I'm telling you.

Fuck's sake. He looked at her.

She raised her cigarette, sucked it in and out of her puckered lips a few times.

You are fucking wild, he said.

She leant her head on one side, looking at him.

Who were these guys? Boys at the school?

God no! They're so immature, even the sixth years.

Who then?

She reached over for her skirt and pulled it on, lifting her bum slightly to get it all the way up. Then she tucked in her blouse, zipped up the skirt, and said, That's for me to know.

And for me to find out?

She shrugged, stubbed out her fag on the ground in between their legs. You don't know them. Who cares anyway?

Do you not?

She paused, leant towards him, looking him in the eye. I care about you, she said. And you care about me. Don't you? You said you did. I just about fainted when you said it and put your hand on my shoulder.

Ha, Christ! So how did it feel when I put my hand on your fanny?

That felt good. But it was that touch on the shoulder that really got me. Your hand was so warm.

141

He looked at her, then jumped up. Speaking of warm, he said, I'm fucking freezing.

She got to her feet too, and put her arms around his waist. Thanks, she said.

You know, he said, We shouldn't be doing this.

Will we come here again?

He looked at her. Yes.

Tomorrow?

Yes.

Rob got a pizza out of the freezer and put it on dual micro/grill for four minutes. He laid a plate and cutlery on the table and sat there, looking across at the microwave on the unit by the sink. Behind the smoked glass the pizza was slowly rotating. Rob picked up his fork and knife and clutched them, forearms resting on the cold tabletop as he waited.

Come on you bastard, he said after a few seconds. Hurry up for fuck's sake.

The fan hummed and the pizza turned. The timer clicked down: 59, 58, 57. . .

Fuck's sake, that'll surely do!

He jumped up, rounded the table, and pressed the button that opened the door. He waited for the pizza to come sliding out on its platter. It didn't. That was the CD he'd been thinking of.

He grabbed his plate off the table, brought it to the mouth of the microwave, and shovelled the pizza off the turntable and onto it. He left the door of the oven open to let the steam escape, sat down at the table, and started to eat.

He cut the pizza into quarters, then into eighths. He slipped the tip of his knife under the point of one of the segments and rolled it up towards the thick end. Then he speared it with his fork and lifted it up to have a closer examination: it looked like a swiss roll, except with cheese and tomato sauce instead of cream and jam. Imagine a cream and strawberry jam pizza! He laughed, and took the chance while his mouth was open and the pizza unawares to stick the roll into his gob.

As he chewed a memory came back to him from when he was a kid. He was sitting at the kitchen table in the Froglands flat, it was teatime, and his dad was yelling, Don't play with your food! And Rob, ten years old, he was shouting back, Why not? I've no one else to play with! Rob grinned now at the thought of his cheek. His dad hadn't found it funny, though. He'd grabbed the back of Rob's head and pushed his face down into the plate of mince and doughballs. Rob screamed, although the food wasn't very hot, it wasn't burning him – he just felt that some kind of protest was required. His dad rubbed his nose in it a second, then let him go. When he straightened up there was gravy all over his face, and particles of mince up his nostrils. Clean yourself up for god's sake, said his dad, and Rob went over to the sink. He was trying not to cry. His bottom lip was stuck out a mile to catch any tears that did escape down his cheeks.

This was as far as the memory went: Rob standing at the kitchen sink and looking out the window as he dichted his face. Down in the street the kids his parents didn't like him to play with were having a game of kick-the-can. His folks thought they were better than their neighbours – cause his dad was *skilled*, a pipefitter, a man with a *skill* for joining up pipes so the gas didn't leak out for fuck's sake – and they didn't want Robert getting over-friendly with the unskilleds' kids and picking up dirt and flechs and bad words. What Rob remembered was standing at the window looking out and promising to himself that when he grew up he'd let no one tell him who his friends should be. No matter where they came from, no matter how unskilled or muckit they were, he'd play with whoever the fuck he wanted.

A hand clapped down on his shoulder, he leapt and yelled.

Rob! It's only me.

Jesus Christ Karen!

She started laughing.

Where did you spring from?

Spring from? I walked in the front door! Where were you, that's the question! Off in some dream world!

I was in Froglands.

Nightmare world, then. . . She squashed in between Rob and the edge of the table and sat on his knees.

Karen! I'm eating my tea!

She put her arms around his neck. Eat me, she said, and went to kiss him.

He turned his face away, reached behind her and picked up a whang of pizza. He brought it round, fingers propping the edges up to stop the toppings sliding off, and tried to eat, but Karen was still nuzzling about his mouth. She laughed as he turned his head away, snapping at the pizza.

You must choose between us! she said in a sultry voice. Either the pizza goes or I do!

While she was speaking, Rob jammed as much of the slice as he could into his gob and started chewing. Karen made a growling noise and seized the crusty end of the slice in her teeth. As Rob chomped, she jerked her head back, trying to tear some of the pizza away from him.

Get your own! cried Rob, his mouth full of dough.

Karen just growled, shook her head from side to side, finally coming away with a mouthful of base and tomato sauce. A long rope of elastic cheese stretched from the piece in her mouth to the piece in his, getting longer and thinner as the two of them pulled in their opposite directions.

It's mine! growled Karen.

Have it, said Rob, and, swallowing the half-chewed stuff in his mouth, nipped his front teeth together, severing the band of cheese and letting it go whacking back across Karen's lips and cheek. Immediately, he leant forward, got the loose end of the cheese in his mouth and gobbled it down, sucking it away from Karen's face, chewing and swallowing at the same time.

For a second Karen just sat there, but then she opened her jaws, as if to start on her end of the cheese; Rob saw his chance, flicked his head back, and it came flying out of her mouth, fragments of bread base still stuck to it, and flopped down his chin and onto the collar of his shirt.

Bastard! she cried.

He sooked hard, and fed the cheese in with his lips. Ah-ha! he said, as the last length of it disappeared. She glowered, making on like she was upset at her loss. He chomped his jaws up and down a few times, then stopped chewing and looked Karen straight in the eye. He opened his mouth wide and slid out his tongue, pushing the mess of cheese and slavers on it right into her face. Ah-ha!

Gyaads! She leant away from him, pushing her hands against his chest. That's disgusting!

He laughed, pressed closer towards her, eyes staring, spit dribbling off his tongue.

Robbie! Gyaad's sake! She held him away with one hand, and wriggled off his knees. Once she'd got her feet on the ground, she dashed towards the sink, making groaning noises as if she was going to chuck up.

Rob laughed: something was coming over him. With Karen out of the way he could get his hands on the plateful of pizza again. He snatched up another slice and stuffed it into his mouth, still laughing. He picked up two more bits, one in each hand, and waved them in front of him.

Karen turned from the sink having wiped some tomato sauce from her face. She grinned when she saw him and shook her head.

You're a mental case, she said.

He tossed one of the pizza slices towards her. She dodged, and it landed on the draining board.

Robbie! Don't!

He threw the other slice straight at her. She tried to catch it, but it slithered through her hands and down the front of her blouse.

God's sake! Robbie Catto!

His hands now free, he took hold of the crust hanging out of his mouth and tore it clear. It's funny, he said, chewed some more, and swallowed. You didn't seem to mind when that bastard Grant was doing it the other night. *His* tongue's alright is it? Eh? Fucking eh?

Robbie. . . what?

So don't go slobbering over my food woman. I don't want your slavers mixed up with mine – I never ken where your mouth's been, or what's been in it.

I don't ken what you're talking about. . .

Get your fangs round his whang, did you?

Robbie! What's got into you?

He didn't answer, just snatched up his plate with the remaining pizza, banged out of the kitchen and into the bathroom across the hallway. He locked the door behind him, put the lid of the bog down, and started eating. He sat there till he'd finished the lot.

First thing, Rob had had to set out chairs in the science video room. Now, two periods later, he was meant to clear them away again. But when he walked in, there were papers and lumps of plastic spread over the front table, and somebody was crouched down by the video machine. Rob hesitated, then walked forward.

Having trouble? he said.

The guy looked round. He had on a spotty bow tie, he wasn't a teacher. Fuck's sake, no teacher could get away with wearing one of those. The kids would never give him peace about it.

I think the cassette's stuck in the machine, the guy said.

Rob went over, looked down. The red light's out: you've got it switched off, he said. You must have pressed off instead of stop, or something.

Oh, said the guy, glanced down at the video again, and pressed operate. The red light blinked on. Then he pressed another button, and the cassette was ejected. He pulled it out, pressed off, and stood up. Thanks, he said.

No bother, said Rob. But are you finished here? Cause I was going to clear the chairs and that.

The guy started shuffling his papers together and piling the lumps of plastic into a hold-all he lifted from under the table. Certainly, he said. Carry on. I'm just a bit behind: not used to talking to more than one person at a time, you see! I got a bit flustered with forty people asking questions and so on!

Rob nodded, and went to start stacking the chairs in the front row. But as he bent to lift the first one, the block the guy was stashing away caught his eye.

147

Here, he said. Is that what I think it is?

Eh. . . The guy looked down. If you're thinking it's a scale model of the female reproductive organs, yes, he said, and pulled the block out of his bag again.

Rob went over and looked at the arrangement of different coloured tubes and bags encased in the plastic, which he now saw was shaped to suggest a waist, spreading out into hips at the base. A cleft nicked out of the bottom showed where the legs joined on.

So that's what it all looks like! he said, and laughed. I did wonder!

The guy put the block back in his bag, and started putting his papers away in a couple of folders. Now you know, he said. As do all the fifth and sixth years. I've been giving them their sex education, he said.

Rob nodded. I mind that, he said. It was all about frogs and spawn attached to reeds. For years I thought women floated a bunch of eggs in the bath and waited for their husband to come along and dribble sperm over them!

The guy chuckled. I hope you know better now, he said.

Christ aye, said Rob. And I'll tell you something: so do the kids. You're too late coming to see them in fifth and sixth year. Because (a) you've got all the smart kids there, and they'll've done it already in biology. And (b) because all the thick ones that left in fourth year had been shagging away for ages before that. Christ, half the lassies probably left in fourth year because they were pregnant.

The guy clicked his video into its case. We see a few very early pregnancies down at the health centre, he said. But they're pretty rare. One or two a year maybe.

Rob sat down on a seat in the front row. You're a doctor? he said. You'll ken my mother-in-law then. Liz: head receptionist.

Of course, said the doctor. She's been there a lot longer than I have.

Christ aye! Rob laughed. She's been there since you guys were giving out prescriptions for leeches. Since they used to do amputations with their bare teeth. In fact, I reckon she's done a few of those herself!

The doctor chuckled, put his folders into his bag and zipped it up. Well, he said. I better get back: I'm doing the lunchtime surgery today.

Rob jumped up. Wait! he said. I've something to ask you.

The doctor paused. About reproduction?

No! I ken all about that! It's my specialist subject!

I haven't got long, said the doctor.

Rob glanced towards the door, checking it was shut, then said in a quiet voice, I was wanting to ask you about loonies.

Pardon?

Well, one particular loony. He's been on my mind, see, but I didn't ken who to talk to about him. But now that you're here. . .

The doctor glanced at his watch.

What are you doing that for? said Rob.

I do have to get back for the surgery.

Aye, but this'll just take a minute. What I want to know is, are loonies allowed to just wander the country these days? I mean, should they not be locked up somewhere?

The doctor cleared his throat. I presume you're talking about people suffering from mental illness, he said.

Aye, that's right, said Rob. Loonies. Weirdos as well, ken.

I'd rather not use those terms, said the doctor. I mean, if

someone had an illness of the kidney – or of the reproductive organs! – you wouldn't call them weirdos. So why use that word to talk about people with illnesses of the mind? What does that say about your attitudes?

Rob took hold of the doctor's elbow. Listen, he said. We're not talking about me. We're talking about folk, mentally sick folk – fair enough – who're wandering the countryside, hanging about outside schools and the like. Maybe they're harmless, or maybe they're not, but what I want to know is: shouldn't they be locked up till we find out?

The doctor sighed. It's a complex subject, he said. And there's a lot of disagreement. But the current practice is to keep people in hospital – locked up, as you would say – for as short a period as possible. Then they're released into the community, and cared for there.

But what if there's no one to care for them? said Rob.

There are CPNs, said the doctor. Community Psychiatric Nurses. And there are supervised hostels – though too few, it's true. Depot injections can be useful, too: the patient sees a doctor or CPN once a month, say, and gets a slow-release dose of whatever medication keeps them on an even keel.

But what if they're dangerous? Never mind caring for the weirdo! Who's going to care for the *community*?

Actually. . .

From what you've said, Rob interrupted, There could be dozens of dangerous lunatics roving the countryside as we speak! Jesus! Think about that! It's scary!

Actually, the doctor repeated, The vast majority of folk with mental illnesses are of no danger to. . .

Something should be done, said Rob. Something *must* be

done! Before innocent people start getting hurt! Before children start getting hurt! These weirdos must be dealt with!

The doctor looked at him. I better get back to the centre, he said after a second, picking up his hold-all.

And I better get out to those woods, said Rob. Fuck stacking chairs! This is a matter of life and death!

I'm going to be more careful from now on, said Rob. See yesterday? I had to go and dunk my head in a sinkful of water! Donald and Billy kept going, You've something in your hair boss, what's that? It was spunk! Drops of spunk that fell there. So. . .

He held the condom out at arm's length, and dropped it amongst the tangled roots of a broom bush.

How about. . . your wife?

I had a shower when I got home. She's working late this week, so I'd plenty time.

She won't suspect anything?

Na.

Not even with that big lovebite on your neck?

What! Rob clapped a hand up, then saw she was laughing. He laughed too. I'll give you a lovebite, he said. I'll bite your bloody tits off!

She acted terrified, pulled her blouse together across her chest.

No, like I say, said Rob, Karen's got this good job, she works late quite often. She's really into it, her job. I mean, her *career*.

Oh yeah.

Aye. Rob found his shorts and pulled them on.

Working late at the office, eh?

Rob stopped. What do you mean by that?

151

Well, it's the oldest excuse in the book, isn't it? Working late! Like you're working over your dinner break!

Some folk do have to work late, you ken. You'll find this out when you have to get a job. I mean, I work late, and I work some weekends: that doesn't mean I'm screwing around.

But you are screwing around.

He looked down at her, grinned. Oh aye!

She stubbed out the last of her fag and got herself dressed. See if your wife's working late, she said as she tied the laces on her trainers. Why don't we go back to your place after school, fuck on a proper bed, save my back getting pricked and scratched by the undergrowth?

Sometimes it's better doing it in weird places, said Rob. It can get boring in the same old bed.

Not for me, said Sandra. I've never done it in a bed.

Have you not?

I've never even slept in a double bed.

Rob shook his head. That's what I'm worried about, he said. Us shagging ourselves senseless and falling asleep, Karen coming home and finding us.

Sandra stood up and came over towards him. She put her hands on his arse and rubbed her groin against his. I bet it's a big brass bed, she said. Imagine it, Rob: you could tie me to the bedposts, ravish me, do what you liked to me. . .

Rob kissed the top of her head. I do do what I like to you.

There must be more, she said. More I can do to please you. Come on, tell me, tell me and I'll do it, I want to make you happy. . . She squeezed herself tight against him.

You are pleasing me, he said. Fuck's sake, I wouldn't be here if you weren't extremely fucking pleasing to me.

There must be more than this. . .

Okay, okay, there's more! He broke her hold on him, paced away a couple steps. There's chocolate bars up the fanny, you haven't done that! That would be more.

Chocolate bars?

Aye! Here's what happens: we're raring to go, right, and I've got this Mars bar in my mouth – my teeth round the wrapper, just like a fucking condom – and I bend you over in front of me, rip open the wrapper, then take the Mars bar down and shove it up your arsehole!

What? She looked almost shocked.

I'll shove it in, ease it in, push it in all the way, till you have a king-size Mars bar right up your arse. Then, ken what I'll do? I'll lie down and get you to crouch over me. I'll lick all the melted chocolate from up and down your crack, then I'll say, Push . . . And you'll strain a little, and Mars bar'll come sliding out of your bum, inching out slowly, and I'll lie there, gobbling it up, chewing it inch by inch, eating every last bit as it slides out your arsehole.

She looked at him, raised her eyebrows. Would you really do that?

Well, you asked for more. . .

I ken, but. . . I've never seen that before. I thought I kent everything – from my dad's magazines – but I've never seen that!

Rob grinned, tapped the side of his head. A bit of brainpower, he said. A bit of imagination. It's amazing what the human mind can come up with.

Well, said Sandra. Will you come up with something amazing by tomorrow?

More than likely.

Same time, same place?
More than likely.

Rob decided he couldn't be fucked rushing back to the school. Let Billy and Don work out what had to be done for a change. They were the jannies, after all, that was their fucking job. Rob was head jannie, and that was different: it meant he had to use his head, to do headwork, to think things through.

So after Sandra had gone off, he just sat there, thinking about school security, and whether some kind of high fence around the grounds might be a good idea.

Watch-towers would be necessary as well, of course, and possibly searchlights for use during evening activities and for early mornings and late afternoons in midwinter. Certainly such a system would ensure the kids' safety, though it would probably be pretty damn pricey. Still, that wasn't his concern. He should put the plan to the rectum in a memo and let him worry about the economics. That's what he was getting paid for.

The only disadvantage about an increase in perimeter security was that it'd make sneaking out to shag Sandra very difficult. Tunnels and gliders were ridiculous, a fucking joke, and he didn't think they used those wooden horses in PE any more. Of course, the head janny would likely be responsible for organising guard rotas, so he could probably arrange something, some kind of blind spot where she could crawl under the barbed wire.

Fuck's sake. And smuggle out Mars bars hidden up her arse at the same time! Rob laughed out loud, then stood up, stretching.

I don't think it's funny.

He turned. A shape in the bushes. Who's that? His hands balled into fists above his head.

Movement. A figure emerged: the ginger-haired guy from the pillbox.

Christ, said Rob. It's you.

Who else? said the guy.

Rob shrugged, laughed. I don't ken. Somebody from school chasing me up for skiving.

The guy looked him up and down. You're a bit old for school, surely. Even with the shorts.

Rob laughed again. I work there, he said. I'm a jannie. Head jannie, actually.

The guy grinned. Jannie mannie, he said. Hello Jannie Man.

Not got your goggles on theday? said Rob, shaking his legs to keep the cooling muscles loose.

Do you think I'm daft? said the guy. I don't need them out here: just when it's smoky in my house.

Oh aye! In your palace!

Aye. Anyway, I've been needing my eyes uncluttered.

Why's that?

The guy hunched the shoulders of his donkey jacket up around his lugs, grinned, then slowly eased the shoulders down and the grin off his face. So I can see all that's going on, he said. If you know what I mean.

Rob looked at him, then glanced about the wall of whins that surrounded where him and Sandra had been fucking. He frowned. What do you mean?

The guy glanced around too. Nothing, he said.

Did you see me? said Rob.

I'm seeing you now.

Aye, but did you see me a while ago?

I saw you three days ago.

Fuck's sake man! shouted Rob. Did you see me half an hour a-fucking-go, here with my fucking. . . wife?

Fuck's sake man! the guy shouted back. Don't fucking ask me what I saw! They're my fucking eyes! You're always on about them – goggles this and goggles fucking that – what's your fucking problem?

I've no problem, said Rob, quieter now, trying to calm the bastard down a bit. I'm just saying I don't like being watched.

The guy turned away. I wasn't watching you, he said. I was watching birds.

Birds?

Aye.

Rob couldn't help himself: he laughed. You're a fucking birdwatcher?

Aye.

Rob nodded. A bird watcher! It's all starting to make sense now! That's why you're hanging about the cliffs. The bunker's a hide. You're a fucking birdwatcher! A twitcher!

You have to watch them, said the guy, turning back to Rob. Ken why? Cause otherwise they'll get you: they'll peck your eyes out and you'll never see again.

What!

It's true. I've seen it. You have to watch them, or you'll never see again. And if you can't see, you won't be able to watch them. It all ties in.

Birds? said Rob.

Aye.

They peck your eyes out?

The guy nodded, slowly, and said, Next time you're lying here, watch it. Or else! His gaze shifted away from Rob's face, and immediately he started, stiffened, and raised an arm to point past Rob's shoulder.

Rob turned and looked out to sea. Fifty yards offshore three ducks, beak to tail, were skimming the wavetops.

Under radar cover, said the guy. A small raid. Sometimes there's whole squadrons.

Rob watched the ducks till they flew out of sight. They didn't spot us! he said, and went to laugh. But the look on the guy's face was so serious that he stopped himself.

There's dive bombers as well, said the birdwatcher. And some that have a kind of flame thrower. Except it's not fire, it's a kind of poison muck. They spray it at you and it burns your skin. That's if you get too close to their HQ.

Rob looked at him. It's an interesting theory you've got there, he said. An interesting comparison: birdlife and warfare.

Comparison? said the guy. It's not a comparison. It *is* warfare.

As Rob crossed the car park towards the school, the Tradesman's Entrance opened and the dominie stepped out. Rob nearly turned and ran, then realised it was too late, he'd been seen, and carried on.

Mr Moran, he said as he passed the last car.

I called in at your office, Mr Catto, said the dominie. Your colleagues couldn't tell me where you were, but at that moment Mr Copeland spotted you emerging from the woods.

Did he?

Moran looked Rob up and down, just like the birdwatcher had. Yes, he said, eventually. Been out running, have you?

God! You wouldn't believe it! Rob wiped a hand across his brow. Running's not the word for it! Chasing, more like.

The dominie frowned. Chasing? he said. Whom were you chasing?

This is it, said Rob, shaking his head. I still don't know: I never caught the bugger! But I'm pretty sure it was that fellow Mrs Ellis saw. The weirdo, mind?

Moran looked past Rob and out towards the woods. I got your memo about Friday night, he said. I thought your suggestions about a task force were, eh, a little premature, but. . . Do you think it was the same chap again?

I really just glimpsed him, said Rob. I was out for a wee jog at lunchtime there – keep yourself fighting fit, Mr Moran, that's my philosophy – when I glimpsed this figure through the trees. A big guy, some kind of coat he was wearing, a big coat. And he was just shambling along.

Did he have his hood up?

Absolutely! Zipped right up! So anyway, I gave chase, I ran after the bastard. I was going to tackle him, ask him what he was doing. Not jump to any conclusions, like, just ask him why he was hanging about the school woods with a big coat on.

Moran frowned, bent his head to listen, his eyes still raised and scanning the woods.

Well, Rob went on, He must've heard me coming, for no sooner had I started running towards him, then he started running away. I've never seen anyone going at such a speed! I'm telling you, he must've been on something, some kind of drug, cause I'm a pretty fast runner, and there was no *way* I could've caught him!

Ah, you didn't catch him then?

Rob sighed, resting his hands on his hips and shaking his head. I'm afraid not, he said. He just seemed to disappear. He ran away in front of me, and then he just disappeared. I'm beginning to think he must have some kind of burrow out there, some kind of lair he can dive into and hide, cause that's the second time he's got away from me. It's frustrating, Mr Moran, it really is! I tell you, when I finally do catch the bastard – pardon my French – he'll deserve everything he gets!

Moran looked at him. I wouldn't like you to get. . . involved in anything, Mr Catto.

Rob made a face. I wouldn't *like* to either, he said. But I might not be able to help myself, ken. I mean, after all this bastard's done.

This is the problem, said the dominie. The fellow hasn't actually done anything yet.

Aye, said Rob. This is where they get you. This is the terrible bit. We have to wait for the pervert to actually start doing his perversions before we can act. We have to wait till he goes for somebody till we can go for him. It's a terrible state of affairs.

Moran nodded, then looked at his watch. Ah, he said. I have a meeting. But, thank you for your vigilance, Mr Catto. Please keep it up. But also, please don't get *involved* in anything yourself. Please let me know any new information immediately, but don't become involved in anything unless it's absolutely necessary.

Absolutely, said Rob. Don't you worry on that score.

Moran turned to go.

Oh, said Rob. What was it you wanted to see me about, anyway?

The dominie paused. Just a minor matter, he said. I had a complaint about some unrepaired hooks in the girls' cloakroom, and also a couple of corridor lightbulbs that had failed and not been replaced. But Mr Copeland and Mr MacBain assured me they'd deal with both matters straight away.

I should think so too, said Rob. Skiving buggers. He laughed.

Moran didn't join in; he just nodded once, and turned and walked away.

When he got home, Rob went and lay down on the bed. He closed his eyes, but couldn't sleep. There was too much racket going on. He reached for the remote control on the bedside unit and switched on the wee telly on top of the tallboy.

The first thing that came up was a kids' programme. On the next channel was cricket. The third channel was another kids' show, and the last one was something black and white. His thumb jerked for the off button.

After a few seconds, he was fed up of just lying there, and switched the telly on again. It was back on the first kids' programme. A girl and a guy wearing stripey clothes were going completely over the top in their acting, their eyes bugging out and their hands waving about. It looked like they were speeding. They probably were! It would all tie in: the actors could only behave that way if they were drugged up, and the kids could only enjoy it if they were stoned too. It was all beginning to make sense. It was also beginning to look like the whole world was out of their heads, except for Rob. He was the only straight cunt on the whole fucking planet!

The one surprising thing was that you didn't see everyone taking the stuff every five minutes. But that could be explained too: depot injections, fucking depot injections like the loonies got. Everyone on the fucking world apart from Rob must be getting hallucinogenic depot injections every month or so, and walking around out of their heads the whole time. There was no other way to explain their crazy behaviour.

Still watching the kids' programme, Rob put a hand down the

160

front of his jogging shorts and started scrunching up his cock and balls. Then he fell asleep.

Rob woke with the feeling he was being shouted at. It wasn't a dream, somebody *was* shouting at him. It was people on the telly. He turned down the volume one bar and tried to work out what they were saying. It was about politics, and the guys in the suits weren't really bawling at him, they were attacking each other. But despite that they seemed to be on the same side, and against Rob; despite seeming to slag off each other they were still smiling, and it was Rob who was feeling attacked. He switched off the telly and lay back.

There was less of a racket going on in his head than there had been earlier, and he was able to think things through a bit. He started from the guys shouting on the telly, moved on to what Billy had been saying the other day about power games and prison, and ended up with the weirdo in the woods.

Every time he thought things through these days he ended up face to face with the guy. Or not face to face, cause he'd never really got a proper look at his face. Face to fucking hood! The guy was at the root of a hell of a lot of stuff that was going on around the school, that much was obvious. Obvious to Rob, anyway. Not many folk seemed to have noticed his connections with drink, drugs, underage sex, smoking, littering, violence, disrespect, porn. In fact, nobody had, except him! But the more he thought it over, the clearer the connections got. And the clearer it got that it wasn't just the kids who were at risk from the weirdo, it was the whole fucking town!

By the time he heard the door downstairs opening, he'd got the whole scenario worked out.

Mrs Ellis was at her window talking to a boy about free dinner tickets. Rob waited till the kid pissed off, then leant over the counter.

I'm needing to find a pupil, he said.

Mrs Ellis screwed her face up. Any pupil, or one in particular?

Rob frowned, as if he was thinking hard. No, it has to be this one particular one, he said. Could you look at the timetables for me?

I suppose so, said Mrs Ellis, and walked away across the room.

It's a bit of lost property, said Rob. It has her name on it. Seems important, so I thought I better give it to her.

She sat down in front of her computer and touched a few keys. Name? she said.

Robert Catto.

She sighed. No, the pupil.

Oh, sorry. It's Sandra Burnett. She's in third year. Like I say, I have something to give her, so. . .

Mrs Ellis typed some words into the computer, then swivelled in her chair. She's in history with Mrs Mackay, she said. She's there till lunch break, so that's another forty minutes. Room 26. Okay? She swivelled away from him.

Thanks ever so much, he said, and headed off towards the history department.

A minute later he was standing in the doorway of Room 26.

Sorry to interupt, Mrs Mackay, he said. But there's a small problem at the school office. Is there a Sandra Burnett in the class?

Rob had spotted her sitting up the back the instant he walked into the room, but now he followed where Mrs Mackay was pointing, and made on not to know her.

Sandra? he said. Could you come with me for a few minutes.

He turned to the teacher. We'll only be a short time, he said. Oh, you might as well take your bag, he said to the girl as she came down towards the front of the class. You might need. . . something.

Sandra went back, picked up her bag, and scowled at a few of her classmates who made comments as she passed them on her way to the front again.

Let's go, he said, and held the door open for her. Then he nodded at Mrs Mackay once more, and went out into the corridor.

Well? said Sandra.

Mind you wanted me to come up with something amazing for theday?

Aye.

Well, I forgot: I'm on canteen duty at dinnertime, we can't meet out by the cliff.

That's not amazing, that's terrible.

I ken. The amazing thing is, we're going to do it now instead. Come on.

They walked quickly away from the history rooms, turned right at the geography junction, and headed down the corridor towards the big staircase. Halfway to it, Rob stopped, glanced behind them, then said, Right, in here! and pulled her by the elbow into the boy's toilets there.

A first year was washing his hands at the sink.

Skedaddle, said Rob.

The boy reached for a paper towel.

Forget it, said Rob. Blow them dry.

The boy scuttled out, glancing up at Sandra as he passed.

We can't do it here, she said. Folk'll come in.

Remember who you're talking to, said Rob, and winked. From the pocket of his dustcoat he pulled out a piece of folded A4. He opened it up and held it flat in front of his chest.

Out of order, read Sandra. Use science block toilets till mended.

Rob grinned, held up a drawing pin, then opened the bog door and pinned the notice to the outside of it. He closed the door, then flicked through his key-chain till he found the right key, and locked it.

When he turned round, Sandra was gone.

There was the sound of pish spraying on water from inside the nearest cubicle.

What are you doing? he said.

I drank a can of juice at break, she said. I was bursting.

He went over and pushed the cubicle door open.

Don't look.

You're getting shy? After everything?

She grinned, looked up at him. Ken what we did in English theday? she said. A story about tinks getting married. Gypos, ken? Ken what they did? The lassie and the mannie both peed into a bucket, then somebody swirled it round and said, Whoever can separate these two pishes, can split this couple up!

What!

Aye!

In English?

Aye.

It's disgusting! They give you that in English? Not much wonder this place is going to rack and fucking ruin!

She pulled a piece of tissue out of the dispenser and reached down to wipe herself. Then she pulled her pants and jeans up, and got to her feet.

So how about it, she said. You pee in there, Rob, and we'll never be parted.

Rob looked down into the bowl for a second, then reached over and pressed the flush.

If I tried to pish thenow, he said, It'd go all over the ceiling.

She put a hand down to his crotch, rubbed it up the length of his cock.

Get the fucking Durex, he said. Now *I'm* fucking bursting!

She slid out of the cubicle. I'll just wash my hands. . .

Don't, he said, and came out of the cubicle after her.

But I've just. . .

I'll kiss your hands clean, he said. I'll lick them clean. You're a dirty cunt, Sandra Burnett, but I'll wash you clean.

He unbuttoned his dustcoat, took it off, and spread it on the tiled floor of the bog.

Billy and Donald were out of the bothy. Rob had read his paper, now he was standing looking out of the window, out into the woods across the car park. Once again they'd been full at dinnertime with kids hanging about, dropping rubbish, smoking. Smoking god knows what. And certainly the woods would be where the kids bought their drugs. It was true that nobody had actually been caught with anything out there, or anywhere in the school, but that just proved how fucking devious they were at hiding the evidence. It was only a matter of time. Rob reckoned that if some kind of seizure wasn't made soon, he should have a word with the police, arrange with them to plant E's on some fifth year or other, who could then be made an example of. The

165

message had to be put across, that was for sure, and if an opportunity didn't arise naturally, one would have to be created.

Rob would be surprised if it had to come to that, though, for it was a well known fact that every school in the land was hoaching with drugs. In fact, it was a wonder anyone bothered going to the chemist any more. They should just drop by their local high school playground and they'd soon find what they were looking for. They'd soon feel a lot better! Or worse. They'd feel a change, anyway, and that was what folk wanted from their prescriptions, that's what was really required, that folk should feel something was having an effect on them, something was working on them. That meant that hallucinogenic drugs were probably more useful than antibiotics. Cause you take a dose of penicillin and what do you feel? Bugger all. No change whatsoever, till a week later you look down and see that the infected gash on your finger has healed up. So what? Give the patient some powerful acid instead, then they'd really know they'd taken some drugs, then they'd really know something was working on them. And they'd completely forget they had a gashed hand, and it'd heal itself anyway, probably.

So it wasn't fair that the kids had all the drugs and the jannies and the teachers had none. It was a disgrace that the distribution of them was so biased. And all because the staff room and the dominie's office were on the other side of the school; they didn't see the ongoings in the woods every dinner time, they never realised what they were missing. But Rob could remedy the situation. He was probably the only person in the whole school – the whole world! – who knew what was going on and could do something about it.

He got hold of his memo book and a biro, and started to write.

FAO Mr Moran, Rector

Dear Mr Moran,

As requested in your recent note, I have impressed on my staff the need for constant vigilance in our enforcement of moral standards. One potential problem has occurred to me this afternoon. I believe we should act quickly to deal with it, before the obvious injustice of the current situation starts to undermine morale and equilibrium in the school. I'm talking about drugs, Mr Moran: the children have them, and we don't.

It is clearly unfair. You are in a position to redistribute the drugs, by seizing them from the pupils who possess them (mostly S4 and above) and giving them out on request to teachers. Perhaps a cardboard carton could be set up in the staff room, from which folk could take pills, tabs, powders and herbs as required. An 'honesty box' next to the carton could raise money for school funds. Needless to say, janitors and cleaning staff would have to be provided for, and it seems only fair that you, as headmaster, should get first choice of whatever narcotics are available.

I hope you find my idea useful. If you would like to discuss the finer details of the scheme, please do not hesitate to call for me.

Yours, R. Catto (Head Janitor)

After signing the memo, Rob put it in an internal mail envelope, pushed the toggle through the hole to close it, and tossed it into the out-tray on his desk.

Then he took off his dustcoat and other clothes, put on his jogging gear, and headed out the Tradesman's Entrance. It felt funny running away when the car park was still full of teachers' cars, and when the upstairs windows still had kids' heads bobbing about behind them. But his drugs idea was something special, he was sure of that; it had taken a lot out of him, and now he needed a rest. He could rest by jogging. Cause it wasn't his body that was tired, his body was fine. It was his head: his head was full of ideas, all shouting to be heard. It was really buzzing, his head, it was like a bee hive.

Aye, that was what it was like, a skip full of bees. Rob had the idea that if he opened his mouth a river of bees would come swarming out and terrorise the town. So he kept his mouth shut. He jogged out of the car park, across the road, and away through the bought houses, all the time breathing through his nose.

Fuck's sake, how was he going to eat his supper? Through a fucking tube up the nostril? Bugger that! Better let the bastarding bees out here, out in the open, not in his own fucking living room.

He stopped running, waited till his heart had slowed its racing, then pointed his face in the direction of the nearest bought house and opened his mouth wide. A swarm of bees didn't come out of him, but a shout did:

FUUAAAAHHHHHHHH!

Rob ran home a long way round, but he was still feeling unsettled when he arrived in the estate. The pieces weren't fitting together, they were still all jumbled up, despite the good jogging he'd given them.

The car was in the port, and when he opened the door Karen shouted from the lounge: Hullo-oh! I'm in here, come and get me!

He stuck his head round the door. She was sittting on the settee, wearing a dress and make-up. You're early, he said.

She put down the book she was reading, and sighed. I've worked late the rest of the week so I could finish early thenight, she said. We're going to my folks', mind?

Eh? No! He stepped inside the room.

It's their wedding anniversary, we're having a meal.

A party?

No, just the four of us. I told you weeks ago.

Rob sat down on the arm of the settee. You could've reminded me.

Why, have you something else planned?

No, it's just. . . fuck, I'd like to have had some choice in the matter.

You did have a choice: you chose to marry me, and that means you chose to visit my parents once in a blue moon. She smiled, tilting her head to one side. Just cause you never see yours.

How can I? They live in fucking Wales. In the middle of a fucking gas refinery or something. I'm not going there: it's likely to blow up at any minute.

Rubbish.

It is not! They do live in Wales.

Aye, and mine live on the other side of town, so we've no excuse.

Jesus. . .

Listen Robbie, I'm not going to argue with you.

Cause you ken you're wrong.

She paused, looked him up and down, then raised her eyebrows. No. Cause seeing you there in your shorts is driving me crazy. She slid along the settee till her head was resting against his bare thigh. Come on, get them off and ravish me here by the rubber plant.

Fuck's sake. Rob jumped to his feet and Karen's head banged down on the arm of the settee. She let out a cry.

Robbie, you mongrel.

He stopped by the door. I think I'll have a shower, he said.

She sat up. Can I watch?

Jesus, what's up with you theday? Sex mad or what?

She got to her feet and went over and leant against him, tilting her face up to his and tickling her fingertips through the hairs on his legs. You never used to complain, she said. I thought I was sex mad and you were sex crazy and that's how we got on so well. She looked at him through her eyelashes.

After a second he sniffed. Did I say that?

She moved a hand over and cupped his balls through the nylon of his shorts. Better than that, she said. You showed me.

He looked down at her, not moving, but when she started to slide her fingers down inside his waistband he gave her shoulders a shove, pushed her away. She looked surprised.

If I didn't say it you've nothing on me. If you think I showed it, tough; that's just your interpretation. Maybe I just meant you were a good ride.

Robbie!

I'm having a shower.

He dashed through to the bathroom and locked the door, turned on the shower and stripped. As soon as he pulled off his shorts and pants the reek of stale spunk and rubber filled his nostrils. Thank fuck Karen hadn't got this far. He stepped into the shower and scrubbed.

When he finished, he switched off the shower. Karen's voice

170

came floating through from the living room. A one-sided conversation. As soon as his back was turned!

He stepped out of the bath, wrapped the towel round his middle again, and went out into the hallway.

Karen! he shouted. Who the fuck are you phoning now?

She stopped talking. He could picture her putting her hand up over the mouthpiece.

Well?

I'm telling my mum we'll be a bittie late, she said. Cause of you jogging too much.

He blinked some water out of his eyes. Really? he said.

Aye, she says to say you're a fanatic, a fitness fanatic. Karen giggled. And to hurry up, the roast's in the oven!

Rob didn't say any more. She had it all worked out, all the angles covered. He'd have to be *really* smart to catch her out.

In theory Rob got on fine with Karen's folks, but these days he was tending to find them a bit wearing. They each had two or three things they were interested in, and whatever a conversation started off about, before long Liz would bring it round to illnesses the population of the town was prey to, or else how wonderful her daughters were and how they were getting on in the world. Rob had never had a day off sick in his life – he'd put that down on the application form for the head jannie job – and he was married to Karen, so he knew exactly how wonderful or not wonderful she was. And the fact that she earned a lot, twice as much as him, was something he couldn't forget either – especially as she never mentioned it. She didn't mention her sister Maureen often either, but Liz made up for that, with updates on her CV in the US every other week.

As for George's subjects, they were even more boring. One was the amount that footballers and other athletes got paid, and how it was a disgrace compared to the tiny amounts earned by folk who worked eight-thirty to five, six days a week, fifty weeks a year – never mind a couple of hours on Saturday afternoons with three months off in the summer. Another of his was about all the latest electrical gadgets he had bought into his shop and how labour-saving they were. Whenever the price of these things came out, Rob felt like chucking up. He felt like pointing out that they cost so much you'd have to work overtime for a year to pay for them: they really *created* fucking labour! But George and Liz had given them more or less a full set of these gadgets for their wedding present, so he couldn't moan, he just had to keep his mouth shut as usual.

This time hadn't been too badly boring though. Rob had got through the meal without falling asleep face-first on his plate, and him and George had polished off most of three bottles of pink wine. Now Karen had cleared away the dirty dishes and was racking them up in the washer, and Liz was serving cups of coffee.

Milk? she said.

No, said Rob.

Sugar?

No, said Rob.

Nothing at all?

No, I like it black. Hot and strong and black.

I'll get some mints then, said Liz, and went back into the kitchen.

George leant across the table. When I was in Suez, in the army, ken, there were women like that.

What, like Liz?

No: hot and strong and black! Eh? Ha! He thumped his hand on the tabletop, making the teaspoons rattle in the saucers.

Rob nodded, raised an eyebrow.

They had plenty energy all right, I'll tell you. Know what I mean? Do it all night for a dollar, some of those darkies.

Rob laughed. George, you're not meant to say things like that any more.

Ha! I know, but it's true.

What's true? said Karen, coming in from the kitchen with her mother.

After Eight? said Liz, putting the box down in front of Rob, and opening the lid amazingly carefully, as if something nasty might leap out on a spring.

Nothing did. Rob took a sweet, laid it beside his saucer, then slid the box over the tablecloth towards George. We were just talking about black folk, he said, giving George a quick wink. Saying how they seem to have a lot more energy than us peely-wallies.

George started to look a bit worried. His eyes flickered from Rob to his wife and back.

At sport, I mean, said Rob. You see them on the telly: they win all the gold medals.

That's true, said Liz.

George was just saying, Rob went on, What amazing stamina the black folk have. Run all night, some of these black women!

I've heard that, said Liz.

I haven't, said Karen, and reached across for the box of mints, which her dad had been dipping into but not passing on.

George took a slurp of his coffee. It tells you a lot though, he said as he put his cup down. I mean, I've got nothing against them

173

as such, I'm not prejudiced or anything. I'm just being realistic here. And the truth is, the darkies are good at sport, but not good at anything that needs a bit of brainpower.

Dad!

No, Karen, I ken we're not meant to say it, but it's true. There's all the footballers, and the runners, and the jumpers – fair enough, give them their due – but, Rob, is there for instance any coloured teachers at the school?

Dad!

Let him answer. George held up a hand for silence. Rob?

Rob frowned, as if thinking hard. No, there's not, he said at last.

I rest my case. George sat back in his chair, folding his arms.

Dad, there's no black folk in the whole town except for three waiters in the Bengal Bay. It doesn't mean anything that there's no teachers. Go down to London or someplace – there's hundreds of black teachers there!

George shook his head at Karen. You're clever, he said, And your heart's in the right place. But you haven't been around the world like I have. I'm talking from experience here. And my experience is, these coloureds are not too well stocked in the brains department.

Good bodies though, eh! said Rob, and winked across the table.

George looked a bit startled. Eh? Oh, aye, I'm not denying that.

Paid well for it though.

What? His eyes were staring.

These black folk that do all the sports – they get well paid for being good, eh?

Too bloody well if you ask me, said George, looking relieved.

Aye, said Rob, with a shake of his head, And it's just rewarding crime as well.

Robbie! What the bloody hell are you talking about?

Don't be crude, dear, whispered Liz.

Well! Karen put down her coffee cup, pressed both palms on the tabletop as if she was about to leap up. Then she sat back. I've never heard such rubbish!

It's true, said Rob. George'll back me up here: ken how the blacks are such good runners? Cause they get lots of practice – running away from the police!

Robbie!

Escaping from the scene of the crime!

That is a terrible thing to say Robbie Catto.

George was nodding. He's right though, darling. It's a fact, you see it in the papers: ninety per cent of the crimes in this country are done by immigrants.

Dad, that is *shite*!

Karen! Don't talk to your father like that!

It's all about drugs, George said. That's what ninety per cent of the crime's about. And. . . and half of these athletes *take* drugs to make them faster! It all ties in, see?

Rob laughed.

The pair of you are drunk and havering, said Karen.

And Liz, said Rob, turning to her, What about AIDS?

What?

Well, you've got all the leaflets at the surgery there, you tell us: where did all this AIDS business start?

Liz frowned, and her cheeks started to go pink.

Karen narrowed her eyes and raised a finger to point at Rob. You just watch your step, she said. Don't go too far boy.

He looked at her and smiled. All I'm doing is asking a question, he said. I'm not going anywhere.

Good, said Karen, and sat back.

You have to admit, though, that AIDS started in Africa.

Och Robbie. . .

Is that right? said George.

God aye! It's rife over there! Then it started to spread. Is that not right Liz?

Well, we do advise tourists to practise safe s-e-x if they go to Africa, she said. But then, we advise them to do that here as well.

That's just for woofters, said George.

Weirdos in the woods, said Rob.

Perverts, said George.

More coffee anyone? said Karen loudly.

Don't change the subject, said George.

Dad. You are getting terrible in your old age. I swear. . .

George shrugged and got to his feet. I'm just saying what we all think, he said, opening a door on the sideboard and taking out a bottle of whisky and two nip glasses.

I do not think that!

Rob laughed, accepted the full glass of whisky George was holding out to him.

And Robbie, I ken what you're doing, so just stop it.

Rob laughed again, then raised his glass. Cheers! he cried. Geordie, Liz: here's to another sixty! He winked and tossed back the whisky.

I'll tell you this, said George. Sometimes it feels like sixty years!

Dad, don't be horrible.

I'm not, I'm just kidding. Your mother kens fine. . .

But look, Karen went on. Here's you and him toasting, and you never even offered us!

George emptied his glass, put it down, and picked up the bottle. Very sorry darling, he said. Do you want a whisky?

You know I don't like the damn stuff!

Elizabeth?

Liz shuddered. Oh no.

George shrugged, then poured himself and Rob another big dram.

God's sake, said Karen, folded her arms, and turned to look out the front window.

Rob laughed, drank his whisky down.

Have another mint, said Liz.

He's had enough, said Karen.

Liz nudged the box over towards Rob, and he took a handful of the wee paper packets out of the box and dumped them on top of his first one, still lying by the saucer.

I think we better get going soon, said Karen.

Do you have to? said Liz.

Karen turned back from the window and put her hand on her mother's where it rested by the handle of her empty coffee cup. It's been a long day, she said.

Of course dear, said Liz. You work so hard.

Rob laughed, and started stacking all his After Eights in a neat pile. Me too, he said. No rest for the wicked, eh?

When Karen was in a roose she always walked fast, whether she was in a hurry or not. When she was happy she was a doddler, even if time was tight. Now there was nothing to rush home for, but she was tearing off in that direction, arms pressed in at her sides, eyes on the pavement. Rob loped after her.

Karen. Hey. Slow down.

She kept on walking.

I want to talk to you.

She didn't slow, but he was right at her heels.

Karen! He put his hand on her shoulder, and she pulled up at once, causing him to crash into her.

You bastard, she said, staggering away from him.

You shouldn't've stopped so quick, sorry.

Back there, you idiot. What did you have to make a fool of dad for?

What?

You were winding him up all through the meal. I saw you. God, and then you start having a go at mum!

I never did.

Christ, dad's enough of a pain for her at the best of times. She doesn't need you getting him all worked up and roaring.

We were just having a bit of a laugh, me and your old man: no harm in that.

All that rubbish about black folk and gays. Jesus, it's bad enough him reading it in his stupid paper without you encouraging him. I just. . . god. . . I give up. She set off down the road again.

Rob was getting a bit embarrassed. The street was silent and empty apart from the two of them, and if anyone looked out their window they'd see at once that there'd been a row, that Karen was sprinting away in a strum.

Karen! he yelled after her. Will you stop fucking running. She didn't even slow down. He set off after her again. This time when he caught up with her he didn't grab her shoulder, he ran right in front and stopped, facing her.

She hesitated, her eyes still lowered, then darted sideways to pass him. He shot out his arm and caught her round the waist.

Let me go.

I want to talk to you.

I don't want to talk to you, you bastard.

Karen, Karen. . . He put his other arm round her too, and tried to bring her close to him, but she leant back and pushed her hands against his chest. Karen, I just want a bosie. . .

Let me go!

Look, he said, and squeezed tight with his arms, Stop fighting or they'll think I'm fucking attacking you.

Let me go and I'll stop fighting.

Jesus. . . He released her.

She stepped back, shook her hair out of her face, glared at him.

Will you listen to me? he said.

I don't see why I should.

Karen. . . I'm sorry. She lifted her chin. But face it: your dad's an old bigot.

Hold on. . .

No, just listen a minute. Listen, then I'll shut up. He's a bigot, and I reckon he should be allowed to be. At his stage in life, he's earned the right to be what he likes.

He's only fifty-five!

The point is, live and let live. Him saying those things harms nobody.

She looked away, then back at Rob. And what about you saying them? You should know better for sure.

I do know better, he said. I was pretending I didn't, just for a laugh. He chanced a smile.

I don't think it's funny, she said.

You know me Karen, he said. You know I know the score. You don't have to be black to be a cunt, I know that. I mean, look at the fucking playground pervert, he's not black. But he is a cunt. He's a weirdo. Nothing to do with the colour of his skin, he's just a sick cunt. Your dad blames blacks for all the ills of the world, but I know it's not their fault. It's the sick bastards who're to blame, the weird cunts, the cunts in hoods on sunny days.

Karen shook her head, then turned and started walking slowly along the road. Rob fell into step beside her.

Even that, she said quietly. Even there, you see, you've changed. Saying things like that.

Like what?

Like. . . like calling people cunts. You never used to do that.

What!

You shouldn't do it, it's not fine.

I've always talked about cunts!

No you haven't. Not to me.

But. . .

You've talked about my cunt. You've talked sexy and talked about your cock and my cunt. Okay. That's alright. That's using the word properly.

So?

So you shouldn't start calling folk you hate after a part of me!

They can't hear.

Robbie! It's not them who mind. It's me. It hurts my feelings.

God's sake, is that all? Rob looked up at the sky. I don't ken why we're arguing about such a little thing.

She stopped. It's not a little thing! My feelings? That's a big thing! Just about the biggest thing there is! Short of breaking my legs, hurting my feelings is the worst thing you can do to me!

Rob took his hands out of his jacket pockets and reached out to touch her arm. She took a step back, and half turned away from him.

Sometimes I think I'd rather you broke my legs than breaking my heart the way you're doing.

Rob put his hand on her shoulder. Hey, baby – breaking your heart? – what are you on about?

Karen moved away and sat on the low flat-topped dyke of the garden they were passing. The windows of the bungalow at the end of the lawn were in darkness. She looked up at him. Her eyes were glistening in the yellow light of the street lamp across the road.

You mean you don't even know you're doing it?

He shrugged.

Jesus. . . that's worse, that's even worse. . .

Well, how am I. . .

Jesus Rob! Sex! For a start, sex!

Keep your voice down.

Well! We haven't done it for ages. Weeks!

He scuffed the toe of his shoe in the pavement grit. We did it in the woods by the school, he said.

Aye, that was the last time – ages ago – and that was bloody coitus interruptus!

You can't blame me for that.

It wasn't even good before it was interruptus! It was nasty! Everything's nasty these days, Rob – *you're* bloody nasty. Something nasty's got into you, you never used to be like that.

God! I don't want to be someone that just mumps and moans, a wife that just moans, a *human being* that just moans, but honestly Rob, you're driving me to it, and I hate it. I hate what you're doing, and I hate me for hating it, and I hate you for making me hate myself.

She brushed a hand across her eyes.

I wish you'd even talk to me about it, but you won't. You just grunt these days. We used to have a real laugh together, we used to talk about things – everything! – but now you just grunt and go off by yourself. I hate it, I can't stand it, I've had enough.

Rob looked at her. It wasn't my fault we were interruptus, he said. It was that fucking cu. . . weirdo. Him in the parka, it was him, he's to blame, I'll fucking get the bastard, I'll kill him!

No! No, Rob, that's not it. . . Jesus!

He watched her wipe tears from her cheeks, and blinked. What is it then?

Will you listen to me?

I am listening! I'm just not understanding. You keep leaping about from one thing to another. First you say something's annoying you, then you say it's not. You're confusing me. Cause it's not easy for me either, you ken. I've only been in the job a month, I've only been in this bloody town a month. It's alright for you, you grew up here, you know it inside out. I'm still settling in, of course I'm a bit shook up! It's a stressful fucking time, not made easier by you acting crazy!

Don't twist it round!

What?

Don't twist it round so I'm the crazy one!

Well I'm not fucking crazy! I'm completely fucking normal,

completely fucking Mr Average. The man in the street, that's me, I'm not fucking crazy!

So why are you snapping and snarling at me all the time? Why won't you touch me? Why are you so moody? Why do you keep turning nasty on my family and friends?

On your friends? When? What friends? I've never been nasty to your friends!

At Grant's party, at the Indian, the way you just walked out! It was rude.

Oh aye! You're more worried about your precious Grant than you are about me.

What?

Wipe his whang on your waistcoat, did he?

What are you talking about?

Rob looked away for a second, then back. Then, his voice quiet again, he said, I told you: I wasn't feeling well.

But to just walk out like that. What an embarrassment!

They were a bunch of smug buggers anyway. I'm glad I was rude to them. They think they're so clever cause they make big dosh from Scottish Petroleum plc. They all look down on me, you ken, they all think I'm a piece of shite cause I'm *just a jannie*.

No they don't.

I know they do. What they don't appreciate is the responsibilities I have. Six hundred kids, and I'm looking after the lot of them. It's down to me, just me, to guard them from perverts and drug pushers and god knows what lunatics. That's what I call responsibility, that's what I call a job: not just sitting around in an office playing computer games all day. But no, no, all they see is me in my dustcoat, me with a brush and shovel, me with a choked lavvie. They don't realise that's just a cover, they don't realise I'm really the kids' fucking guardian angel.

Karen stood up from the dyke, shaking her head. You've lost me, she said.

He jolted, stepped over to her, leant into her face, shouting: Lost you? Who to? Who've I fucking lost you to? If I've lost you, who's won you Karen?

Shut up, will you?

One of those fucking smug oilers, eh? Of course it is, it's fucking obvious! Probably that fucking Granny Grant, eh? I bet it's him, the shit, I never liked the look of that slimey shite of a bastard!

Rob. . . She tried to move away from him, but he kept pace with her, half turned towards her, shouting in her face.

It doesn't matter who it is really. They're all the same. They all hate me, and they've poisoned you against me. That's it, eh? That's fucking it. They reckon you're too good for me, eh – just a fucking janitor, no match for an assistant fucking credit controller at Scottish Pefuckingtroleum. Ha! And your mother, she thinks the same too, eh? You can't deny it, and neither can she. Christ, I feel sorry for your dad sometimes, even if he is an old fart. I bet he's not good enough either, eh, I bet that's what you think, you and your ma. I'm not good enough, and he's not good enough, and when the two of us get thegether and have a bit of a laugh, well, that's just fucking atrocious. So there's you, there's your mother, there's all your office friends, your fifteen grand a year oily pipefitting bastard fucking roughneck mud-engineer roustabout bastards who're sticking their drill-bits up your CUNT, all of them too, the whole lot of you, you're all against me, all a-fucking-gainst me, you bastards, you bastards, you bastards, you bastards. . .

Stop it. Rob, stop it. You're scaring me. She pushed him away from her, and this time he didn't come close again, he just looked her up and down, sneering.

I'm scaring you? Is that it? Jesus, is that what I'm doing? Well you're making me fucking sick.

She took a step away from him, backwards, watching him. I don't know what you are, she said. Whether you're sick, or drunk, or what. I don't ken what you are.

He laughed. I'm a man. I'm a man.

Whatever you are, I don't like it.

She took another couple of backwards steps, then turned, and ran off down the road.

Rob stared in the window of Karen's dad's electrical goods shop for a long time. He thought about chucking a brick through it, but by the time that occurred to him he'd been looking in at the fridges and hoovers and tellies for twenty minutes. Two or three cars had passed, and a strolling couple, quiet like they were sober, despite it being so late. In other words, he'd been seen. You can't stare in a window at midnight for twenty minutes and not be suspected when the bastard's found smashed three seconds later. The only way to burst a plate glass window is to do it completely spontaneously, without even looking at the fucking thing. He'd seen kids do it a couple times at his last school. You just have to stroll past and toss in your brick like you're dropping a sweetie wrapper. Aye, you can get away with murder if you don't look like a murderer.

He walked further along the street, past a laundrette with

mould-speckled net curtains, and a shop called Petmania, which had kittens and mice in adjacent cages in the window. He squinted at the animals, trying to make out if the mice looked scared and the cats frustrated, or whether they'd got used to each other, but it was too dark. The street was an old narrow one, used mostly for servicing the back doors of the shopping street next over, and the lamps were very spaced out. A couple of them weren't working at all. He left the pet shop and walked on.

Towards the end of the street, the air became filled with an amazing smell of curry. Rob stopped, sniffed the air, and looked across at the dark buildings on the other side of the road. One of them had a tall silver chimney coming out of a boarded-up ground-floor window and beanstalking away up the wall towards the cloudy sky. Rob thought for a minute, imagined a street map of the town in his head. That would be the back of the Indian restaurant where him and Karen and the bastard oilers had had the birthday meal. That was another window he could put in.

He was about to walk on when there was a noise, a clatter in the shadows at the foot of the chimney. Something amongst the dustbins. A rat, probably. He turned away, but hadn't gone more than two yards when there was another, louder noise, a scraping. The rats weren't big enough to shift the bins around, surely. He hoped to Christ not. He peered into the shadows but could see nothing except different angles and thicknesses of blackness. If it wasn't a rat, what the fuck was it scranning the bins at half past midnight? Jesus. . .

He took a sideways step in the direction of the nearest working lamp. Then another. Then another. Then stopped. One of the lumps of black had moved. He stared. Nothing. He strained his ears. Nothing.

Then there was a long sigh of breath exhaled.

Rob's heart stuttered.

Hello jannie!

Rob leapt. The voice had come from an area of shadow away to the right, yards from where he'd been staring. He turned to face the speaker, as best as he could judge.

You're out late and alone, said the voice, and now it started to sound familiar.

Who's that? said Rob. There was no answer.

Then a figure emerged from the darkness and walked towards him. It was a stocky figure in a dark parka with the hood up over its head.

Rob took a step back.

Who's there? he whispered.

The figure stopped at the edge of the pavement, no more than three feet away, but its face still completely shadowed. Rob could hear it breathing: his own lungs had seized up.

There was a long silence, then, It's me! said the figure, and reached up to push back its hood. For a moment Rob couldn't think. Then it clicked.

It's you, the birdwatcher!

That's right.

The one with the goggles.

I don't have my goggles now. They're at home. I've my armour now.

Rob almost laughed with the relief of seeing who it was, but he managed to hold it in. Your what? he said.

My armour. This coat, it's armour-plated, nothing can get through it. Same with the helmet. He jerked a thumb over one shoulder towards the hood hanging down at his back. Usually I keep the helmet on at all times during the hours of darkness. You never know when an attack might come. But seeing as you're a friend and ally, I think it's okay to take it off. Bread?

He thrust a lump of something out towards Rob. Rob's hand reached out and took it, raised it to his mouth, and stopped it there. It smelt strange and charcoaly.

What's this? he said.

It's bread, from the restaurant there.

The Bengal Bay?

The one where the drunk people go.

Rob sniffed the bread. It's naan.

No, it's bread. Taste it.

Hold on, said Rob. Did you take this from the bin?

It's not stealing, said the guy. I don't steal. It's thrown away and I rescue it, that's all.

Aye, but is it alright to eat?

It's fresh. They make it every day, you know. They don't throw out much, they chop it up and use it the next day. But bread they throw out, every night. It's good. Try it.

Rob held the naan out to the guy. No thanks, he said. I've had a big meal already thenight.

I'm starving, said the guy, taking the bread back and stuffing it in his coat pocket. Come on, he said, and started off along the middle of the road at a great speed.

Rob watched the guy scurrying away down the street, something tugging at the roots of his brain. Then a flashbulb went off in his head, the rest of the world went black for a second, and he screamed after him:

Fucking sick bastard!

The guy stopped where he was, turned, and walked back

towards Rob, slowly. He halted ten feet away, reached up, and pulled his hood over his head again.

I'm know I'm sick, he said. That's why I was signed in for a while. But I thought you were a friend, I didn't think you'd turn against me for being sick.

Rob took a step towards the guy, his hands rising from his sides, his fingers gathering into fists.

I don't hate you for being sick, he said. I hate you for being a sicko. For hanging about the school playground, for spying on me and my wife when we were screwing in the woods. That is sick, that is fucking sick. I hate you for that, I should kill you for that you fucking sicko.

That wasn't me, said the guy.

Don't fucking lie! I recognise the fucking hood! It's all making sense now, you fucking lying bastard – birdwatching my arse!

I keep my head down, keep a low profile, stay out of trouble. I don't go bothering folk or children.

Are you saying you haven't been hanging around the school woods?

Yes.

Yes you have been hanging around, or yes you're saying you haven't?

The guy took the lump of naan out of his pocket and started chewing on a corner of it.

You're sailing close to the wind pal, said Rob.

The guy swallowed. They're my woods, he said, My garden. They abut my property. They go all the way over to the school, where I let the children play, then they come back and abut my home again. So I must be allowed to come and go. I never hang around, I come and go, that's all.

And spy on whoever you find you're passing?

I try and pass quickly and quietly, without the couples being disturbed, or even noticing me.

Couples?

You're not the only one with something to hide.

Don't talk about me! cried Rob. It's you we're sorting out here. Come on, get your fucking helmet off, let me see your face.

The guy reached up slowly, and pushed the hood off his head.

That's better, said Rob. Let's be straight with each other here. What you're saying is, there's loads of folk screwing in the woods, and you get your kicks from watching them. That's it, isn't it, you fucking sicko: you're not a birdwatcher, you're a Peeping Tom!

Usually all I see is a pair of male buttocks going up and down. That doesn't give me any kicks.

Where are the women then?

They're under the men. If the men weren't there, it would just be women lying stretched out under the trees. That would be different.

I bet it would you pervy bastard!

But I've never seen that yet.

Rob looked at the guy. Then he turned away, walked a few steps across the road, stopped with his toes in the gutter, and stood, thinking. He could hear the guy clear his throat and scratch himself, but there was no sound of him trying to sneak away while Rob's back was turned. He had nerve, Rob had to give him that, the sick bastard definitely had nerve. Rob walked back into the middle of the road, stopped, and gazed into the guy's pupils for a long time. He shuffled his feet, looked away. As soon as he did, Rob asked him what his name was.

What's yours? said the guy.

You know me: I'm the jannie man.

Well, I'm the bunker man.

Rob stared at him again. Okay Bunker Man, he said eventually, I take it all back. You're not as sick as I thought.

No, I can look after myself.

I bet you can.

Come on down the seafront with me, Jannie Man. People buy fish suppers and eat half of them sitting in their cars then throw the rest in the bins on the prom. Sometimes the chips are still warm! Feasts! He started walking bouncily, almost skipping, along the street.

Rob hesitated, then followed. I'm not needing food actually, he said after a minute.

You can't get by without it.

I ken, said Rob. But like I said, I already had a big feed thenight.

Do you want a roof for your head then? Come back and stay at my place!

The pillbox? No, thanks but no, Bunker Man. I've got a house. Up on the council estate. My wife's there now, she'll be waiting for me.

Even though you had a big fight?

Rob stopped. Here, how the fuck did you know that?

Why else would you be walking about the empty streets in the wee hours of the morning? said the guy, and stopped under a street lamp.

Rob drew back his head and looked at him; the light beaming down from above made it look like his ginger hair was blazing. You're a pretty smart cunt, eh?

Bunker Man screwed up his eyes. I keep a good lookout, he said. I watch people a lot.

191

We've already talked about that, said Rob.

I see what they get up to. I observe but don't intervene.

Rob looked at him. I bet you'd like to though, eh?

Like to what?

To intervene.

What in?

Well, I don't know. In something a bit sexy maybe.

I'm an observer, that's my mission. I'm not allowed to interfere. Anyway, I have to keep up my guard, and as soon as you start doing things, you get distracted, you can't keep up a proper watch any more.

But what if you knew you were safe? What if there was a girl, say, that you knew you would be safe with, what if she was lying in the woods or somewhere, waiting for you?

I don't know. He walked off.

Rob followed. What if I was hidden somewhere, watching over the pair of you. Not watching you doing anything, like! Just similar to what you do: observing from closeby somewhere, watching your back, guarding from any approaching dangers.

I don't know.

I bet you'd love to get involved in something sexy for once, eh, instead of just watching and wanking.

I do not do that.

Oh no?

No, no.

Prove it.

What? How?

We'll work out a deal, Mr Bunker Man.

What kind of deal?

I provide a girl lying in the woods, or out by your house if you'd

192

like that better. That's my side of the deal. And your side is, you have to fuck her brains out. Okay?

Bunker Man didn't reply. Rob's fingers fidgeted in his jacket pockets, and found something crinkly in the left one: the stack of After Eight mints Liz'd given him.

Here, he said. Are you still hungry?

Starving.

Seeing as you're a pal, Rob said, Have these. He stopped, Bunker Man beside him, and held out the pile of mints on the palm of his hand. Delicious these are, he said, and grinned.

Bunker Man looked at him, then down at the mints, and picked up the top one in its crackly wrapper. He raised it to just below his nose, and sniffed, his eyes on Rob.

You take it out of the wee bag.

Bunker Man blinked. I'm not stupid, he said, and put the sweet away in a pocket.

I ken, said Rob, watching him zip up. You're fucking smart, you are.

Bunker Man made his fingers into a grab and lifted the pile of mints from Rob's palm. Are you not wanting any? he said.

Rob shook his head. They're for you. He smiled.

Bunker Man dropped the sweets into the side pocket of his parka. Then he unzipped his top pocket again, took out the first mint, threw his head back, and let the After Eight slip into his gob. He chewed. Sweet, he said after a few seconds. So sweet. I haven't tasted sweetness for a long time.

Rob laughed. This girl's sweet, he said.

Bunker Man ran the tip of his tongue over his lips, first all the way round clockwise, then all the way back the other way. What girl? he said.

193

The girl I want you to fuck.

Bunker Man was frowning. I don't know about that, he said.

Rob sighed. Are we friends or what?

There was a pause. What if she doesn't like me?

Don't worry. She'll love you.

Will she?

I'll tell her all about you, she'll love you.

I don't know. . .

And you'll love her. She's got beautiful thin ankles.

I better be careful, said Bunker Man. I still don't know my own strength, exactly.

Those ankles could snap like twigs, said Rob, and laughed.

He had wondered if the latch might be locked from the inside, but his key turned and the door opened and he stepped into the dark house. He kicked off his shoes, and nipped into the bathroom for a wash, pish and brush of the teeth. He hummed to himself as he scrubbed the toothbrush about.

Then he went up the stairs, opened the bedroom door as quietly as possible. The curtains weren't completely closed. Yellow light from the lamp outside cut across Karen's clothes scattered on the floor, and the covers that curved up over her hip and shoulder. She lay with her back to the empty side of the bed, his side.

He started to undress. As he pulled down the zip of his breeks, Karen stirred, and when he let them fall to the floor, she raised herself a fraction from the pillow and turned her head in his direction.

Who's that? she said, sounding three-quarters asleep.

Who were you expecting? He took off his socks and boxers and chucked them towards the laundry basket.

Rob?

Yeah. He stood there, his back to the window, looking down at her.

I was worried.

The sleepiness of her voice excited him for some reason. I went for a walk, he said. His cock was starting to harden. He reached down and gripped it, chugged his fist up and down a couple times.

What are you doing? she murmured.

He waited without answering, but she didn't say anything else. He pulled back the downie and wriggled over towards her, pressing himself against her back, his arms circling round to hold her neck and her belly.

Mm, she went.

He brought his right hand round from in front of her, gripped his stiff cock again, and steered the end of it down against her buttocks. He pushed one finger along between till it found her arsehole, then guided his cock along the finger till it touched the knot of muscle there.

Relax, baby, relax, he whispered into her hair, and started pushing his cock into her.

What. . .

He put his hand back round to just above her cunt, and held it there so her hips wouldn't slide away when he shoved. And now he did shove, hard against her, she made a noise, waved a hand, still all but asleep, and he clenched his teeth and thrust as hard as he could, and the head of his cock was grated as it started to penetrate the valve of her arse, and she screamed, leapt away from him and out of bed, and stood there, naked, looking down on him, her face screwed up in a fury.

That's another thing you do, she shouted. You always try and put it up my bum when you're drunk!

She grabbed an edge of the downie, yanked it off the bed and wrapped herself in it, then stomped off out of the room, down the stairs, and into the lounge.

Neither of them had ever slept on the settee before. This was a historic night.

Rob found Donald in the games hall, refereeing a game of five-a-side for the youth club. The next time play stopped, Donald called out, Look, lads, here's Mr Catto come to supersub! Already stripped for action!

Rob waved away Donald's suggestion. Just passing through, he said.

The footballers had glanced up for a second. Now they were concentrating on the free kick that was about to be taken. Donald peeped on his whistle then crossed the hall towards Rob, keeping his eye on the ricocheting ball all the time.

Thought you were jannying, ref, not reffing?

Ach, one of the leaders is off sick, so. . .

Job descriptions, Don, watch the job descriptions.

Donald grinned, turned away from play to speak to Rob. There was a thump of ball against brick and a roar of Goal! from half the players. The other half immediately started shouting, No way! Miles outside the post! and calling on the referee for justice.

Donald winked at Rob, gave a blast on his whistle, and trotted off towards the goalmouth. Both teams crowded round him.

Who's in control here? shouted Rob from the sideline. Come on, let's get this sorted!

Don bent to pick up the ball, whistle gripped in clenched teeth, then gave a series of peeps, showing with signs of his hands that he was going to do a bounce-up. The team that thought they'd scored started howling.

Come on ref! shouted Rob. Let's have a proper decision – goal or no goal? – none of this sitting on the fence!

Donald looked up at him, winked again, then blew his whistle once more and raised the ball over his head in both hands. Rob turned and left the hall.

He went along to the bothy, got a key out of the box on the wall, then headed back towards the school office. He paused at the door, glanced down the corridor, then back towards the bothy. There was no one about. He opened the door and went in.

The carpet on the floor of the office was thick, and the room seemed quieter and warmer than the rest of the school. He stood just inside the door and looked around, keeping his breathing quiet and slow. The heat was making him sweat, and he could quite clearly hear his heart thudding. He felt like he was breaking into the place, for fuck's sake! Bad enough kids crawling in through windows and smashing their school up – imagine the jannie being caught doing it! Terrible!

But he wasn't going to smash the place up. He stared at the computer for a few seconds. It looked so easy to use, just like a telly, but he didn't even know how to switch the fucker on. It was always a bit of an embarrassment when kids started rabbiting on about them, assuming he knew what all the jargon meant, expecting him to be interested in the latest programme they'd seen or whatever. They might as well have been talking Martian for all he knew about it. One time he started telling a bunch of them how when he was at school there weren't any computers, but they all thought he was joking. So he told them how one day in his fourth year, just before he left, the maths department got one delivered, and set it up in the book store. Every maths class that day got filed in to look at the thing, sitting on a wee desk up the far end of the store-room. None of the teachers knew how to work it, so it just sat there, and the kids shuffled past it, half scared it might start speaking to them, or screaming, Exterminate! and poking out a laser gun.

The lucky thing was that half the staff *still* didn't know how to work the computer, so most of the pupils' files were stored on good old paper as well as the machine. It was just a matter of finding the right filing cabinet, and even that wasn't too hard. There was a whole wall of them, right enough, but Mrs Ellis had them all labelled with different coloured cards.

Rob stepped from one cabinet to the next, reading the cards as he passed. He opened one with a pink label and flicked through the dividers, but they contained information about kids that'd already left. The next one had pink labels too, so he ignored it and passed on to a couple with green cards. Within seconds he'd found what he was looking for, the Bs were in the top drawer, and there was only one Burnett in the school: Burnett, Sandra Daniella.

His lips were dry. He picked the couple bits of A4 out of the divider and read them. One had a copy of a week's timetable with all her classes written in. The other had her address and phone number, and some details about her folks and their daytime contacts. He wetted his tongue and ran it over his lips, then sat down in Mrs Ellis's swivel chair and picked up the phone. He pressed 9 for an outside line, then dialled her number. There was no answer. Fuck, he said to himself, but his mouth was so dried out he could hardly speak. He circled his tongue around inside his cheeks and worked his molars against each other till he had a mouthful of spit.

Hello?

Someone had picked up the phone. He opened his mouth to speak but it was full of spit, and a slaver dribbled out onto the mouthpiece. He swallowed, wiped his mouth with the back of his hand.

Hello, said the voice again. Who's there?

He thought it was her. Sandra?

Aye?

Say it's a wrong number if you can't talk. Just hang up.

There was a pause. It's alright, she said at last. There's just me in.

Thank god for that. He leant back in the swivel seat.

Is that you? she said.

It's me, Badman.

She chuckled. Badman? Is that what you call yourself?

Aye, that's my codename.

Oh aye? I ken who you really are!

Shh!

Well, Badman, how are you theday?

Feeling bad, he said. Very bad. I'm feeling very very bad.

That's good, she said.

Are you feeling bad too? he said, and he felt his cock start to twitch.

I always feel bad, she said, and laughed again.

Fuck's sake, he said. His cock was completely hard now.

What?

I want to fuck your brains out, he whispered.

What?

Fuck, he said. I want to fuck fuck fuck fuck fuck fuck fuck you.

She was silent for a second, then she let a breath out. I want you to, I want you to fuck me.

I'm going to fuck you. I'm going to fucking well fuck you, you little fucker. I'm going to fuck your cunt, your beautiful cunt, I'm going to fuck it. You're a beautiful cunt and I'm going to fuck you.

I want you to, she said.

Will I come over to the cunt's place?

No!

I ken where it is.

They'll be back in half an hour.

That's not long enough for the fucking you're going to get.

Em. . . He heard her breathing. How about the school?

No, I'm there now, there's too many folk. Wait. . . He leant back in his chair, thinking. I'll meet you at the cliff path, he said. The usual place. But then I've got a new place in mind. I'll take you there, baby. I'll fucking take you there and fuck your brains out.

Hey, you're a bad man, mister!

I'm a very bad man.

And I'm a bad girl.

You're a very bad girl.

I'm the worst girl in the world.

You're worse than me. You're the fucking worst. That's why I'm going to fuck you, cause you're fucking bad and you deserve to get fucked. Completely fucked.

I deserve to get fucked.

Too right you do. And I'm the one to fucking do it.

I need you, Badman.

I'll be there in fifteen minutes.

I'll run. I'll be waiting for you with open arms.

Good.

And open legs.

That's good, fuckbird, that's the way I like them.

I love you, Badman.

Fuck fuck fuck fuck fuck fuck fuck. He hung up.

Before leaving the office he'd photocopied the files with Sandra's details on them. He could feel the folded paper creasing and uncreasing in the pocket of his shorts as he jogged.

At first he thought he'd beaten her to it. She wasn't waiting where the pathways joined, nor coming along from the direction of the town, as far as he could see. He stopped, looked at his watch, then gazed back the way he'd come on the off chance she'd decided to take a strange route through the woods. No sign.

Then he heard a stirring, and what sounded like a giggle being muffled by a fist. He made on not to have heard anything, sighed, and turned back to the main path again, putting a bored look on his face. As he turned, something moved at the edge of a whin bush, just off at the sea side. He watched the spot, without seeming to, and after a few seconds could make out an elbow in a blue denim jacket. He took a step in the direction of the elbow, faking a glance at his watch again, then suddenly let out a roar and jumped sideways past the bush and fell on the girl crouching there.

She screamed then grunted as his weight knocked the breath out of her, then squirmed underneath him to turn and get her face out of the dirt. He wouldn't let her turn, pressed her down onto the ground with one hand between her shoulder blades and the other on her arse. She tried to speak, so he pressed down harder and her voice was stifled. Then he moved the second hand down and under her skirt and squeezed one of her buttocks hard, the tips of his fingers gripping into the crevice of her arse.

Guess who? he said, putting on a gruff voice.

She spoke, but her mouth was still shoved against the ground. He eased up the pressure.

Whoever it is, she said. He's a bad, bad man.

He grinned. Got it in one! he said, and let go of her.

She rolled over and looked up at him. Oh, it's *you*!

Who else?

There's a lot of bad men about, you ken.

He frowned. Not as bad as me. I'm the worst. I'm *the* Bad Man.

She smiled. Hello Bad Man, she said.

Hello bad girl.

He leaned forward, put one hand behind her head, the other out to one side to support himself, and looked down into her eyes.

I used to love weekends, she said. Cause they meant no school. Now I hate them, cause I don't see you. Or that's what I thought. She grinned. Now I love them again. But I love. . .

He lowered his head and kissed her, before she could finish the sentence. After a couple minutes he broke away and looked down at her some more. Come on, he said. Come away to my castle. I'm going to lock you in the dungeon and only let you out at fucktime.

Fucktime, she said. When's that?

All the time.

Sounds good to me.

Oh, this old place, she said.

You ken it?

Everybody kens it – everybody used to come out here to drink or smoke their hash or whatever.

Used to?

Aye, they just do it down the High Street now. Nobody gives them hassle like they used to. Nobody gives a toss.

Watch out for the garden wall!

What?

He stepped ahead, moved a couple of the stones aside, and ushered her through. They walked on to the bunker.

I've done the place up a bit, said Rob.

Done it up?

Well, me and a friend of mine. He's done a lot of it. He might be there just now, actually.

She looked at him, frowning. I thought we were going to screw. I don't want any spectators!

Rob faced her, held both her hands in his. Don't worry. He's probably not there. And if he is, I'll just ask him to leave us. Okay?

She nodded, pouting, then raised her head and kissed him.

Wait here, he said.

He left her, and strolled round to the front of the pill-box. There was nobody there, and the slot window was blocked on the inside with what looked to be a bit of carpet, so he couldn't see if Bunker Man was at home. He'd have to go inside.

The zigzag corridor between the concrete walls had been completely cleared out. There was no rubble or rubbish, and no trace of the rotting sheep, thank fuck. Another piece of old carpet had been hung in the door space. Rob tried to knock on it, but it just sagged in where his fist hit it, so he lifted one edge of the carpet aside, and called in.

Hello? Anyone about? It's me: Jannie Man.

There was no reply. Rob listened, but there was nothing to hear inside the bunker, just the faint noise of the sea slashing the bottom of the crags.

His eyes were getting used to the dark of the place. All the old shite was gone. There was a pile of driftwood in one corner, fresh ashes in the hearth, a worn nylon shoulder-bag with clothes spilling out of it, and a flowery sleeping-bag lying on top of a row of upturned plastic fishboxes next to the fire.

He ducked out of the place, nipped down the corridor, and stuck his head round the edge of the entranceway. Sandra was standing with her hands stuffed in the tight pockets of her jeans, a fag jutting up from her lips.

Took your time! she said when she saw him.

Come on, he said. It's not the Ritz, but if I get my way you won't be looking at the decor.

She brushed against him as she passed. You always get your way, she said.

With you I do.

It's good to know I can please *someone*, she said, dropping her half-smoked fag on the floor of the corridor.

He crushed the smouldering cigarette under his foot, then reached past her and pulled the carpet-door to one side. Welcome to Fuckingham Palace, he said.

She laughed, and stepped inside.

Rob insisted that they both take all their clothes off. They'd never done it anywhere sheltered enough to strip properly before. She mumbled something about not wanting to, about puppy fat, but he wasn't listening, he'd already unfastened her jeans and was sticking his hands up inside her T-shirt, lifting it towards her head. Once he was naked too, they fucked on top of the fishboxes, her going completely mental as usual as soon as his cock went into her.

A second before he was away to come, Rob remembered he hadn't a Durex on. He jerked himself out of her, just in time for spunk to go sluicing up over her belly, chest and neck. She yelled, bucked against him more, so he pushed two fingers up her cunt and jabbed away with them while his damp cock, so hard now it was hurting him, dug into her side.

Suddenly she curled over so his fingers slipped out of her, and she took his cock into her mouth and held it there. The tip of her tongue circled the hole at the end with tiny movements that felt like hammer blows. He howled, she kept on licking, breath stuttered out of him.

He screamed. It was killing him, the feeling of it.

He leapt off her and stood at the side of the dead fire, crouching down and cupping his balls in one hand, the other held out in her direction to ward her off, to show he was alright.

After a few seconds he straightened, wiped the tears away from his eyes, and looked at her. She'd got inside the sleeping bag and was lying there, one hand down between her legs, the other holding the flap of the bag open. In the half-light he could see small glistening patches across her skin.

Look, he said, and pointed at them.

Come in beside me.

You're covered in spunk.

So? Come on. . .

If it was my wife I wouldn't go fucking near her, he said. I'd be sick. Jesus! The thought of her skin touching me!

I'm not your wife, she said. Come in.

You're a dirty cunt, he said. I'm going to break your bones in pieces and suck out the shit from inside.

Come in beside me, she said. Hug me and I'll hug you. Come on, we need a hug.

He looked at her for a second, then did what she said.

Rob woke up feeling cold and with pains in his back. Not much fucking wonder. He was lying in a derelict gun-bunker on a bed made of fishboxes.

His right arm was numb. Sandra's head was resting on it, her face pressed into the side of his chest. The only warm part of his body was where her breath was touching his skin.

He examined her. She looked very soft, very young. When she was awake and in control of her face, it was full of sharp angles – eyes, cheekbones, jaw – and she behaved like that too. Now she was sleeping, all the sharpness had gone out of her, and she was – well, she wasn't behaving like anything, she was unconscious, but she looked very young. She looked like a kid. He didn't like her looking like that. He felt like he'd been tricked somehow.

He eased his arm out from under her head, lifted the flap of the sleeping bag, and stood up. She murmured something, but he didn't reply, and it wasn't till his belt-buckle clinked as he stood over her finishing dressing that she opened her eyes, focused on him, then yawned. When the yawn ended, her mouth settled into its hard-edged line again.

Morning, said Rob.

Were you going to run off and leave me?

What? No. He shrugged. I woke up, felt a bit cold, so. . .

She pulled the sleeping bag up to her chin, shivering. Aye, I ken what you mean.

He grinned at her. Are you getting up then?

Not with you watching.

What! After what we just did? You're shy again?

You could wait outside. I bet the sun's blazing down, and here's us stuck in the black hole of Dunnottar.

Rob considered, nodded, and walked out of the bunker.

It was sunny outside and the wind had dropped to almost nothing. He stretched his arms into the air, opening his fingers wide, feeling the sun's heat on the palms of his hands. Then he let them fall, yawned, and strolled round to the front of the pillbox. Far out at sea, right on the fracture-line between water and sky, sat a long flat ship, with a bridge like a turret at one end.

I don't think I like you any more.

Rob turned, raised his eyes. Bunker Man was kneeling on the edge of the roof, his hood up, a glum look on his face.

Hullo there, said Rob, quietly. I did look for you earlier to ask if it'd be okay, but you weren't about, so. . .

I was at the bird cliffs.

Seagull for tea is it?

No. Eggs.

Rob looked at him. What are you doing on the roof?

I was watching you.

What!

Through the smoke hole.

You fucking. . . you fucking pervert!

You call me a pervert? said Bunker Man, and laughed.

What are you saying? What did you see? There was fuck all to see!

I saw you sleeping with the girl.

Sleeping?

Aye.

Is that all?

I saw what you were dreaming, too.

For god's sake. Rob turned away, looked out to sea. It was very blue in the sunlight, almost the colour of the school uniform shirts that nobody wore except in old photos. Something thumped behind him: Bunker Man jumping off the roof.

He came alongside. Could you swim it?

What? said Rob. The sea?

Aye. Could you swim it?

Well. . . it depends how far.

To the other side. To England.

England? England's not over there. It's not over the sea at all.

Yes it is.

Rob shook his head. It's not.

Why's the castle pointing in that direction then?

What castle?

This one. He jerked his head over his shoulder. My castle.

The bunker? That's against, eh, the Germans. The Nazis.

Now Bunker Man was shaking his head. No, he said. It's against England.

Look, I'm telling you. . . said Rob.

Whose fucking castle is it?

Yours! Yours!

So I say who it's against, okay?

Okay, okay!

It's bad enough you coming sleeping in my bed. . .

I owe you one, right?

You do.

I ken I do. I'll pay you back. Anyway, it's all part of the plan: you wait and see.

Bunker Man stared at him, opened his mouth to speak.

Robbie! It was Sandra, shouting from round by the entrance passage.

Bunker Man froze, looked at Rob with panic in his face, then pushed him away, flapped his hands towards the entrance, and scuttled off in the opposite direction.

Rob watched him for a second, then turned away, Hull-o! he called, and started walking towards her.

She was leaning against the wall in the sun, smoking, looking older again. Thought you'd pissed off for a minute, she said. Then I heard you talking to yourself.

Eh? Oh, aye! Aye.

What time is it? she said, leaning her head back into the sunshine, closing her eyes.

Rob checked his watch. Just after twelve. We must've slept nearly an hour.

She nodded. Do you have to be back?

Not really. The wife's used to me going away jogging. How about you?

Her lips were closed in a tight line. I don't have a wife.

No, but. . .

And I wish you wouldn't keep going on about yours.

He shrugged, then realised her eyes were still closed. Sorry, he said. But the main thing is, I don't have to be back at all. I mean. . . forget her.

Sandra leant off the wall, smiled at him. Will we go for a walk then?

Okay, but where? We can't go into town.

No problem. We'll go further along the cliffs. There's beaches and everything: wee coves where we could lie down and not be disturbed.

He nodded. You're the boss, he said.

They headed north along the cliffpath. At first it was wide and well-trodden, but the further away they got from the town, the narrower and rougher it became. Sandra took hold of Rob's hand, but to begin with he pulled away from her grip.

What if somebody sees? he said.

Nobody comes this far out.

But if they did – Christ, even us being together!

They walked a step apart and almost silent for five minutes. Then Rob stopped, turned, put his arms around her shoulders and kissed her. Then he took her hand and they walked on.

Nobody comes this far out, eh?

She shook her head. Not many.

Only us bad folk with something to hide.

Aye. She laughed.

The path was narrow. Walking side by side made them keep banging into each other. Rob put his arm around her shoulders, tried to see if that was any easier, but it just meant they were banging into each other all the time instead of occasionally. Plus it felt really fucking strange having his arm around the shoulders of anybody else but Karen. The funny thing was, he'd been sucking Sandra's tits, and sticking his fingers and cock up her cunt, and he'd never once thought of it as being different from Karen, or the same as Karen. In fact he'd never thought about Karen at all. But now this wee thing, this wee matter of Sandra being a couple inches shorter than Karen, and the way that made his arm ache a bit when he put it round her shoulders, that reminded him it wasn't his wife he was with. It made the image of her keep flichtering into his mind; she looked furious and also fucking heartbrokenly sad.

Rob was beginning to feel guilty. He didn't like the feeling.

He took his arm from around her, and stuck his hand in the pocket of his jacket. She linked her arm through it, and looked up at him. That made him feel even worse. He took his hand out of the pocket and let her hold it again.

Listen, he said, stooping to get under the branches of a half-couped tree. I'm not going to go on about it, but I just want to get it straight between us from the start.

There's one thing very straight between us already, she said.

Aye, that's what I mean. It's sex between me and you, pure sex, right, nothing else.

She squeezed his fingers between hers.

I fuck your brains out and you suck my cock, he went on. That's all there is to it. It's nothing to do with. . . fuck.

With what?

I'm married, right, said Rob, in a quiet voice. I'm not even going to say I love my wife, cause that doesn't matter, it's irrelevant. What matters is me and you having a fucking good time together. What matters is (a) Nobody must know, (b) I'm not leaving my wife or anything, (c) It's nothing to do with love.

Sandra let go of Rob's hand while they scrambled up a rocky slope in the path. He looked at her as they reached the top.

I'm being straight with you, he said. I'm honest, always honest, too honest some folk would say. The point is: if you want love, forget it. It's sex you'll get from me. If you want love, fuck off now, don't waste my time. If you want fucked, stick around: I'll fucking shove it up you till your eyes water.

For a few seconds she didn't reply, just looked down at the path sloping away from them through the rocks. Then she took his hand again, and pulled him onwards. Pure sex is fine, she said. I like it. I mean, you know where you are with it. Like when you're fucking me, I know you're fucking me, and I know we're both having a good time.

Aye. A great time.

But if you or anybody started saying they loved me, well, I'd just start worrying. I mean, how could I be sure they weren't lying? Just saying it cause they thought they should? I mean, what is love? You can't see it, you can't hold it – everyone talks about it, but no one's ever shown me a bit of it.

Messy stuff.

When your cock's inside me, when you're holding me tight, when you're squeezing the breath out of me, I can feel all that, I can be sure about it, I love it.

Rob nodded. I reckon it's good to talk about all this, he said. To be honest from the start, ken? I mean, folk waste so much time lying to each other, pretending to be things they're not, behaving ways they think the other person wants them to. And it never works. You can't hide your true self for ever.

Whereas me and you. . .

Me and you should be honest from the start. Well, that's what we are being. It's a new way of doing things. It means we're going to have a really good time together.

She tickled his palm with the tip of her pinkie. I know we are.

Cause we can be honest about our desires.

Our desires! That sounds good!

And if we say what they are, that's the first step in making them happen.

Talking about steps, she said, slowing. If we take a few off to the sea side here, we should be able to scramble down to that wee bay, and we'll never be found. We could make something happen there.

Lead on, he said, and laughed.

The path veered inland round the head of the bay, but they cut off it and started down the steep grassy slope towards the sand. It was too sheer to run down; they had to go sideways, leaning back on one hand for support and balance, occasionally gripping onto a broom bush or a clump of reedy grass to steady themselves.

Glancing across the curved beach as he scrambled down, Rob saw that it was littered with big cubes of concrete, some half-covered in drifting sand, all crumbling at the edges. They lay in a rough line across the mouth of the bay, halfway between the sea and the boggy area of grass and dockens that separated it from the neep park inland. The blocks looked like they'd been tossed up on the shore by the waves, but Rob knew that couldn't be the explanation.

Sandra reached the beach first, and gave a whoop as her feet touched the sand. She headed off along it in a gangling run, her arms and legs flailing out at angles like she was trying to shake them off. Rob sprinted after her, caught up easily, and launched himself forward to grab her shins in a rugby tackle the mannie Jackson would've been proud of.

Sandra screamed as she hit the sand, then laughed as Rob started untying the laces of her trainers and pulling them off her feet. She got up onto her knees and started crawling away, heading for the nearest concrete cube. Rob crawled after her, laughing too, and as she came into the lee of the block he shouted, Stop! If we stay behind this, no one'll see us from the path. We could do anything.

She stopped, stood up, and watched him as he covered the last couple of yards towards her on his knees. What did you have in mind? she said.

Desires! he cried, jumping to his feet.

Oh those! Are you going to tell me first, or just surprise me?

He laughed and advanced on her, pushed her back against the side of the concrete block, one hand on each shoulder, then bent his head and kissed her. She pushed her tongue into his mouth and let it lie there, not stirring, till he closed his teeth and gripped it. He slowly increased the pressure of his bite, watching her face as he did so. After a second her eyes opened and looked into his. He moved his lower jaw from side to side, still nipping with his front teeth. Her eyes opened wider. He released his bite for an instant, then clamped it shut again, harder than before. Her eyes were staring now, and she was making whimpering noises down in her throat. He couldn't take any more of it, he just had to let her go and let the laughter out.

He gave a final sharp nip, then opened his jaws, jumped back, and roared.

Sandra just stood there for a moment, a shocked look on her face, her tongue still half out. Then she drew it in, blinked the water away from her eyes, and said, That was fucking sore, you bastard!

He laughed some more.

It's not funny!

You should've seen your face, he said.

She wiped a hand across her mouth.

I'd like to see you explain that to your folks! Sorry mum, sorry dad, my boyfriend bit my tongue off in a fit of passion. I tellt him to give me a lovebite and he got the wrong idea!

She looked at him.

Of course, he went on, if you'd no tongue you couldn't've told them what happened – you wouldn't be able to speak! Ha!

Sandra looked away, shrugged. What's the difference? They don't listen anyway.

Rob paused, sighed, then stepped up to her and put his arms around her. He rested his cheek on the top of her head, and the sweet smell of her hair filled his mouth.

What's that perfume you're wearing? he said.

I'm not wearing any.

Nothing at all?

Are you saying I smell?

In a good way! You smell amazing. Of life! You smell of fucking youngness and life! He breathed in deeply. You're young and you're alive, what more could you ask, eh? Tell me that! No, I'll tell you: nothing. Cause there *is* nothing more. You have it all, Sandra, you have it fucking all.

She lifted her face and looked up at him. Do I?

Yeah, you fucking do.

I don't feel like I do, she said, lowering her face again, and pressing it into his chest. I don't feel like I've anything really.

You do, you fucking do!

He felt her breath hot on his skin through the cotton of his T-shirt.

I've got you, Rob. You're the only thing I've got.

He didn't speak.

You're the only thing I have that matters. If it wasn't for you I

215

don't ken what I'd do. I'd jump in the sea and swim straight out, keep going till I couldn't swim any more. Thank god I have you. Thank god.

She clasped her arms tight around his waist, pushed her face hard into his shirt. She was breathing in shudders, and the sound of it was giving him an erection.

Listen, he said, and twined his fingers into the back of her hair. Listen. I'm glad I have you too. I care for you, Sandra, I really do.

Rob. . .

That's why I wouldn't want you to get pregnant. Not now. I mean it would cause all sorts of problems.

She let out a sound that was half laugh, half sob. You're not joking!

That's another thing I should've said earlier. If you did get pregnant, you couldn't let on it was mine. No way. I'd arrange it so somebody else got the blame. Tell some remedial halfwit to come to the bothy, have you half undressed inside, then you'd grab him, shout rape, and I'd come running in, give him a battering, and save you. And he'd be too thick to know he wasn't to blame for the bairn!

He pulled down on her hair till her face was tilted up towards his. She was half smiling, but also blinking again, trying to get rid of the tears in her eyes, trying not to let him see them. That made his cock so hard he knew for sure she'd be feeling it, through his shorts and her jeans even.

But it would be better if it didn't come to that, he said. There's something we can do. I should've got some more johnnies, I ken, but I just. . . forgot. So. . . trust me Sandra.

I do.

I mean I could've bitten your tongue off, but I didn't, I was only kidding. Trust me.

Rob, I do. She stretched up and kissed him on the tip of the nose, then on the chin, then on the lips.

Turn around, he said.

She turned.

Put your hands out against the block.

She leaned forward.

He unbuttoned her jeans and pulled them and her pants down below her knees, where they jammed.

Raise your right leg.

She did, and he yanked the jeans and pants off over that foot.

Now spread your legs wide, he said. And bend over a bittie more.

She pushed her backside out towards him. He eased his jogging shorts down, then unbuttoned the wee buttons on the front of his boxers. Relax, he said. His cock was sticking out the boxers' spaver; he let the end of it touch the skin of her backside, while he raised a finger to his mouth and covered it in saliva. Then he pulled his hips out of the way, lowered the wet finger, aimed it at the pink twist of her arsehole, and shoved it in.

She cried out, the muscle tightening around the second joint of his finger, and he had to press a hand on her shoulder to stop her turning around.

Trust me, he said, moving the finger in a fraction further. Hold on to the block and relax. Trust me and relax.

Her head fell down between her propped arms, and the sphincter loosened its grip slightly round his finger. He shoved it in further, the full weight of his body behind it, then pulled it half out, worked it around a little, then pushed it in hard again.

217

Relax, he whispered. Trust me Sandra, you'll enjoy it if you relax.

Slowly he pulled the finger out, pulled it right away from her, then lifted it in a circle towards his nose. He sniffed. There, he said. That wasn't too bad, was it?

No, she said, quietly.

I bet you enjoyed it, eh?

She didn't reply.

You're so good, Sandra, he said. So good at being bad. He worked up a mouthful of spit, dropped it into the palm of his hand, then rubbed it over the end of his cock. Relax, he said. He aimed for her arsehole again. You'll like this, he said, and thrust forward. One movement, and the bulb of his cock was inside her arse. She made a noise, he didn't know what. He moved both hands down to the front of her pelvis and pulled her back against him, pulled her onto his cock, held her there for a few seconds. Then he began to fuck, pushing in and pulling out, slowly at first, then faster, faster, till his legs were slamming against her buttocks, her elbows were locked to stop him crushing her against the concrete block, his cock felt like it was pushing right up into her guts.

You fucking cunt, he was shouting. You bad bad cunt, you fucker, oh, you fucker. Take that, you fucker, take that, you cunt. Jesus fuck, you bastard, you fucker, you cunt, you fuck, you. . . ah!

As he came he gave a mighty shove, lifting her off her feet for a second, then setting her down again for a couple of final thrusts, before he let go of her hips, pulled his cock out of her arse, and turned away from her.

She didn't say anything.

After a few seconds he glanced round at her. She was beginning to fit her foot through the loose leg of her jeans.

Girl, he said. My cock's filthy. It's covered in spunk and shit. If you really loved me you'd get it clean. Wouldn't you?

She pulled up her breeks. I thought we weren't bothering with love, she said. I thought it was pure sex between us.

Love can be useful sometimes, he said, reaching out and taking her head in both his hands.

They walked along the beach, weaving in and out of the concrete cubes.

My dad used to take me here when I was young, she said.

When you were young?

Aye, when I was a kid.

He looked about at the grey sand, the scrubby sides of the bay with the bog where they met, and the crumbling, stained blocks. Surely there are bonnier beaches for a picnic? What about that big one on the other side of town?

She nodded, sidestepping to avoid a spear of rusty iron that jabbed out from one of the blocks at waist height. We went there as well, she said. We went to all the beaches. It's my dad's hobby, you see.

What, beachcombing?

She laughed. No! These things. She slapped her palm on the side of the block they were passing. Defences. He's writing a list of all the wartime coastal defences on the east side of Scotland. He's been doing it for years. He's obsessed.

That's well seen.

He goes away every weekend to a different part of the country, taking photos, measuring angles. There's thousands of the things, and they're all on his list. He did all the beaches close to home first, ken. So when I was young, when I was a kid, we'd come out here, count the blocks, measure them, work out how much they weighed, what size of tank could push them aside. He'd take photos of them from all angles, me standing beside them in my swimming costume for comparison. . .

But why bother? They're just lumps of concrete.

Not to him. He loves them. He says they're historical monuments. They should be preserved and the folk who made them should be remembered.

Christ's sake, what is he, a history teacher?

Ha! No! He's not interested in history apart from these things. He's the caretaker at Saint Andy's.

The old folk's home?

Aye. He fixes the heating and helps in the garden. Mends their zimmers and stuff, I suppose. And here, you'll like this: the old mannies come down to his wee office to complain sometimes, but they always leave with a smile on their face. Ken how?

Cause he says he'll fix the problem.

No, cause after the old mannies have yelled at him, told him what needs fixing, and are going out the door, he says, Could you look up for a second Albert? So Albert looks up, and sees that above the door my dad's pinned a centrefold from one of his magazines, some sexy girl with everything on display. And of course the old buggers love it, so they always leave the office grinning from ear to ear.

And their tongues hanging out.

My dad reckons some of them make up things to complain about, just so they can come down and have a look at his latest naughty girl. That's what he calls them: his naughty girls.

Rob was laughing. Maybe I should try that in the bothy at school. Mind you, I think some of the teachers wouldn't approve. They'd say I was corrupting the morals of the pupils or something.

Is that what you're doing to me, corrupting my morals?

Christ no. Yours were corrupted long before I came along. You're past the point of corruption, are you not?

She shrugged. I suppose so.

You're wild, girl. Your morals are invisible to the naked eye. You deserve everything you get.

Sandra looked at him, then stepped away from his side. She stared down at the sand for a moment, then did her gawky run off along the beach and round the back of a cube further down the line.

Rob laughed and strolled on, eventually coming upon her crouched on the sand with her back to the block, her chin in her hands.

She looked up. I wouldn't have sex with just anyone, you know. Just with you, cause you care for me.

He rolled his eyes. What about the others?

What others?

Come on Sandra. I can tell when somebody's been fucked, you know. And you've been well and truly fucked. You told me yourself. Two guys at a time, you told me.

She blinked. Oh yeah. I did tell you that.

So don't make on you didn't know the score when you came along flashing your gash at me.

Is that what I did?

Don't act the innocent now. Too late for that. You had your hands on my tackle before I could say John Thomas.

Well. . .

Admit it girl: you wanted somebody to fuck your brains out, and you chose me.

She stood up, sliding her back up the block, still leaning away from him. Aye, I chose you, she said. I wanted to talk to somebody, and I chose you.

Talking. Is that what you call it? Pure body language, that's what you talk.

She held his gaze. Sometimes maybe if you start with that, you can get round to the proper talking later on.

Aye. Well. Like now. We're talking now.

But not about. . . not about what I want to talk about.

Well, what's that then? Come on, spit it out. I can't hang around here all day, you ken.

She looked away. It doesn't matter.

No, come on, seriously. We had a good fuck, so we surely should be able to have a good chat too. I mean we're civilised human beings, eh? What's on your mind Sandra?

It's. . . nothing.

He shook his head. That's what I thought.

They walked back towards town, not saying much till they approached the taing with the pill-box at the end of it. A thin stripe of smoke was trailing up out of the hole in the roof, drifting inland with the slow breeze. Rob grinned to himself: Bunker Man would have his goggles on.

He slowed. Listen, he said.

What?

Mind how you were saying you wouldn't have sex with just anybody?

It's true. I ken they say I'm slack but it's not true, I hate them.

But anyway, you said you would with me cause I cared for you?

Yeah.

Well, seeing as I care for you, and I'd never ask you to do anything if I thought it'd hurt you, would you trust me if I asked you something?

I already trusted you, and look at me, I'm walking like a cowboy.

But what if I asked you to trust me again?

Well. It depends what for.

What if I asked you to sleep with somebody else?

She didn't answer for a while, then she said, Sleep?

Well, fuck.

She was silent again. Eventually she said, Is it your wife? A threesome, like?

Rob laughed. No, I don't reckon Karen would be into that.

Frigid is she?

Well. You could call it that. Pretty fucking icy these days.

What I'm saying is, I don't just sleep with anyone. I mean, if you were involved, and. . .

This is a friend of mine, said Rob. The one who helped me do up the bunker, in fact. He's a really fine guy, but he's shy, ken? He's never had a ride in his life, he's that shy.

A virgin. I thought they were killed or cured by the age of five.

Well not him. And I just know it would really cheer him up, really do him a lot of good, really bring him out of himself, if you would let him fuck you.

Rob, she said after a moment. I can't believe you're seriously putting this forward. This is somebody I've never met?

You'd mind him if you had.

I've never met him, and here's you arranging for me to go to bed with him.

I thought maybe back in the bunker there, actually. We could go there right now.

What?

You'd have nothing to worry about. I'd be there too.

It is a threesome! Another man and me, you kinky bugger.

Here! Shut it! I wouldn't be joining in, just watching. Nothing kinky at all.

She shook her head. I don't think so.

I wouldn't even be watching, really. I'd just be standing by. So if he got out of hand I could smash his head in.

No, I don't like the sound of it.

For fuck's sake Sandra. What's one more squirt up a cunt like yours? It'd make no difference to you, but it'd mean the world to this guy. He'd die happy after fucking you.

What do you mean, a cunt like mine? Are you saying I'm a slag?

No, no. I'm saying you're into sex, that's all. Why not? There's nothing wrong with that. I'm into sex as well. If you asked me to fuck your friend for a favour, I'd do it right away.

If you fucked my friend she'd probably fall apart into a pile of bones, she's that skinny.

I wouldn't care, I'd do it anyway, I'd quite fancy that.

Well that's you. I'm different. I like to feel something about whoever I'm fucking. I mean to say, it's about the only time I get to feel anything these days. I'm not keen to give up my one chance of getting some happy feelings.

Jesus Christ.

What?

All this talk about feelings. Why do women always go on about their fucking feelings this and feelings that? Ken what feelings are? Feelings are things invented by women to give them an excuse for behaving unfuckinglogically.

Rubbish.

I've got a feeling right now, I'll tell you: the feeling I'd like to slap you across the fucking face, fucking chin you, you bitch.

It's funny, that's a feeling a lot of men get.

With you? I'm not surprised. Christ, you're a cunt on a stick, right enough, but you're a fucking annoying wee bitch as well. I've never hit a woman before, Sandra, but I could fucking belt you. Sometimes I could punch your fucking face in. And you deserve it, that's the thing, you fucking ask for it.

One minute you say I'm asking for sex, the next I'm asking for a kicking.

It's the same thing with you: punching and fucking, it's all you're good for in this life. That's why you were put on this earth: to be punched and fucked and like it.

No!

Come on, admit it.

It doesn't have to be that way. I'm going to change.

Rob rubbed his hands over his face for a few seconds. When he dropped them he spoke in a calm voice. Are you saying you won't help me, then?

I thought you were different, Rob, but you're not, you're the same, you're worse. I'm not going to help you, I'm going to help me.

She glared at him for a second, then jumped off the path and into the woods, going crashing off through the trees and undergrowth in the direction of the school. Rob tensed his

225

muscles to race after her, then changed his mind, relaxed, and let her go.

Rob was already in bed when she came into the room. He watched her undressing. Compared to the girl she looked broad. She wasn't broad really, she was slim, but there was something more solid about her, and she had hips and a chest. Compared to Sandra she was much more solid.

What are you looking at? she said, pausing on the point of unfastening her bra.

He closed his eyes. Are you not sleeping downstairs thenight, then?

Why should I get a crick in my neck?

Through his eyelashes he watched her take the bra off and pull on the baggy T-shirt she slept in during the winter.

You're the one causing trouble, she went on. Why should I suffer cause you're a stirring bastard? *You* sleep on the settee.

She got into the bed, careful not to touch him, and lay on her back looking up at the ceiling, a calm set to her face.

I don't want to sleep on the settee, he said.

Fine.

I'm sleeping right here.

Fine fine fine.

He waited. Are you staying?

It's my bed too, you ken.

So you are?

Rob. I am sleeping here, in the bedroom. Okay?

Good.

Good?

He sighed.

No I'm sorry Rob, but for a minute there I thought you said it was good I was sleeping here. It seemed like you were saying you wanted me here almost. Surely not. I mean, that doesn't sound like the Robert Catto of recent days.

Rob sighed again. I'm sorry, he said.

What for?

Well. . . whatever it is I did to upset you.

You don't even know, do you?

Know what, for god's sake?

You don't even know why you should be apologising. You don't even know what it is you've done wrong.

Well. . .

This is the worst bit about it, the worst bit about *you*, Rob: you don't know when you're in the wrong. I don't think you're putting it on, I think you really do believe you're right all the time and everybody else is in the wrong. It's a joke, the world's unfunniest joke. Think about it Rob. I mean even by the laws of probability, you're bound to be wrong sometimes: everybody is.

Rob thought for a few seconds, then said, But what if somebody tried really hard to be right, to get things right? What if they tried hard to do the right things, and also to get everybody around them to stop doing wrong too? I mean that would work against the probability rule. It would be somebody taking control of their life and trying to be right always – not just drifting along right half the time and wrong the other half, cause some statistic says that's the way it's go to be.

Karen groaned. Do you really think you're in control of what you're doing, Rob?

Aye. Cause I am. Everybody is. Everybody has to choose between the right and the wrong, that's what I think. If they choose right then they're right, if they choose wrong they deserve everything they get. That's what I think. It's a free choice all along the line.

Aye, but there's something you're missing out: the effect your choices have on other folk. Say I choose to be nice to you, treat you like I love you and trust you.

Rob snorted.

No, but if I did: that's my choice. But if you then come along and you choose to treat me horribly, treat me like you hate me, like I sicken you, like you want to hurt me – well, that kind of interferes with the choice I made, doesn't it? It doesn't matter what I choose if you come along and mess it up.

Rob sighed, swung his legs out from under the downie, and stood up.

What are you doing?

I'm choosing to go for a pish, he said. And I hope that choice doesn't mess up your nice little life too much. I hope it doesn't mess up anything but the lavvie pan. He left the room and went down to the bathroom.

By the time he came back upstairs, Karen had switched the lamp out. It was just as well. Standing in the glare of the bathroom, he'd noticed that his cock was red-raw. The chances of Karen wanting a close-up look of it in the near future seemed pretty slight, but still it was good to know she wouldn't catch a glimpse of it and maybe start asking difficult questions. Maybe he should get in first anyway, mental attack being the best form of mental fucking self-defence.

Karen, he said as he slid in beside her.

What?

Are you awake?

228

No, I'm talking in my sleep.

It's just. . . I wanted to ask you something.

Go ahead, Rob. You can't make things worse.

I just wondered where you were theday, that's all.

Where *I* was?

I tellt you where I was: out jogging.

For six hours? Where did you run to, Aberdeen?

No, I tellt you: I dropped in at the school, had a blether with Donald, then went up the coast a bit. But not that far. Anyway, we're not talking about me. I was asking you. . .

I already tellt you too. I waited till three and you still hadn't come back from your morning run, so I thought, sod him, and I went off to the supermarket by myself.

And then?

And then I went round to Susan's and we had a cup of coffee. And by the end of it she told me she thought I needed a drink, so we cracked open the wine box I'd just bought and got wired into that. Next time I looked up it was nine o'clock, the wine was nearly done, and Susan's mascara was all run from laughing so much. So I got a taxi home.

You're sticking to that story, are you?

It's not a story, it's true.

Well well. And why were you laughing so much?

What! I can't mind every daft thing we said!

Give me an example then. I mean what were you talking about?

Jesus Christ Robbie! I was probably talking about you half the time, saying what a total bastard you are. That's probably why she reckoned I needed a drink. To drown the sorrows of life with you. Aye. That was it. Thank god I have good friends like Susan, good woman friends. I used to have Mo to talk to, and now I have Susan, thank Christ. Cause no matter what you treat me like, what shite you spout, I know that if I go to her and tell her, she'll believe me, she'll talk it through with me, she'll understand. Why? Cause she'd been through exactly the same crap. Why? Cause she's a woman.

Fuck's sake, said Rob, and rolled over.

That's right, she said. Turn away from it, turn away from me. Cause you can't stand to think of me like that: you can't face it. Ken what Susan says our motto should be? Women of the world unite: you have nothing to lose but your chaps. She started laughing. Good, eh? But you can't face it, can you? You just couldn't believe such a thing was possible, that's why you're getting the hump now.

I'm not getting the hump.

Well it looks like that to me.

I'm just. . . jealous, that's all.

Jealous? Don't start that again. I thought we sorted that out the other night, after you had your wee brainstorm about Grant.

No, not jealous in that way. I mean jealous of this thing you have of other women understanding you, of automatically being on your side. Christ, I wish I had somebody on *my* side.

What? All the men in the world are on your side.

No they're not.

You're saying men aren't on the same side as each other, versus all the women?

No way. Maybe men are against women, but they're against each other as well. This is it, Karen: if I walk into a pub full of men, or into the bothy at work, or if I bump into some guys I know down town, well, I don't feel I'm with *allies*. I feel I'm with *enemies*. Christ, every man is a rival to every other man.

Come on. A rival for what? For getting the best woman? Don't give me that knights in shining armour crap.

No, not that kind of rival. Just a rival in the fight to keep on *living*. Every man is an enemy of every other man, a competitor, a rival. We all hate each other. You can't relax for a second for fear of getting stabbed in the back. That's what being a man's like. Not much wonder I'm jealous of this thing you women have – this trust, and this helping each other. Christ, I could do with some of that, but no chance. Me against the world, that's what it is. The whole fucking world against me! Not much wonder I'm fucking. . . fucked up. Christ, it's battle stations twenty-four hours a day when you're a man.

It doesn't have to be.

That's the way it fucking is.

Well what happens if you just wave the white flag, refuse to fight? What happens if you just surrender?

Rob closed his eyes to stop the tears springing out. You die, he said. Surrender equals death.

Because it'd been a late night, Rob didn't wake till nearly ten. Karen was already up and about though; he could hear her banging and thumping down below. He got dressed and went down, drank orange juice out of the carton, then took an apple from the bowl in the middle of the table. He bit into it, juice ran down his chin, and he chewed.

Karen had spread newspapers on the work surface by the sink and was using a screwdriver to prise the lid off a paintpot. He watched her as she turned the tin round a fraction, levered at the lid, turned it again, worked the screwdriver again. When she was three-quarters finished, he leant off the table, went over beside her, and tried to open the cupboard under the sink. Her legs were in the way.

Excuse me, he said, through a mouthful of apple.

She took a step sideways, and he opened the cupboard. There was a bin fixed to the inside of the door; the top of it swung up automatically as the cupboard door opened. Rob bent over and spat the half-chewed apple into the bin. The bag crackled as the apple splattered down inside it.

Fucking disgusting, said Rob as he straightened up.

What is it, a worm? said Karen.

No. This. Rob held the remains of the apple under her nose. What does that remind you of?

An apple.

No, it *is* an apple. What does it *remind* you of?

She shrugged, lifting the lid off the paintpot with the tips of two fingers.

Come on. It's obvious.

Rob, I'm busy. I don't have time for silly buggers. I'm doing the living-room today. I've already pushed all the furniture into the middle of the floor.

Look at it, he said, waving the core about in front of her eyes. Just fucking look at it. You ken what it's like? Human flesh. It's fucking disgusting, but that's what it is: apples are like wee balls of human flesh. Look at the feel of it. And the juices leaking out. And the colour of it — the same colour as your face.

Karen sighed.

Every time you eat an apple, said Rob, it's like taking a bite out

232

of a human body, a girl's body. A girl's thigh. Her inside thigh. He clicked his teeth together.

Karen was stirring the paint with a length of cane. She gave it a final whirl, then lifted the stick out and wiped the paint off it on the inside edges of the tin.

Right, she said. I'm going to get rollering. I'd appreciate it if you didn't hang around my elbow talking shite all day. I've had enough of it, Rob. I've had enough, full stop.

She went out. Rob gazed at the apple for half a minute, examining the line where his teeth had punctured the red skin and dug through into the white flesh beneath. This was where the comparison broke down: a bite out of Sandra's thigh would surely not behave like that. It wouldn't be neat and clean, the skin cutting off in a tidy line, the meat underneath staying put where it was, leaking a bit of juice maybe, but nothing drastically sottery. The skin of a thigh would tear and shred unevenly. Flesh beneath would be mushy and messy. There'd be blood fucking everywhere. If human flesh was really like apples, folk would be going around taking lumps out of each other all the time. What could be more natural? A girl like Sandra, you'd strip her off and there'd be chunks missing from her shoulders, from her tits, maybe one from a buttock, and certainly quite a few bites around her inner thighs.

Rob imagined the feeling of a lump of Sandra's flesh sitting on his tongue. It was a feeling that gave him an erection. He swallowed, and could feel the juicy chunk of her slipping down his throat.

He dropped the last of the apple in the bin, took a drink of water out of the tap, then walked to the hooks in the hallway and put on his denim jacket. He felt in his inside pocket. The photocopies with Sandra's number and address on them were still there. He pulled his set of car keys out of his jeans pocket, then remembered the car wasn't in the port.

Fuck, he said to himself. Then he paused, considered, nodded. I'm going to get the car, he shouted, as he went out the door.

Rob rang the doorbell. Nothing happened. He took a step back and looked up at the first-floor windows. The curtains were still drawn in one of them. He waited a second, then leant forward and rang the bell again. He couldn't hear it ringing, but that didn't mean it wasn't, of course. Nothing worse than keeping your thumb pressed on the button and all the time the folk inside hurrying to get out of the bog or down the stairs, cursing the annoying bastard at the bell. Even if it is their fault they don't have one that works decently in the first place and they deserve every ring they fucking get.

He took a step back again and stood with his hands behind his back. Above the door was a half-circle of glass with a picture of a lighthouse painted on it. Beams of yellow light rayed out from the top of the tower, and when they reached the edge of the glass they changed into letters, spelling out words in a foreign language: IN SALUTEM OMNIUM.

The door opened.

Morning, said Rob, and smiled at Susan standing there, rubbing her eyes.

Rob. Eh, hello. What time is it?

Time all good folk were up and about, that's for sure.

It's Sunday.

It's cold as well. The wind fairly gets you down here on the front, eh?

Aye. Well. She turned and walked off into the house. You'll be coming in then, she said over her shoulder.

He closed the door behind him and breathed in the warm air of the hallway. It smelled of plants growing and of female skin.

I was looking at the picture above your door, he said, as he followed her through to the kitchen. Did you do that?

Me? No. It came with the house. This place used to be the shore station for the lighthouse out on the Rock. The families of the men who were offshore lived here. It was kind of a signal station too. They used to hoist flags up a pole on the roof, ken?

Rob scraped out a chair and sat down at the big pine table.

Coffee? she said.

I just came to get the car, he said. I'm not staying.

Is that a no?

Rob looked at her, the way her hair was still tousled from being slept on. No, I'll have one. Great.

She filled the kettle and put it on the gas, then started getting mugs out. She was telling Rob about a big brass telescope the families used to have. They'd look out of the upstairs windows to see what signals the men had up on the Rock, ten miles out in the shipping lanes. That way they'd know if anyone was sick, and what stores they needed next relief.

Rob wasn't listening to her. He was watching the back of her as she moved about in front of the unit. She was wearing a loose sweatshirt and tight leggings.

Susan told him she'd found the telescope in a press when she moved in, and she had it set up at the window upstairs. Of course, there were no signals to see these days: the lighthouse had been unmanned for twenty years.

Rob looked hard as she bent over to get milk out of the fridge,

235

but for the life of him he couldn't make out the lines of her pants under the material of her leggings. So quite likely she wasn't wearing any for fuck's sake the fucking slag. He looked away.

The words round the edge of the fan-light are the motto of the Rock lightkeepers, she said. In salutem omnium. It means, For the safety of all.

She put a mug of coffee down in front of him, then sat at the opposite side of the table with her own. She raised the mug to her lips then laid it down without drinking. She stood up, went over to the window, picked a Marlboro out of a pack on the sill, and lit it.

As soon as Rob saw the fag in her lips he thought of Sandra. As soon as he thought of Sandra he thought of fucking, he thought of fucking Susan on the breakfast table, her leaning forward, him shoving in from behind, her with one tit in a bowl of cornflakes, milk dripping off the nipple, the other tit lying on a plate of toast, melted marge and marmalade sticking to the curves of. . .

You're a dirty bastard, said Susan.

He started. What? Why?

She blew a long jet of smoke up into the air and watched it disappear before looking back to him.

Karen's a gem, she said. She's brilliant. And she really loves you. If you'd been here yesterday you'd've seen how much she loves you. But what do you do? You treat her like shit. You ignore her. You give her a hard time about her work – really you should be giving her a medal for what she gets through.

She took a drag, held the smoke down for a couple seconds, then blew it out in his direction. He didn't react.

You're a bastard, she said. You don't deserve her. But I'm

helping you cause she loves you – god help her – and I wouldn't want to see her hurt for the world.

She tapped some ash off her fag, and sighed.

Give her a bit of time, Rob. Give her a bit of yourself. That's all she's asking. Not all of you, just a bit of you. Give her it soon or. . . She shrugged. Or it might be too late.

Good coffee, said Rob. So smooth and mellow! Not a hint of that bitter aftertaste you sometimes find in instants! What was that about a telescope?

I've known Karen since she was a wee lassie, said Susan. Did you ken that? I used to work with her mother, aye, Liz, up at the health centre. That was my first job when I left school, filing and reception there. Karen used to come in and see her mum after school and stuff. She used to think I was all grown up and trendy – I did as well! – course I was only sixteen at the time, I knew nothing, absolutely nothing. But Karen must've been just. . . ten, so it was all relative, I suppose. Nowadays I'd say you know nothing, absolutely sweet FA, till you're well past thirty. Thirty-six, maybe. But that's cause that's how old I am now, probably!

Rob looked at her. Some folk know a hell of a lot by the time they're sixteen, he said. Younger, even.

Aye, said Susan. And some folk never learn nothing, no matter how old they get. She widened her eyes at him over the rim of her mug.

I bet you think you know me really well, said Rob. You probably watch me through your telescope, watch me walking down the street, and you think you know me well. But I promise you: you know nothing. Anything you know about me is *nothing*.

Susan pulled her seat in closer to the table, leant forward across it. Karen talks to me a lot, she said. She always has done. When I was working at the hospital in Aberdeen and she was at the college we used to bump into each other. I mind her telling me one time she was going out on a date with a janitor. I told her not to throw herself away, but. . . here we are, five years later, me and Karen ended up in the same office, me and the janitor chatting over a Sunday cup of coffee. All friends together.

You're so fucking smug, said Rob.

And it's cause we're all friends I'm giving you this advice, this friendly advice.

Rob laid his hands flat on the tabletop, then gathered them up into fists. I don't want your advice, he said in a quiet voice. I don't want you sticking your nose in my affairs.

She gave a laugh. So it's affairs now, is it? You're a worse bastard than I thought, Rob.

In my business, he said. You have no fucking business sticking your nose in my business, or in my wife's.

Karen's a friend of mine, she said. If she comes to me like she did yesterday, greeting her eyes out, I'll talk to her as long as she wants. And I don't care if you approve or not.

I'm not talking about approving, said Rob. I'm talking about, if I hear of you sticking your nose in my business again, if I hear of you putting ideas into my wife's head, I'm going to come round here, I'm going to get the big brass telescope from the window, and I'm going to jam it up your cunt. Then I'll have a good look around, see what signals you're showing, see how you like having *your* life poked about at.

Susan put down her coffee cup. If you're not out of here in five seconds, I'm phoning Karen and telling her what you just said.

Threats now, is it?

And then I'm phoning the police.

Ha! You think they'd believe you? A woman like you? The signals you send out? A woman with a pair of spunk-stained fucking pants at the top of her flagpole? We don't need a telescope to see what those mean!

One. Two.

Rob stood up, jolting his chair so it fell backwards onto the tiled floor, and raised a finger to her. Fuck you, he said.

Three. She stood up too. Four.

One day I'm going to fuck you, he said. I'll fuck you so hard your eyeballs pop out. And I'll catch them in my mouth like peanuts and swallow and carry on fucking.

Five. She left the table and crossed the room towards the phone on the wall.

Rob walked away from his fallen chair, down the hall and out the front door. As he paused to unlock the car in the short driveway, he looked back at the white-harled house. Susan was standing in the doorway, her arms folded, the painted lighthouse beaming out its message above her head.

He pursed his lips into a kiss, blew it towards her, then got into the car and churned up the gravel as he drove away.

Rob stopped the car at the first phone box he came to. He got Sandra's details out of his jacket pocket, shoved in some money and dialled the number.

It was picked up on the first ring. Yeah? said a man's voice.

Rob almost put the receiver down, then he brought it back up to his mouth, and said, Is that the Bunker Preservation Society?

The what?

You know, the old bunkers and gun emplacements and that, are you the guy that. . .

Oh. Aye. That's me. It's not a society really, it's just me.

Well listen. You ken that one just out of town, on a long spit of land?

Which side of the town?

Eh, north.

1940 vintage, two six-inch guns, guarding the northern approaches to the harbour.

Whatever. Well, did you ken there's a guy living there just now?

Living there?

A dosser. He's biding there, lighting fires, putting up doors. He's really wrecking the place – taking it to pieces.

There was a silence.

I mean, it's a historical monument, eh? said Rob. He shouldn't be allowed to just move in there and wreck the place!

No, said Sandra's dad. But listen, who am I speaking to anyway?

Me? Oh. I'm just a walker. I was walking past. And I saw him. I saw smoke. And a sledgehammer. He's probably knocking the place down or something, I don't know the details.

Listen. Thanks for letting me know. I mean, I don't ken how you got my number. . .

Don't mention it.

Aye. Well, there's nothing we can actually do, legally. . .

They're useless, aren't they, the police? When you really need them, they disappear. They're a fucking joke! But you get slagged off if you take the law into your own hands and sort the bastards out. It's a sign of the times. Terrible.

Maybe we should go out and have a word with the guy.

A word? A word's no good! Half a brick in the face, that's what this cunt needs.

Well. . .

He's probably blowing the place up as we speak. Hitler couldn't do it, but this fucker. . .

You're right, you're right. We'll sort the bastard! Where'll I meet you?

Eh. . . Rob cleared his throat. I can't make it right now.

This afternoon then?

I'm busy all day as it happens.

Oh.

But don't let that stop you. There's no time to lose. Go yourself! Aye, and give him one from me, he deserves all he gets, as far as I'm concerned.

Okay. I'll go right now. But listen, what did you say your name was? I'll ring you and let you know how. . .

Don't waste time on me! Get going! Nail the sick bastard!

Aye, but. . .

Rob hung up. He got 30p of unused coins back.

He drove quickly through the town and into the small council estate just inland from the school. He parked at one end of Sandra's street and waited. After about ten minutes a square-headed man in his mid-forties came out of a house halfway along. He was carrying some kind of metal tool-box and scowled around as he walked over the square of grass in front of the house. He got into an Escort parked by the pavement and drove away. As his car came past, Rob bent over, pretending to be looking for a cassette in the glove compartment.

As soon as he saw the Escort turning out the end of the street in his wing mirror, Rob got out of the car, walked along the pavement and up to the door of the house the guy'd just left. The number matched the one on the sheet in his pocket. He looked up and down the street, then reached out and rapped the door with his knuckles. His heart was racing. It had been ever since his row with Susan. He made a point of taking a pace back off the doorstep, for fear of launching himself on top of Sandra as soon as she opened the door. Better to wait till they were inside, away from the gaze of the toddlers and grannies who were loitering in the street.

The door opened. The woman was Sandraish, over forty, Sandra's mother. He'd completely forgotten about her fucking mother.

Well? she said.

Eh. . . Jesus! said Rob. How about Jesus, eh? What a bastard!

She looked him up and down. Are you Jehova's Witness?

Me? No!

Oh. What then?

Well. . . wrong number. I'm at the wrong house. Sorry to bother you.

Rob took a step backwards, his shoulders up in a fixed shrug, a grin hanging half off his face. Then he saw somebody coming into the hallway behind the woman and peering out past her: Sandra. He stepped forward again. I see you have children, Mrs, eh, Mrs. Great. I wish I had one. They're a blessing, aren't they?

You are Jehova's.

No, honestly, I'm. . .

Sandra, is this a friend of yours? He's havering enough he might just about qualify.

Sandra came forward to her mother's side. Her eyes were

242

staring, her lips parted. No, she said. Not at all. It's Mr Catto, from the school. The jannie.

Hello Sandra, said Rob. How are you theday?

Look, said her mother. Is this something to do with the school, or what?

I'm collecting for the Janitors' Relief Fund, said Rob. Would you like to make a contribution?

Not really.

Oh well. . .

I mean, my man's a janitor too. Not much sense in giving you money to give back to him, is there? Especially as I bet he'd only get half of it back.

Well well, quite right.

What was the name? The Janitors'. . ?

Relief Fund.

I've never heard of that before.

No, you wouldn't have. It's new. Just set up.

I'll mention it to my. . .

Don't bother, please!

Well. . .

Okay, I'll be off. See you tomorrow then, Sandra? At school, I mean? Just in passing, nothing in particular, but see you probably, eh?

I'm a bit sick actually, she said. A bit. . . sore. She cast her eyes downwards, then looked at him again, flickered her eyelids.

Well, I hope you're better by themorn, said Rob, backing down the path. It wouldn't be the same without you! School, I mean. . .

He left them staring after him, walked quickly down the path and away from the house, right down the pavement, all the way to its junction with the main road. Then he minded on the car, and went back up the street towards it, whistling under his breath, wondering what the fuck he should do next.

I don't like the colour, said Rob.

You chose it!

I never did. I'd never choose that.

Oatmeal it's called. She took a step back and looked at the wall she'd just finished.

Lumpy porridge, more like.

Mind, we got it at the supermarket a couple weeks ago? I've been waiting for you to make a start, but I can't wait for ever. Probably do a better job myself anyroad.

Rob shook his head. Should've done it all white, he said.

She bent over and lay the roller in the ribbed section of the tray. I don't believe you sometimes, she said. You're too much, Rob. She came over towards him, wiping her hands on the sides of the old jumper she was wearing. I suggested white! I was all for it! Brighten the place up a bit, I said. You said no, cause it would show all the dirt. You said we had to get something off-white cause white would show every fingerprint, every speck and smudge!

Rob looked at her, blinked. Did I say that?

Standing in the supermarket!

He nodded. I was right.

What?

White would show every bit of dirt, but *that's what I want*. I want to see every little stain, every particle of muck. See it straight out and wipe it off, that's what I think. The whole house should

244

be shining fucking white, that way the first sign of any dirt we can clean it up, wipe it out.

Jesus, Rob.

None of this business with filth building up in the corners, piling up by skirting boards, gathering everywhere, deeper and fucking deeper till we're smothered in the fucking stuff. Get it out in the open. Let's get a good clear look at it! Then *stamp it out*.

Karen was standing right in front of him. She had a hand up over her eyes. When she let it down he saw that there were tears making her eyeballs glisten.

Robbie, what are you doing? she said.

He looked away from her and around the lounge, at their settee and hifi and telly corralled into the middle of the floor, shrouded in sheets.

Just giving my opinion about things, he muttered. If that's still allowed.

Of course it's allowed. But but how come all your opinions have changed? I mean it's not just the colours, though that's a big enough pain in the neck when I'm trying to get our home sorted out. I wish you'd just say, Oh aye Karen, that's nice, nice bit of painting in the lounge, my dear. But all I get is, I want to see *dirt*. I want to see *filth*.

Rob pushed past her, yanked away a sheet, and sat down on the settee next to the CD rack. He lifted that onto the floor, leant forwards, and pressed the on button on the telly. Nothing happened. He pressed the button a couple more times: still no sign of life.

It's broken, he said. Dead.

Karen sighed, leant back against the door frame. It's just

unplugged, she said. I had to unplug it to move it away from the wall. You can plug it back in if you want to.

Rob shrugged, sat back in the settee, stared at the blank screen.

What is wrong with you? she said.

Rob didn't reply.

Talk to me.

Rob sighed. Where's the remote control? he said at last.

A sound like a quiet scream came out of Karen.

It's un-fucking-plugged, she whispered.

Rob jumped to his feet. I didn't ask if it was plugged in, he shouted. I asked where the fucking remote was! Jesus fucking Christ. He strode up to her, gripped her upper arms, shook her. This is the fucking problem with you, he said into her face. You try to be too clever all the time. I ask you (a) and you answer (b). You always have to be clever. You can't just have a normal job, a make-some-cash-to-live-on job, you have to have a high-flying, impress-the-folks-and-neighbours job, a humiliate-the-husband job. And you can't just have blether-over-a-pint friends, you have to have fucking super-slag bitches like Susan MacfuckingAlistair to pour your heart out to, to fill your head with all sorts of shite. What's wrong with talking to me, for fuck's sake? Why go to her? Why not tell me your problems?

Tears were coming into her eyes again. Rob. You are my biggest problem.

He looked at her for a second, then pushed her away, pushed her hard against the doorframe. No, he said. I don't think so. If there is a problem, it's not me, it's the rest of the world.

Rob, stop, she said. Stop and think.

You think I'm a problem, you think I'm a bad man. You don't

know how good I am. You don't know that your friend Susan tried to get off with me this morning.

No she didn't.

Answered the door half naked.

I don't believe you.

Flashing her tits at me while she made a cup of coffee. Suggesting threesomes, me, you and her.

Never.

And when I said no, she says, Oh well, just you and me then Robbie, and goes for my cock, she grabs my fucking cock.

Don't talk this dirt. I don't believe a word. She'd never say that.

He let go of her and turned back into the lounge. She's a menace, he said. She's dangerous. A woman like that, living by herself there.

She's not by herself. Tara's there during the week. It's just at weekends she stays with her dad.

Rob put a finger out and stroked it down the half-dry paint on the wall, leaving a long grey streak. I fear for that girl, he said. I worry about her.

You shouldn't worry, shouted Karen. There's nothing to worry about. And anyway, it's none of your bloody business to worry about somebody else's kids.

That's what they want you to say! he shouted back, whacking both fists against the wall and resting his forehead on it. Jesus Christ woman. This is what's wrong with the world today. Everybody kens there's bad things going on, but no one'll face up to them. Everyone says, Not my business, nothing to do with me. While evil rules everywhere!

He turned to her, and he could feel tears in his own eyes now too.

I say, NO, he said. No to turning a blind eye, whether it's feminist fucking lesbian slags like your friends, or drug pushers in the playground, or perverts shagging dead sheep and children in the fucking pillbox. We can't let them off. We can't pussyfoot around trying to see their point of view, to understand their sad fucking emotional problems. Look at the bastards. Judge them right or wrong. Give them a fair trial, then fucking condemn them. Stamp on them. Wipe them out! It's the only answer. Rid the planet of the cunts.

For half a minute they stared at each other, then Karen came towards him, her hands open. Rob, she said, You need help.

Yes. I need help to stamp the bastards out. You're right! So you'll help me? You're on my side? I knew you weren't completely evil, otherwise why would I've married you in the first place?

No, Rob. . .

Let's start, he cried, seizing up the roller and paint tray, and stepping over to the window.

What are you doing?

He dipped the roller in the paint, then raised it, dripping, to the window, and started covering the glass in long crisscrossing strokes of oatmeal emulsion.

What the fuck are you doing? she shouted.

This'll be our HQ, said Rob, painting away. We need secrecy. No one to see in, to see what we're doing. Just slits for us to see out. And defences too, we'll come to them soon. But for now let's block out the windows. Stop the evil bastards from spying in.

She stepped over and tried to grab the tray away from him, but he gripped it tight.

Get your own, he said. Start on the kitchen.

Rob, she said. Stop this. You need to stop, to calm down. This is our home, not a castle. We don't need a castle, there's no one out to get us. We've no enemies out there.

What? WHAT?

Put down the paint.

Everyone's out to get us. Everyone's our enemy. It's us against them!

She tugged at the tray again, his grip was loose, and it went flying out of his hand and against the top of the settee. Paint ran down the blue velour.

Stop! he cried, and thrust the roller into her face. If you're not with me, you're against me, you're one of the fucking enemy, the enemy within. He edged away from her, his back to the window, heading for the door. Jesus, how did I miss it for so long? A spy within my own HQ. Not much wonder they're always getting the better of me. You're fucking giving them inside information. You're a traitor, a fucking traitor. Who can I trust? No one. No one!

He backed out the door, at the last instant hurling the paint roller at her head for cover, and sprinting out the front to the car.

Rob didn't know how long he'd been sitting at the desk, but when he looked up it was dark outside the window. The car park was gone and all he could see was his own blurry reflection and the pool of desk, memo pad and pen, illuminated by the lamp to his side. He looked down at what he'd written.

FAO Mr Moran, Rector

In recognition of the janitorial staff's recently established role as guardians of moral good in the school, I propose a change to our uniforms. Eventually peaked caps, camouflage jackets and leather holsters should be issued. With regards to this last item, there is, of course, no need to arm us immediately (though I believe that caretakers in many urban American schools have been given weapons, with a very positive effect on corridor discipline.) But they would be an impressive accessory, handy for holding a notebook and pencil, which could be whipped out and used for recording details of pupils' names and crimes.

As I say, that lies in the future. Meanwhile, I suggest our position be reinforced – both in our own minds and in those of the children – by the design of a logo that could be embroidered onto the chest of our dustcoats. Maybe the art department could be involved in the final design, and the home economics department in the sewing. I have in mind some suitable graphic, such as a crossed dustpan and drainrod. Under this would be the new motto I propose to adopt as our 'mission statement'. As a Latin scholar, I am sure you will require no translation.

Then, in big letters that he'd gone over so many times the biro had torn through the paper in several places, Rob had printed:

IN SALUTEM OMNIUM

Rob said the words out loud, laughed, then stopped. Something had moved outside the window. He gazed into the dark, saw nothing but his own reflection staring back. Then his reflection broke into a broad grin. Rob hadn't started smiling, just the reflection. Its eyes were rolling too. Rob brought a hand up in front of his face and reached out towards the glass. His reflection threw its head back and cackled, then jerked to one side.

It wasn't his reflection: it was Bunker Man. Now he was

250

cupping his hands round his face and pressing them against the window to shade his eyes as he gazed into the bothy.

Rob's frown eased away and he started to smile back. He pointed at Bunker Man, then moved the pointy finger back towards himself, to inside the bothy. Bunker Man stuck his tongue out. Rob raised his eyebrows and repeated the pointing. Bunker Man gave the window a foot-long lick with his grey-scaled tongue. Rob laughed and stood up, pointing along in the direction of the Tradesman's Entrance. Then he left the bothy, went along the corridor and opened the door into the car park.

Bunker Man was still licking the window. He looked round as Rob swung the door wide. Working late, Jannie, he said.

No rest for the wicked, said Rob, and laughed. Anyway, I'm not really working.

Bunker Man stepped away from the window and came lumbering towards him. What then? Playing?

Eh?

If you're not working, you must be playing. It's logic: there's no way out of it.

Rob chuckled. So I'm playing! He stretched his arms and yawned. What about yourself? What are you doing hanging around the school at this hour?

I'm not hanging anywhere – I'm passing by, nothing more. Been out hunting all afternoon, and not a sausage.

No sausages, eh? said Rob. Dear oh dear.

Nothing else either. I had half a pizza for breakfast, I held it up with two sticks over the fire till it warmed. That's it all day: I'm starving! Thirsty too. Sunday's not a good day for scranning: no drunks chucking pokes of chips away.

It's a shite of a day, said Rob. Ken why? Cause on the seventh day god had to stop for a crap.

Bunker Man grinned, sidled a step closer. Don't have any more of those square bits of chocolate, do you? They were great!

Rob laughed. I've none of those, but if it's grub you're after you've come to the right place.

A grin spread across Bunker Man's face, and when Rob stepped back and waved him to go inside, he didn't hesitate.

Come away through, said Rob, and led the way to the bothy.

It's warm in here, said Bunker Man as they walked down the corridor. It's clean too, you can smell it. It smells like a hospital.

They reached the bothy.

Rob chuckled and lifted the supermarket carriers off the easy chairs. He nodded towards Donald's. Sit, he said, and lowered himself into his own one. Hungry, eh? Fuck the warmed up pizzas tonight, pal! Tonight we're feasting!

He couped the first carrier bag of groceries onto the floor between their feet: out poured tins of tuna, garlic bread, salad tomatoes, orange cheese, melted ice cream, marge, tinned tomatoes, chicken soup, yoghurt with fruit and muesli, mince, tortilla chips, shampoo, potplantfood, tampons.

Rob looked up. Bunker Man's mouth was hanging open. Rob laughed and reached for the next carrier: assorted peppers, six pack of Bud, 100-watt bulbs, bag of flour, box of eggs, packet of chocolate digestives, net of onions.

You bought all this for me? said Bunker Man.

Rob shrugged. Not exactly. It's been in the car since yesterday afternoon, he said. But I reckon you deserve it as much as anyone. I'm starving!

Wait though. Rob tipped out the last bag: bottle of gin, carton of orange juice, kitchen roll, bag of Mac Red apples, baking tatties, fruit teabags, thawed crispy pancakes, jar of fish paste, bread with grains on top.

Right, said Rob. Let's get stuck in and build up our strength!

Rob sliced bread, spread it with marge, then chopped up a couple onions and made sandwiches. He handed one to Bunker Man and took a bite out of his own.

Bunker Man wasn't eating. Do we not get a bit of cheese in this? he said after a while. Cheese and onion, that's a proper flavour. Onion by itself isn't.

Rubbish, said Rob, chewing. Bollocks. Cheese is just fat, solid orange animal fat. Who wants a slab of that in their gob? Not me! But onions are good for you, good for the blood. It's a well known fact.

Is that right?

Aye! Onions put zing in your blood, they're famous for it. I'm always eating them: onion rings, skirlie, French onion soup with croutons, chicken dopiaza in the Indian. And look at my blood! It's louping in my veins!

Is it?

God aye! Tuck in!

Bunker Man lifted the top slice of bread and peered inside. Are you sure?

Rob sighed. Okay, he said. Seeing as it's your feast, you can have some cheese. But I wouldn't touch it with a bargepole. Or a bunkerpole, come to that.

Bunker Man gazed at him for a second, then shut the sandwich and took a huge bite.

You can have cheese, said Rob.

Bunker Man shook his head, said something through a full mouth.

It's no bother, said Rob, looking around for the Scottish cheddar. What did you say?

Bunker Man did a few big chews, then mumbled through half a mouthful: It's not bad. He swallowed again. Zing! he said.

Aye, that's another thing, said Rob. Onions are meant to make you greet, right? But did you see tears in my een just then? No way! Cause I eat so much of the buggers I'm immune! I never greet any more: onions are like a jag against greeting.

That's good, said Bunker Man. That's what I need.

I'll tell you something else, said Rob, finishing his sandwich. I saw a hypnotist once. I was on holiday in Spain, and I saw this guy in an English pub. He gave a girl an onion, then he hypnotised her and told her it was an apple. And she ate the whole damn thing, saying how sweet it was! Everybody was killing themselves!

Suicide?

Eh? No, laughing a lot. That's what killing yourself means: laughing a lot.

Right.

But the point is: eating an onion's nothing to me. I just went, *So*? and walked out of the fucking place. I'd rather eat an onion than an apple any time!

Bunker Man looked round at the food spread between them, then reached forward and picked up the bag of Mac Reds. Alright, he said. You take one of these, Jannie Man, then I'll hypnotise you and convince you it's an onion.

Rob looked at him, then at the apples, then at Bunker Man again. Then he burst out laughing. He threw his head back and roared. After half a minute it turned into a squeaky chuckle, then he gasped for breath and was back into a big hooting laugh. He waved his hands about in front of him, helpless, then brought them up to wipe away the tears that had sprung from his eyes.

Rob was giving Bunker Man a guided tour of the school. They started in the bothy, with Rob pulling open the filing cabinet, and snatching out the sheaf of memos he'd written over the past couple weeks but not handed in to the dominie. He explained that he had given Moran a few, but didn't want to overwhelm him with the number of his good ideas. If he did that, his cover as a simple jannie might be blown, and the mission he was on would be put in jeopardy. Bunker Man asked what the mission was and Rob replied that it was to do with rooting out evil wherever it appeared, stamping on the first traces of it anywhere in or near the school. After all, the schoolkids of today were the adults of tomorrow, and it was his belief that seeds of evil had to be stopped from entering the pupils. If they weren't stopped, the result would be a vast blooming of filth and wrong-doing and perversity throughout the town – throughout the country! – in years to come. For operational reasons, Rob couldn't go into detail about how his mission was proceeding. Likewise, he couldn't disclose the exact contents of his memos, most of which had a bearing on the same matter. But he told Bunker Man not to worry, that before long he'd know all about it. And he laughed. Bunker Man looked at him for a second, then started laughing too. Rob filled a carrier bag with apples, chocolate biscuits and sixpack, and led the way out of the bothy and away down the service corridor.

He took them into Moran's office and let Bunker Man sit in the big leather chair behind the desk. Then he pointed out the files in Mrs Ellis's office and told Bunker Man how they contained the official information about all the pupils. He went on to explain how he had been compiling another, secret set of files on the pupils, which contained details of all their drug habits, sexual peccadillos and criminal records, including those offences that their bribery and/or masonic connections had got them off.

Rob opened a couple of bottles of beer, gave one to Bunker Man and took a long swallow from the other, then set off along the main corridor. They turned down the corridor of sweat and went through the girls' changing rooms into the games hall. Rob started howling, throwing his head back and howling like a wolf. At first Bunker Man looked terrified and started to back away, but Rob stopped for a second and told him to listen to the echoes, that they were fantastic, that it was like being in a giant cave, an enormous bunker. And when he started howling again, Bunker Man listened, then grinned, then started howling too. The pair of them stood there in the dark of the big hall and howled and hooted and roared.

They dumped their empty bottles in a bin in the changing-rooms, opened new ones and went on up to the canteen. They sat there for a while, eating an apple each. Rob asked Bunker Man what the apple reminded him of, and Bunker Man said after a moment's thought that it reminded him of a child, with the seeds of evil already planted in its heart. Rob was so impressed by the answer that he immediately chucked his core away across the canteen. It bounced off a table and skidded out of sight. Bunker Man followed suit, but his apple flew further and banged into the metal shutters that were pulled down over the serving hatch. You still don't know your own strength, do you? said Rob.

Heading towards the history department, Rob needed a pish, so stepped into the bog there. He finished his second bottle of beer while standing pishing, and tossed the empty into the bin as he left. Bunker Man did likewise.

They headed along past the maths classrooms, then the modern language department, and stopped by the fire escape at the end of the corridor. Rob opened the last two beers, then used his fishtail key to disable the alarm trigger and pushed open the fire escape door. They stepped out and stood on the metal platform at the top of the stairs, drinking and looking out over the car park and the woods.

This is a fine place you've got here, said Bunker Man.

Thanks, said Rob. I think it's time for you to leave.

What!

You heard me.

But I like it here.

Sorry, said Rob, and took a drink. As I say, I have various things going on, and I can't afford to let anyone get too close to them at this stage. Even you.

I never get to stay anywhere I like, said Bunker Man.

Bollocks, said Rob. Where you are doesn't matter. It's what you do there that's important.

Bunker Man drank and frowned for a while. Aye, he said at last. You're right there.

I'm always right.

Quite often.

Always. Always.

Well, said Bunker Man. What should I do when I get home then?

Wait, said Rob. And soon you'll find out. Something'll tell you. Or someone. Might well be me. I'll tell you what to do, and then you must do it. No hesitation or repetition. And no questions.

Will it be part of the mission?

Aye. We all have a part to play in that. Cause there's a lot of parts, and they all have to be played by someone. And you'll do as well as anyone.

Bunker Man finished his beer and grinned at Rob. That's good, he said. That makes me feel good.

Here's something else that'll make you feel good, said Rob. Watch this.

He drew back his arm and tossed the bottle as far across the car park as he could. It popped and smashed on the tarmac.

That'll jag some bastard's tyres in the morning, said Rob, and laughed.

Now me, said Bunker Man.

He threw his bottle hard, and it flew for a long time into the darkness, finally landing with a thump, another, fainter, thump, and a crash.

All the way into the woods! said Rob.

It must've hit a stone or something out there.

Aye. Ha! That'll jag some bastard's arse next Friday night!

Then Rob gave him the packet of chocolate digestives, slapped him on the back, and pushed him down the first step of the fire escape. Bunker Man was slow at first, and looked back over his shoulder a couple times. Go home, Rob said the first time, and the second time he just waved. And Bunker Man went on down the steps to the car park, and away into the darkness.

Got you, said Rob. Cunt.

Back in the bothy, Rob opened the bottle of gin. He drank

straight from the bottle, then poured some into a mug and mixed in orange juice. That was much better. Just cause the world was falling to fucking pieces, didn't mean civilisation had to go out the fucking window.

After a couple mugs, Rob had an idea. He reached for his memo book and wrote a note to the dominie suggesting that in future sex education lessons should be given to much younger kids, certainly as young as third year, and that a practical element should be involved. In a PS he added that he would be willing to volunteer as an adult technician in these experiments.

Then he got out his cock and wanked. He wiped the spunk off the desk and carpet with the memo he'd just written, crumpled the whole thing up and stuffed it into the filing cabinet under W. In his head that stood for Wank, but he decided that if anyone asked it would be better to say it was for Wipe.

He moved to his soft chair and drank gin and orange till he fell asleep.

Rob woke on the floor, lying amongst packets and tins of food. He blinked his eyes against the light pouring in through the bothy window and wiped his hand across the slaver that had slimed his chin. He sat up, looking round at the crushed packet of tampons, the squashed tomatoes and at the flattened loaf of garlic bread he seemed to have been using for a pillow. The open carton of orange juice was sitting to one side of his chair. He reached out and shook it: not a drop left. Beside it was the gin bottle: that was empty too.

He stood up, slowly, grabbing onto the back of Donald's chair for support, and staggered over to the sink. He lowered his head and drank from the tap. After a couple seconds he cowked, spat out water, and straightened up. He'd had his mouth at the hot tap. He went down again, aiming carefully this time, and letting the water run good and cold before he started drinking.

After he'd had enough, he left the tap running and ducked his head under it so water ran down both sides, over his ears, down his cheeks. He clawed the water into his hair with both hands, then stood up, spluttering, and circled his dripping palms over his face.

He stretched, gazing up at the clock on the wall. Seven thirty-five. At least twenty minutes before anyone else would appear. He got down on his hunkers and started putting the groceries back into the carrier bags.

When the bags were full, with the empty orange carton and gin bottle and the onion skins in one to themselves, he carted the lot outside to the car park, got the hatchback open, and dumped them into the Fiesta. He closed the door and lay back against it, eyes closed, letting the clean air of the morning soak into his skin, hoping some of it would penetrate as far as his brain.

When he opened his eyes again, he noticed a streak of brown glass particles across the tarmac a couple yards away, with a few bigger shards and bits of label at the end of it. Jesus Christ, he said to himself, stepped over, and stooped to pick up the big jags. He walked over to the edge of the woods and laid them down at the base of the first tree he came to. Then he picked up a foot-long stone from nearby, carried it over, and laid it carefully on top of the glass. There was a quiet crunching sound.

Rest in pieces, he said, and laughed, then put a hand up to his forehead and massaged it.

Back inside, he got the statutory first aid kit out of its drawer, took four paracetamol with more water from the tap, and headed off into the depths of the school. It was essential that he removed all evidence of Bunker Man's presence in the building the previous night. That meant getting their bottles out of the bins they'd been dumped in and disposing of them well away from the place. There was, of course, the bottle he'd thrown away into the woods. But the chances of that being found were very small, and anyway, they'd heard it smash to smithereens: no fingerprints could survive that, surely. But the bottles in the bins were another matter.

The vinegar reek in the corridor of sweat just about made him boke. Luckily, the girls' changing room smelled of deodorant and sweet shampoo, and at first that seemed better. By the time he'd fished the two bottles out of the bin, though, it was beginning to feel like he'd swallowed a bottle of talc, and he hurried out of the place and along the corridor and upstairs. At first he walked in the direction of the canteen, but then remembered they hadn't finished any bottles there. The apple cores didn't matter: any of the kids could've dropped them. The wee bastards would be much more careful about leaving beer bottles lying about, though, and Rob didn't want a fucking investigation being started into whose they were. Best just to get rid of them completely before Billy or Donald or a cleaner or anybody noticed them.

In the history bogs. That's where the others were.

He turned away from the canteen, feeling the drugs starting to clear his head now, and checked his watch as he passed the geography classrooms. It was nearly ten to. The others would start arriving any minute. He'd better nash on.

The bin in the bogs was just about empty, and when he peered in through the swinglid he couldn't see them. But they had to be there. He glanced at his watch again, then got a good hold of the bin, upended it, and tumbled the contents out onto the tiled floor.

The two bottles bounced down amongst a few screwed-up paper towels, a Coke can, a ripped comic and a used condom. For fuck's sake! He went to grab it, then stopped himself, picked up one of the paper towels instead, and used that to lift the doob. Half the spunk seemed to have dried out or disappeared, but there was still a white gob lurking down in the teat of the thing. More than enough for DNA fucking testing.

Fuck's sake, the evidence was all around. Just when you thought you were winning away from the enemy, just when you thought you'd just about got clear and free, up crops a little bit of evidence, a little snare that could drag you back into all the mess you were trying to get away from. Thank Christ he'd found the fucker before anybody else did – knowing his luck it would've been some biology teacher who'd've set her sixth-year boffins to work dissecting the stuff first period.

He got hold of one of the bottles, and lowered the Durex into it, then let go. The end of the doob flopped and caught the neck of the bottle, and a small spray of spunk spirked out over the back of his hand. His head hung, and he let out a great sigh. Whenever he worked with bin bags, he always ended up with sticky fingers: now he knew what caused it.

He stood up, put the Durex bottle and the non-Durex bottle over by the door where he'd laid the other two, and started scooping the rest of the rubbish back into the bin.

The first classes of the day had just started, and the jannies had all come back to the bothy. Rob was meant to've worked out earlier in the morning, or on Friday afternoon, what needed doing around the school, but he hadn't. So now Billy was looking at a paper and Don was sitting with his feet up, while Rob leant over the desk, making notes of bits of possible work on the back of the Internal Vacancies sheet.

He would print something out, like RAKE BLAZE PITCH, or TEST ALARM SYST, or FILL BOG SOAP DISPS, but after a second's thought, each of them seemed wrong and pointless. Either the jobs had been done a day or two before, or else their regular time was just a day or two ahead; some of them required an empty school and could only be done after hours, others were just plain fucking stupid. Rob went through the whole list he'd written and put a line through each item. Then he scribbled all over the page.

Billy looked up from his paper, over to the clock on the wall, and back to Rob; he was about to say something, when there was a knock on the door.

Rob pushed away the piece of paper and turned towards the door. Come in, he said.

The door half-opened, and somebody sidestepped in. It was Mrs Ellis from the office. Mr Catto, she began, but Rob stood up and came towards her rubbing his hands, a big smile on his face.

Mrs Ellis! What can we do for you? Not often we see you in these parts! Not often we see you out of the office, actually. What do you reckon, lads? I think she's got Radio 4 playing through those stethoscopes of hers, that's how she never tears herself away: she's addicted to *The Archers*!

Mrs Ellis frowned. Mr Catto. . . she said again.

So serious! So serious! Oh! He suddenly froze, flicked a glance over each shoulder, then drew closer to the secretary. Don't tell me, he whispered. It's another lurker. Is it? You've seen some other pervert with a parka in the car park. Or was it a bugger in a blazer? A wanker in a waistcoat maybe? Or a flasher in a fucking. . . flakjacket in the French department, excuse my French? Leave it to me, Mrs Ellis, I'll sort the rascal out, never fear. I'll see to him no bother! So don't you worry your grey little, scabbit little head: I'll find this new deviant and stamp him out, I'll get him, I promise, I'll get the cunt!

Billy and Donald burst out laughing. Rob spun round. What's funny? he said. What're you laughing at, you bastards?

Mr Catto, said Mrs Ellis loudly.

Rob spun back round. Her face was beaming red, and her lips were pressed together in a line.

Mr Moran would like to see you in his office straight away, she said.

Me? said Rob.

No, the man in the bloody moon!

Oooh! went Rob.

Summoned to the headie! said Donald. Smacked wrists for Robert theday!

Rob straightened up, gave the lapels of his dustcoat a swipe, and buttoned it. I doubt it, he said. I strongly suspect that Mr Moran is going to offer his congratulations for a new scheme I've been working on. I sent an outline to him on Friday afternoon.

Well, well, said Billy. Is there no end to young Robert's talents?

You ain't seen nothing yet, said Rob. And neither's he! He stepped over to the filing cabinet, yanked open the top drawer, and lifted out a sheaf of pages, covered in writing. I've been working on a few ideas over the past couple weeks, he said. I had another one last night, actually. Maybe now's the moment to present it – to hit him with all of them! He walked to the door, and crooked his elbow towards Mrs Ellis, as if expecting her to link arms with him. Shall we take our leave of these fine fellows? he said.

Mrs Ellis ignored him and strode out of the bothy. Rob shrugged at the others and followed her.

She was surging ahead towards the main corridor; he hurried to catch up.

Do you know what this is about? he asked her as they approached her office.

Mr Moran asked me to fetch you straight away, she said. That's all I know, and that's all I have to say to you.

I reckon you'll soon know a lot more, said Rob.

She didn't reply.

That'll put a smile on your face, he said.

She knocked on the door that connected her office to the dominie's one. I doubt it, she whispered, her teeth gritted, then opened the door. Mr Catto to see you, Mr Moran, she said, then stepped sideways and back, pulling the door shut behind her, leaving Rob alone in the big sunlit room with the rector.

Moran was standing facing out the window, his hands clasped behind his back. Rob watched the back, but it showed no sign of turning; Moran stood absolutely still, staring outside. Rob looked out the window past him, but there was nothing going on there either, just the empty tarmac of the playground with the bus turning circle to the left and some trees beyond that shielding the school from the bought houses. Or the bought houses from the school.

Rob turned his head away and glanced around the office. He'd been in the dominie's room loads of times, but – apart from last night – usually by himself; quite often he came in and sat in the big leather seat after school hours, or on a Saturday, farting and swivelling it round and round till he was dizzy. But he'd only been in the room along with Moran two or three times before. So he was looking around trying to spot anything different about the place, any secret compartments maybe pulled open from the desk, any confidential files taken out from their hiding places and lying about. But the only difference he could spot was that the dominie's black cloak wasn't hanging from its hook by the bookcase. That was because he was. . .

Mr Catto, I'm a man who can take a joke.

Moran had turned to face Rob, and was standing glowering at him, his hands still behind his back.

As well as the next man, he went on. But some jokes aren't funny, they're sick. He looked Rob in the eye. Dangerous, even.

Rob cleared his throat, but didn't speak, just raised his eyebrows for Moran to continue.

On the desk, said the head. What do you see?

Eh. . . Rob flicked his eyes over the big leather-topped desk in front of him. A phone.

No.

Aye there is! A green one, look.

No, I know there's a phone, I know perfectly well. But there's something else.

Pens. A big diary. A dictionary.

No! I'm talking about your memo, Mr Catto!

Ah! Rob looked at the desk again. I can't see it, he said.

Moran took a couple steps over and stuck out his hand to point at a memo sheet covered in big black scrawls.

Rob bent from the waist to peer at the note. That's not my writing, he said.

Not your writing? You signed it!

Did I?

There. Moran turned the page to face Rob, and pointed to the bottom right-hand corner of it.

Rob nodded, shrugged. Funny, I don't recognise the writing at all.

Moran sighed. Maybe you could read the first few lines, Mr Catto. Maybe that will refresh your memory.

Rob picked up the paper, frowned, looked over at the rector. It's hard to read, this writing, he said.

Try.

Okay. He cleared his throat again. Dear Mr Moran, Blah blah blah, moral standards, blah blah blah, obvious injustice, blah blah blah I'm talking about drugs.

Enough!

Blah blah blah pills, tabs, powders and herbs. . .

Stop! Mr Catto, do you admit now that you are responsible for writing this?

Aye, I mind now, I did write it. I recognise those blah blah blahs!

Moran didn't laugh. He sighed, and sat down in his big leather chair. He didn't tell Rob to sit. I can take a joke, he said. As you may have heard, I've written the school panto for the past four years. But this memo isn't funny. It's sick. And it's dangerous. I hope that no one has seen this barring Mrs Ellis and ourselves?

I doubt it. I wrote it on Friday and dropped it in the office, but. . .

Good. I'm relieved about that.

Mr Moran?

Yes?

267

It's just, the tone of your voice, some of the things you're saying. . . Tell me if I'm wrong, but, did you not like my idea?

Moran stared at him, leant the chair back at an angle.

Rob laughed. It tilts as well as whirling! he cried. Fantastic! I didn't ken it tilted!

Moran leant forward again. Are you feeling alright, Mr Catto?

Me? Well, I'm a bit downcast, like, a bit depressed that you didn't like my idea about the drugs, but apart from that. . . He grinned. I'm fine!

Very well. Moran stood up, took a couple steps away from the desk, then turned to face Rob again. I want you to consider this a verbal warning, he said, slowly.

What? I mean pardon?

If you want me to repeat this warning in the presence of your union representative I will do so. Mrs Ellis can fetch Mr MacBain in half a minute.

No, I don't need that, I just need. . . an explanation!

Moran's brow puffed up, and he almost shouted, An explanation? You write letters – barely legible, as you have just admitted – making *wild* allegations of drug abuse among the pupils, advocating the spread of such substances to the staff, and even implying. . . Moran stepped up to the desk, thumped his fist down on it. You even imply that I might use these supposed drugs myself! He held out his hand towards the memo, and Rob passed it over. How did you put it? Let me quote: You, as headmaster, should get first choice of whatever narcotics are available.

Rob shrugged. Well, if you're not interested. . .

Of course I'm not interested! None of my staff is interested!

And I sincerely hope *you* are not interested in such illegal substances!

I'm not at all, really, Mr Moran. More of a Becks man, myself! It was just seeing all the kids outside in the woods, ken, all out there taking the stuff – that's what put the idea in my head.

This is the worst of all! roared the head. Your description of widespread drug abuse among the pupils: it's absolute fantasy! There hasn't been a single instance of a child expelled for possessing drugs. And believe me, that's what would happen: immediate expulsion.

But it's a well known fact, Mr Moran: every school in Britain has. . .

Not my school. And if you value your position here, you will never make such insane allegations again. Imagine the board of governors getting hold of such rumours. Let alone the press. It would be an unmitigated disaster if stories like this started circulating.

But the kids in the woods. . .

If any child is suspected of possessing any kind of drug – including alcohol – they must be dealt with immediately and severely.

Rob nodded. Batter them, you mean?

No! I mean they should be brought to me and I will take the next step. Who do you think you are, Mr Catto, judge and jury?

In salutem omnium, said Rob.

Where on earth did you get *that* idea, Catto?

That memo you sent me. . .

That I sent you? It was you who sent me the memo, and don't forget it. Moran strode away towards the window, stared out of it for a second, then turned to face Rob again. Don't forget your role in this school either: you're a janitor, Mr Catto, nothing more. He turned to look outside.

Rob felt in the pocket of his dustcoat, and pulled out the sheaf of memos. Mr Moran, he said. I've got some more ideas. . .

I don't want to hear them.

I've been working hard on them. . .

Moran's hands clenched behind his back. But not at what you're supposed to be doing, Mr Catto! I've never seen the school so run down and filthy. Get out of here and sweep a few floors.

Rob went to answer back, then stopped himself. He headed for the door, stopped before opening it and turned. You'll regret this, he said.

Not as much as you will, Mr Catto. Now please, get to work.

I'll get to work alright, said Rob, and crumpled the memos back into his pocket.

Rob's face was burning as he stepped out of the dominie's office, past Mrs Ellis at her computer, and off down the service corridor. He walked quickly to the bothy and banged open the door. Billy and Donald looked up.

How did it go? said Billy.

What did the old rectum want? said Donald.

Rob's eyes thrashed around the room. Have we got an axe in here? he said.

An axe? It must've gone *really* bad! said Donald, and laughed.

What do you want an axe for? said Billy.

Never you fucking mind! Who's the fucking head around here? Me! And I'm asking if we have a fucking axe, a hatchet, anything.

No, said Billy.

Fucking great, said Rob, and slammed back out of the bothy.

He headed for the main corridor and turned right, just about running. He went down the corridor of sweat, then through the swinging doors and up the stairs there in great leaps. Both hands out in front as buffers, he battered through the double doors at the top and into the canteen. It was big and quiet, and completely empty. It was too early for the cooks to be setting out jugs of water and trays of cutlery and sliding up the serving hatch; they'd still be sweating away in the kitchens. Rob threaded between the rows of chairs and tables across to the far side of the room, where he thumped his fist once on the kitchen door and strode in.

The place was brightly lit and noisy, with music jangling out of a radio and ringing back off the metal worktops and the pans and trays sitting on shelves round the walls. The cooks were all women, and all wore blue nylon overalls and blue hats pinned to their hair. A couple of them were scraping tatties over at a big double sink. Another couple were arranging raw sausage rolls in lines across a baking tray. And Mrs Phillips the head cook was over by an array of microwave ovens, reading an instruction booklet with a frown so deep her eyebrows had disappeared behind the frames of her pink-tinged specs. Rob stepped in front of her.

Have you got a chopper in here? he said.

Mrs Phillips closed the booklet, her pinkie slipping in between the pages to mark her place. Hello Mrs Phillips! Hello Mr Catto, How are you theday then? Not bad, yourself? Och fine, now what can I do for you?

Have you got a chopper?

The younger cooks scraping tatties giggled, and Mrs Phillips looked past Rob's shoulder at them. I have a CLEAVER if that's any good, Mr Catto.

271

A cleaver? Is that like a chopper? Anything like that – a hatchet kind of thing. Anything with a handle and a big sharp blade. A cleaver: aye, that sounds just the job.

Do I take it you want to borrow a kitchen cleaver?

Aye, I do. And I need it quite quick, so. . .

Mrs Phillips nodded towards a thick wooden butcher's block under the window. From a rail above it hung silvery hooks, a couple of saws, and a shiny chopper with a blade nearly a foot long, and a hole in its nose for a hook to go through.

Rob stepped over, lifted down the chopper, setting all the hooks on the rail jingling, and cradled the flat blade in his left hand.

It's heavy, he said.

Aye, and sharp. And I'd like it back like that if you don't mind. She reached up and adjusted her specs, peered through them at Rob. What are you going to be using it for, anyway?

Well, what do you use it for, Mrs Phillips?

Och, we hardly need it these days. We used to do a lot of our own butchery – cutting up pork chops and the like – but nowadays everything comes ready-cut and wrapped in plastic.

Great, said Rob.

But I still want it back!

Sure, said Rob, and turned and walked out of the brightness of the kitchen.

He retraced his path through the corridor of sweat, swinging the heavy chopper back and forth by his side. It had good momentum to it; it felt like once you started hacking, it'd be impossible to stop, till you'd cut down everything in its path.

He turned into the main corridor. There were a couple pupils dawdling along at the far end, so he slipped the blade of the chopper into the pocket of his dustcoat. The handle stuck out, but it could've been a screwdriver or a hammer or anything. Okay, you could do a lot of damage with those too, but not the right kind of damage, and nobody would scream out if they saw you walking through the school with one.

The kids passed him, stopping dawdling, walking purposefully for a few steps as they approached him. Once past, he could hear them starting to muck about again, but he ignored them, and kept on till he reached the hatch into Mrs Ellis's office. He didn't wait for her to get up from her typing seat, but dug his nails down the edge of the glass window and slid it open himself. Then he let his hand rest on the wooden grip of the chopper.

Can I have a word with Mr Moran? he said.

The secretary shook her head. He's in conference, she said. With someone from the examinations board.

Rob nodded. Do you think he'll pass?

Mrs Ellis had come over to the window and slid it half shut, as if she was afraid Rob might launch himself through the gap and start molesting her. He grinned at the idea, but stopped himself from laughing.

He's busy for the rest of the morning, she said. I could make an appointment for this afternoon?

He leant off the counter. No! It doesn't matter. That'll be too late. I'll just have to do whatever I was going to do, and he can find out after instead of before. I'm sure he'll approve. If he doesn't, he should. Anyway, what am I? A kid? Do I have to ask for permission to breathe?

I don't have time for this, she said, and slid the glass almost closed.

Make time! he said loudly. We should all make time, then there'd be a lot more to go around!

She shut the window and turned away. Rob shook his head, and felt for the photocopied sheets in his inside pocket.

Moran doesn't really want to see me, does he? said Sandra, hurrying to keep up with Rob as he strode away from the door of the classroom.

Sometimes I think you've got a brain in your head, said Rob.

Thanks very much!

Not that I care. There's too much emphasis put on being clever in this school – in this world! But does being clever make you happier? Does it make you a better person? I don't think so.

She nudged him. Where are we going?

In fact, half the time it makes you a worse person: just cause they're smart, with an office job and a big wage, they think they can treat somebody not smart, a jannie or something, like shite. They think they can just ignore you!

Rob. . .

Shush.

They were turning into the service corridor. He walked past the bothy on tiptoes, then went on to the boiler-room door, unlocked it, and held it open.

In here? mouthed Sandra.

He glanced past her down the empty corridor, then nodded, and hustled her in.

It was very warm in the boiler-room, and the noise of the burner and the big fans blowing hot air away through the school roared and hummed back and forth between the breeze-block walls. The sprung door clucked shut, and they were standing in pitch blackness. Rob felt something touch his hand – Sandra moving closer – and his cock started to uncurl. Her hair tickled across his cheek and her lips went to his ear.

Where's the light?

He hesitated, then stretched out and found the wee safety torch hanging from its nail by the door. His fingers closed round it and his thumb switched it on. He lifted the torch and swung it up into her face, then around the walls of the room. Its beam was powerful but narrow; it illuminated a patch of wall or boiler or body, and left the rest in darkness.

This isn't the rector's office, she said into his lug.

It's the Badman's office, said Rob.

He is a bad man, the Badman, she said. I'm still hurting from Saturday. My mum thought I was getting piles the way I was shuffling my bum about on the seat.

He bent towards her face, and his lips touched her forehead. He kissed it, then moved down and placed his mouth over each of her eyes in turn, then the tip of her nose, then her mouth. She threw her arms around his neck, gripping tight.

I'll give you one more chance, Badman, she said, But you have to be good to me. She went to kiss him.

Before her face reached his, he turned it away, and pushed her back from him. He raised the torch and shone it in her face.

I'm always good, he said. That's the whole point.

She came close again. Do you not think folk might start to suspect? she said. I mean, if you keeping hauling me out of classes every other day.

As long as I don't do it to the same teacher twice we'll be okay.

But what about folk in my class? Did you not hear Shirley Young going, Again! when you came just now.

Ach, fuck Shirley Young!

You better not fuck Shirley Young, she said, smacking a hand against his thigh. It's me you fuck, nobody else, I'm the only one, the only one worth fucking, the one only worth fucking.

Rob grinned. Fuck the lot of them, he said. Including you. *Especially* you. And he moved to kiss her, his hands slipping down over her backside, then round the front, one moving up to feel for the buttons of her blouse, one leaving her body, reaching out to one side, searching for somewhere to lay the torch.

Hold on a minute, he said after a second, and pushed her away. He set the torch on top of the burner unit, positioned so its beam shone against the wall, some of it reflecting down onto the floor. Then he took off his dustcoat and laid it down in the patch of light. The cleaver clanked on the concrete floor.

What was that? said Sandra.

Never you mind, said Rob. Get your kit off.

In the half-light, he watched her unbutton her blouse from the top button down. Then she undid her bra. It was one that fastened at the front, and as she opened the fastening, the two pouches fell away to the sides, and her breasts emerged, the nipples casting shadows in the torchlight. She pushed her chest out. Rob had noticed her doing that before. It was like she was trying to make her tits look bigger. He leant forwards and took her left nipple in his mouth, keeping his hands out of the way while she shoved down the skirt she'd just unzipped, and her tights and pants with it.

She put her hands round the back of his neck as he sucked her. Are you sure nobody'll come in? she said into the top of his head.

He moved his mouth up to kiss her again, trailing a slaver over her skin and collarbone. Nobody ever comes in here, he said.

276

Except for us in a minute or two! And another thing is, with this big bastarding fan going, we can make as much noise as we like, and no one'll hear us. You can scream as loud as you like, but no one'll hear a thing.

She moved her lips along the line of his jaw. Are you going to make me scream? she said.

I'll do my best, he said, and squeezed his arms tight around her waist till she laughed and wheezed.

When he let her go, she went down onto her knees and started undoing his belt, pulling down his spaver, and tugging at the tops of his breeks. She turned her face up to him as they dropped to his shins.

Do anything you want to me, she said, As long as you do *something*.

He looked down at her. She was playing with the tops of his boxer shorts. You're fucking weird, he said. What goes on inside you? What makes you do the things you do?

She kissed his cock through the cloth of his boxers. I wanted to tell you on Saturday, she said. It's hard to talk about. Know what I mean? The hardest thing to talk about is the inside of your own head.

Fuck's sake, said Rob, and put his hands onto the girl's shoulders and pushed her face away from his groin. I don't give a toss what's between your ears, he said. It's what's between your legs that's important. She tried to move her mouth back towards his cock, but he pushed her away again, harder this time.

She paused, looked up at him, then moved backwards, and lay down on the dustcoat, her hands cupped to cover her cunt. You know what I have between my legs, she said, and smiled at him. Slowly she opened her folded hands, and parted her legs a little.

Rob felt blood exploding in his head and along the length of his cock, and he fell onto his knees on the edge of the coat. He put his arms out to the sides to steady himself, and gazed into the dark gash and bush in front of him.

I want to get a closer look today, he said. I want to know what goes on inside a woman. I want to see if you have the seeds of evil in you.

He shuffled forward on his knees until the left one bumped on the blade of the cleaver in his dustcoat pocket. Then he stopped, slid his left hand down under the soft material of the coat, and touched the wooden handle and the smooth metal joined to it, with the tips of his fingers.

Rob, she said.

He jolted. What?

That light's shining right in my eyes. Could you point it somewhere else?

Fuck's sake, he said, but moved his hand out from under the coat, reached up for the torch, and took it from off the top of the burner. Look at this. He stuck the torch in his mouth, bulb end first. He sucked in his cheeks and rolled his eyes, wobbling his hands about in front of him like a monster.

Sandra started giggling, then laughing. She held one hand across her chest, and pointed at him with the other, laughing her head off.

He was grinning too much to hold the torch in his mouth, so took it out and handed it to her. Now you, he said, and she lowered the penlight into her pursed lips.

Her cheeks were lit up bright pink, with darker patches round her lips and in lines up to the wings of her nose. She narrowed her eyes to slits and ran the torch in and out of her mouth a few times, wriggling her hips, making on like she was in extreme ecstasy.

278

Rob's cock had settled down a bit while he was kneeling, but seeing her doing that made him completely hard again. He held his hand out for the torch.

She wouldn't give it to him, she was moving it in and out of her mouth faster and faster, wriggling about on the floor, making exaggerated moaning noises. At last she acted an orgasm for herself and the torch, and slowly, slowly, pulled it out of her mouth for the last time. She stopped it an inch from her lips, then stuck out her tongue and gave the glass lense in front of the bulb a long lick. Then she held the torch out towards Rob.

He took it, but didn't point it at anything in particular to begin with. He stuck his thumb in his mouth for a second and got a film of spit around it, then put his hand between her legs, resting the wet thumb on the lips of her cunt. He rubbed the thumb up and down, lightly over her clit, more heavily over her hole, so soon his thumb had pushed through and was inside her. He moved it about in there, round and round as well as in and out, and now he brought the torch up and trained it on her face. He watched her reactions, repeating movements which made her draw breath or bite her lip. After half a minute he was moving his hand in a rhythm, and her hips were pressing back against him. He moved the light away from her face, and trickled it down over her breasts, her belly, through her pubes, and onto the white flesh inside her thighs.

Once more he raised the torch and placed it in his mouth, letting slavers coat the lense and the top half of the plastic case. Then he withdrew his thumb, pressing the heel of that hand onto her mound and stroking the soft skin around it with his fingers. He lowered the torch to between her thighs, the beam pointing straight up between them, illuminating the small glistening lips of her cunt and the tangled fair hair above them. He moved the torch closer, and stopped rubbing her. With the thumb and finger of his free hand he parted her lips wide, and bent his head to look up where the torch was shining.

What goes on in there? he said to himself, and peered some more. After a few seconds, frowning, he pushed the bulb end of the torch right up against the gape of her cunt.

Immediately she jerked half upright. No!

He motioned her to lie down with his free hand.

No, she said again. Rob, don't get any funny ideas.

Trust me, he said, without looking up.

She reached out, as if to knock the torch from his grip, but he raised his free arm and blocked her, then gently pushed her back onto the floor.

And he eased the torch into her cunt, pushing the bulb end past her lips and right inside, then wriggling it about a little, shoving some more, pushing the torch inside her till more than half of it was hidden.

He took his hand away and gazed at the end of the torch. It looked like she had a black plastic cock growing out of her. He looked at her cunt and belly: the mound with the hair was dark, but the skin on each side was lit from within, and up above it was pink too, a glowing pink with darker patches. By the time his eyes reached her navel she wasn't glowing, she was in darkness. He glanced up at her stretched out in front of him, but her face was hidden in the dark. He looked back to her glowing belly.

I can see inside you and outside you at the same time, he said.

He gripped the portion of the torch that was sticking out of her, pulled it out a little, pushed it back in, all the time watching the patches of pink glow change across her skin.

She said something, but too quiet for him to hear.

He pushed the torch as far in as it would go. He put the flat of his hand against the end of it and gave it a dunt, but it was knocking against bone or something.

She made a noise.

What? he said.

That hurts! she said loudly, and it sounded like there was a greet in her voice.

Rubbish, he said. It can't. I'm being gentle. Anyway, it's only a wee bit thicker than my thumb, and you never said that hurt.

Take it out, please.

I want to see what goes on inside you, he said. What makes you do the things you do. And if I find those seeds, I'll take them out: you'll thank me in the long run. So relax, enjoy it. I bet you are enjoying it, aren't you? Aren't you? Say you like it, come on, tell me, I know you do.

Please take it out. She seemed to sob. I'll shout for help if you don't.

He laughed. Nobody'll hear you, he said.

She started screaming, he pulled the torch out and dropped it on the coat to one side, then threw himself on top of her. Her scream hiccupped as his weight knocked the breath out of her, then started again. His cock felt as hard as the torch had been, and he rammed it up her cunt, not gentle now, but battering away, trying to break through something, to break through whatever barrier it was between them, to break through and be really inside, in her skin, in control of her. His face was right next to hers, he could see her lips quivering in the light from the torch on the floor, feel her breath on the side of his face as she screamed, weakly.

For a moment she turned her head and looked him in the eyes, and in that instant the burner and the fan switched off and he came and her scream and his echoed around the boiler-room.

Then they both fell silent.

Break time, he whispered. Heating goes off.

Rob stuck his head out the boiler-room door, then ducked it back in. Wait a sec, he said.

I can't find my clothes.

Jesus. . . He put his head out, glanced up the corridor again, then reached round and switched on the boiler-room lights. He shut the door and stood with his back to it, watching her fasten her blouse, then start to pull up her pants.

She paused, looked up. Have you got any tissues?

I've got some memos. But the paper might be a bit hard on your cunt.

She shook her head, and pulled up her pants, grimacing, then her tights and skirt. She crouched to pick something up from under the burner – the torch – and handed it to him. He examined it.

Have you got your period just now?

It's not due for another week. Why?

Give me my coat up, will you?

She picked the dustcoat off the floor, brushed it down a couple times with the flat of her hand as she held it, then passed it over. He draped it over his left arm and wiped the torch on it, the sides and the bulb end. Then he flicked the light on and off a couple times.

Doesn't seem to've harmed it at all, he said.

She had finished straightening herself up. Can I go now? she said in a quiet voice.

He glanced up at her, then turned away and hung the torch on its hook. You don't have to ask me, he said. It's completely up to you, nothing to do with me. He turned to face her, getting into his dustcoat. You can go whenever you like, he said. Frankly, my dear, I don't give a fuck.

There was a payphone in a booth in the main lobby. Rob got his money ready on the way there, and half a second after yarking open the door he was sticking it into the slot and dialling Karen's work number. The phone rang twice then was answered.

Good morning Scottish Petroleum Christine speaking how may I help you?

Credit control please.

The internal line rang with pairs of bleeps. After three of them, a male voice said, Credit Control.

Mrs Catto please, said Rob.

A hand was put over the mouthpiece at the other end. Rob could still hear the guy hollering across the office: Karen? Where's Karen? The hand was removed and the guy's unmuffled voice said, Just trying to find her. Can I say who's calling?

No, said Rob.

Pardon?

You can't say who's calling, said Rob.

Oh. . .

There was a click on the line, then, Karen Catto here, said Karen.

There was another click: Rob was alone with her.

Hello? she said after a moment. Karen Catto speaking.

Still Rob didn't say anything.

Are you still there? Karen said.

I'm here, said Rob. You can't write me off yet.

There was a silence, then Karen's voice changed. Rob? Is that you? Her lips were closer to the mouthpiece, and her voice was softer, more Scottish.

Listen, said Rob. About last night. . .

Jesus Rob! Where were you? I was sick! I'm sorry for yelling, honestly, I'm sorry. I mean I don't ken what's wrong with you, but. . .

Listen, said Rob. Listen: I'm sorry for running out like that. I stayed at the school.

The school. Of course. God. She laughed. I couldn't think where, Rob. You won't believe it: I even phoned Susan after what you were saying. I think I offended her, somehow, asking if you were there at midnight. But never mind, never mind, I was that worried, I. . .

Listen, said Rob. I don't have much money to talk now. Let's meet and sort this out once and for all.

Aye, that's good, let's. . .

When's your dinner break?

One to two.

He glanced at his watch. Can you make it twelve to one theday?

Eh. . . aye. The wonders of flexitime.

Right, said Rob. We'll meet up, and I'm sorry, and we'll sort this out, we'll talk it through and settle it once and for all. Okay?

I hope so Rob. Cause I still, you know, I do. . . She whispered: I love you.

Rob winced, closed his eyes, didn't reply.

Hello? she said after a couple seconds. Are you there?

Aye, he said. I was just. . . thinking. He cleared his throat. Twelve o'clock then.

Great. I'll see you. Oh! Where?

What?

Where'll we meet?

Eh. . . neutral ground, he said. We'll meet out the cliffpath, by that old bunker.

The one where we. . . ?

Aye. There. Happy memories. And we'll not be disturbed. We'll sort things out once and for all.

Rob ran through the woods in his dustcoat. Within a few seconds the cleaver was jumping about in his pocket, the blade jabbing him in the thigh, the whole thing threatening to bounce out as he ran. He didn't want to lose it, that was for sure, and he didn't want it to tumble out and cleave his foot either. The rest of the way through the woods, he ran holding the chopper in his right hand, occasionally swiping out at branches that overhung the narrow way.

He reached the clifftop path, and turned along it, parallel to the sea. He slowed to a walk, getting his breath back, settling himself. As he drew level with the taing, he checked his watch: quarter to twelve. He had made good time. He slipped the chopper back into his coat pocket, and pushed through the bushes onto the short green grass beyond.

Coming towards him, carrying a bulging nylon holdall, was Bunker Man. His hood was up, his parka was zipped to the snorkel, and he was walking fast.

Stop! cried Rob.

Bunker Man didn't react, kept on walking.

Oi, said Rob, as the guy approached him. It's me, Jannie Man! Your fellow midnight-feaster!

Bunker Man raised his hooded head so Rob got a glimpse of staring eyes at the end of the dark tunnel of the snorkel. Then he walked on.

Oi! called Rob again, and stepped sideways, arms outstretched.

Bunker Man's way was blocked. He stopped. I'm leaving, he said.

You can't, said Rob. I need you. You can't leave.

I have to leave.

But why? said Rob. Things are looking up: we had a good night! It was a laugh, eh?

And when I came home, my house was wrecked.

What!

Between when I left for food yesterday afternoon, and when I got home in the middle of the night, someone came here and wrecked my home. I couldn't see how bad it was till this morning. Now I know it's terrible. They tore down my door and curtain, they threw my firewood store in the sea, they kicked my clothes in the mud. They wrecked my home.

Jesus Christ, said Rob. I bet I ken who that was.

I tried to fix it up, said Bunker Man. But it was hopeless. It's the same old story: I get somewhere I like and they won't let me stay, they chuck me out. They go on with their lives and forget me, put me out of their minds. If I'm not out of my mind, I'm out of theirs. I can't win.

Rob reached out a hand and gripped Bunker Man's shoulder. Listen, he said. What if you could get revenge?

I don't want revenge.

Rubbish! Everybody wants revenge! *I* want revenge!

I want to leave, said Bunker Man.

What if I told you, said Rob, that the person who trashed your home is coming back, will be here any minute?

I better leave, said Bunker Man. I might have a tantrum. And I don't know my own strength when that happens.

There's nothing wrong with temper, said Rob. It's good to let things out.

I better leave.

Rob patted Bunker Man's arm, then reached down and took the holdall from his hand. No, he said. It's too late to run. You better stay here and fight. He put his free arm around Bunker Man's shoulders. Come on, he said. Back to the castle. He took a step towards the pillbox, pulling Bunker Man with him. It's time to stand and fight, he said. Stand up for what you believe, *fight* for what you believe. He dragged Bunker Man on a couple more steps.

I just want to be left alone though.

You never will be, said Rob. You're never going to be left alone. She's going to follow you for the rest of your life. She's going to hound you. She's going to pester you. She'll never let you have a minute's peace. She'll wreck every home you try to make. She'll try and wreck your *life*.

She? said Bunker Man. A woman did that?

Of course a woman! cried Rob. Who else? A treacherous fucking woman!

A woman did that? he said again.

Aye!

Bunker Man stopped walking, turned to Rob. But *why*?

Why? Why? Eh. . . Rob glanced down at his watch: five to twelve.

Why did you do that? wailed Bunker Man.

Cause she's coming here! said Rob. I wanted to see how long we had.

But why? Why? Why's she coming here? Why's she wrecking my life?

Because, said Rob, taking hold of Bunker Man's elbow and tugging him on down the taing, Because she loves you. She told me herself. She's in love with you, she's obsessed by you, she can't get you out of her mind. She wants to have you, to control you, she wants to rule your life. And if she can't do that, she's going to wreck it instead.

It's not fair! cried Bunker Man. I don't even know her. He started sobbing.

Come on, said Rob, Let's get out of sight before she comes, in behind the ramparts. They stepped over the garden gate, and on a few more steps towards the pillbox.

Maybe I should talk to her, said Bunker Man.

No, said Rob. Talking's no good. I've tried talking. It doesn't work. The time for talking is past. There's only one thing that'll work with this woman.

What? Kill her?

You won't have to do that. Just fuck her. That'll be even better. She's sex mad. She wants you to fuck her. She'll act like she doesn't, but she does. Women are always doing that, eh?

I don't know.

They were at the entrance to the bunker. Rob reached out and brushed his hand round the fur trim of Bunker Man's snorkel so the hairs were all lying the same way. He narrowed his eyes and looked at the effect, then nodded.

She loves you, mind? he said. She'll act like she wants you to leave her alone, but that's all a game. After all, she won't leave *you* alone, will she? No, what she really wants is for you to fuck her brains out.

Why does she not just say that then?

Dear dear, said Rob, shaking his head. You don't ken much about women, do you? They like it to be a bit of a fight.

Do they?

Aye. It shows you're really keen on them, if you're prepared to use a bit of force.

Will she fight back, then?

Not if you get in first. You've got surprise on your side, that's the great thing. Rob put both hands on Bunker Man's shoulders, and stared down the snorkel tunnel into his eyes. You get in this bunker, he said, Round behind the entrance-way, and you wait. And when you hear her saying hello you shout hello back. And when she walks in to the bunker, her eyes won't be used to the light. That's your big chance. Pounce on her, knock her down, caa the legs from under her. She'll never know what's hit her.

Then what?

For fuck's sake man. Then you fuck her. Do I have to explain that too?

No, no, said Bunker Man. You don't. Don't shout.

And if anything goes wrong, said Rob. I'll be standing by. Look what I've got.

He pulled the chopper out of his pocket and held it up between them, turning the blade this way and that, so sunlight gleamed off the polished metal.

Bunker Man reached up and touched it, stroked a finger along the side of the sharp edge. What's it for? he said.

It's for emergencies, said Rob. But I doubt I'll have to use it on her. Not if you do your bit. He pointed the cleaver down towards

Bunker Man's cock. That'll sort her better than any axe through the head, he said.

Bunker Man looked at him. Are you sure?

Rob grinned. Trust me.

Rob was getting worried, and Bunker Man was getting impatient.

Rob checked his watch. It was quarter past. Okay, fair enough, five minutes for her to drive from the office down by the harbour, another ten or fifteen to walk out the cliff this far. She wasn't not coming, she was coming as quickly as she could. She wouldn't let him down on this one: she never let him down on things like this. That was one of the most annoying things about her: how fucking dependable she was all the time. Actually, it was good that Bunker Man was getting fed up waiting. All the more likely he'd be in enough of a rage to follow through when he finally did get a hold of her.

Once again, Rob edged round the pillbox till he could see back along the taing. There was movement in the bushes, a figure pushing through them: Karen, at last. He jerked his head out of view, flattened himself against the concrete wall, and took a sideways step seawards. But he couldn't resist having another look at her.

He moved his head out a fraction, so half his eye could see round the angle of the wall, and for one second he watched her coming quickly along the taing. She was wearing her work shoes, and their heels weren't ideal for trekking along clifftops. Also, she had a short tight skirt on that didn't leave her legs much room for movement. And her hair was blowing about in the wind off the sea, strands of it flicking across her face, catching between her lips, getting in her eyes.

He pulled his head back, took a deep breath. From the way she was moving, and what he could see of her face through the flying hair, he could tell she was upset, she was worried. Usually when she looked like that she wanted him to give her a hug, to tell her everything would turn out fine, that the two of them were a good team, that between them they could face up to any problem and beat it. That's what she looked like now to Rob, and it was hard for him not to act on that feeling, despite everything she'd done to him, everything she'd put him through. But he pressed himself back against the concrete wall, made no move towards her: the time for those feelings was past. Now was the time for action. And Rob's first action was to stay out of sight till Bunker Man had struck. Then he would show himself, come to the rescue. In salutem omnium. He would do his bit, just as Karen was, without knowing it, about to do hers. He edged back to the sea-side of the pillbox, and crouched down.

He didn't hear her footsteps approaching, but suddenly her voice called out from close by: Robbie! Where are you?

Again he felt a surge of desire to answer her, but again he rode it out and kept his mouth shut. For some reason, Bunker Man was keeping silent too.

Robbie! she called again, then said something to herself that he couldn't make out.

He couldn't understand why the fuck Bunker Man wasn't calling out like he was meant to. If he didn't make himself known, the whole plan would fail. It wouldn't even fail: it just wouldn't happen.

Robbie Catto! she shouted, and he thought she was coming nearer. Robbie? Hello!

Immediately a voice boomed inside the bunker. Hello!

291

Hello! Karen called back. Are you inside the damn thing?

Hello! Bunker Man shouted, his voice muffled and echoey.

Karen laughed. Hold on, she said. I'm coming in.

Rob clenched his fists, and waited. There was the faint sound of her work shoes clacking on concrete down the zigzag entrance way, then silence. Rob closed his eyes, raised his face to the sky, brought his clenched fists up to his chest.

There was a crack, a yelp of pain from Karen, a scuffle, then another crack, and a thud. Wood whacked down on bone and flesh, and Karen yowled. Bunker Man was shouting something: Thin ankles! Thin ankles!

Rob could hear it all quite clearly, coming out the slit window above his head. But hearing wasn't enough, he wanted to see too. Now something was being dragged across the floor of the bunker. Rob needed to see what. He couldn't afford to miss anything. If his punishment was going to be justified, it was essential for him to catch Bunker Man red-handed, in the act.

Ducking double, Rob ran to the far side of the slit window. Then he straightened up and carried on round the north side of the pillbox, where there was a low pile of rubble, rubbish, and festering bones. He scrambled up it, got a grip on the top of the pillbox with both hands, and jumped, hoisting up first one knee, then, with the leverage that gave him, the whole of his body.

He lay flat on the roof for a few seconds, then raised his head. Just in front was the smokehole. Through it, Rob could hear Bunker Man speaking. He couldn't make out any words, and the voice was one he hadn't heard him using before, full of growls and barks. At first Rob thought that he was actually impersonating a dog, for some reason, but then it clicked: the barks were bursts of laughter. He'd never heard Bunker Man laughing before either.

Rob got up on his hands and knees and crawled over towards the smokehole. He leant over it and peered down into the dark interior of the bunker with one eye. To begin with, he couldn't make out what was going on, but his vision gradually got used to the weak light coming in through the slit window and he could see fine.

Bunker Man was completely naked. His broad back was covered in freckles and ginger hair, and it was bent over Karen, who was stretched out on the row of fishboxes in the middle of the floor. Bunker Man had one hand over her mouth, and he must have been pressing down hard, for she didn't seem able to shout out, let alone move her head clear. Rob hoped he wouldn't go so far as to break her neck; that would be unnecessary, even counterproductive. His other hand was working on getting Karen's pants down. Her skirt was of some stretchy material, and he'd pushed that up over her hips. But now he was having difficulty getting the pants and tights down, because Karen was kicking her legs about, trying to knee his balls as he bent over her, not lying at peace for a second to let him get her undressed.

It was frustrating to watch. Rob really wanted to nip down and get a hold of her thin ankles, hold her still and give Bunker Man a fair chance to get a crack at her. But he couldn't allow himself to join in like that. It would wreck the whole plan. It was essential that he just watch and wait till there was definitely a rape in progress, and he had a valid excuse to smash the weirdo's sick brains out.

Karen was putting up quite a fight. Rob was glad he'd warned Bunker Man that might happen. He was still starting to get agitated, though. Rob could see big muscles moving under the pale skin of his back. Suddenly he lifted his hand from Karen's mouth, letting the scream she was halfway through burst out so loud that Rob jerked away from the smokehole. An instant later, Bunker Man slapped her hard, and she fell silent.

Rob peered into the bunker again. Bunker Man must've stunned her, for now he was pulling down her tights and she wasn't resisting at all. He paused when they reached her ankles, unbuckled her shoes, then yanked them and the tights off and threw them to one side. Then he took hold of her pants in both hands and ripped them in half down the front. She didn't even flinch, just lay there. Knowing what she was like, she was probably starting to enjoy the whole thing. Either that or she was unconscious.

Bunker Man had stopped. He was staring at the mass of dark hair between her legs. Rob wanted to shout out, Don't stop now! Do it! Do it! But he bit his lip and stayed silent, though he was beginning to think he wouldn't be able to keep from whooping for much longer, it was all going so well. He didn't know how long he'd be able to keep just watching, either: his cock was hard as concrete and he could feel blood thumping through it as he lay belly-down on the roof. If Bunker Man didn't fuck her soon, he felt like he'd have to jump down and get stuck in himself.

But now Bunker Man was finally getting his act together, lumbering round to between her legs, reaching out and gripping the flesh around her cunt with one hand. The other hand was wrapped around his cock. Slowly he leaned forward over her, bringing his two hands together, aiming his cock towards her cunt.

His buttocks clenched, he groaned, and he was inside her. That seemed to wake her up, and she started struggling again. But he was spurred on by her writhings, and started thrusting into her from his hips. She was shouting and screaming at him, her eyes bulging with rage, her head jerking from side to side, but he seemed not to notice. He was working to a rhythm of his own, grunting some sequence of words or sounds over and over as he fucked her. She started punching his face and the sides of his head, and without breaking rhythm he moved his hands up from waist level and gripped her elbows, pressing them down onto the fishboxes. He couldn't hold her legs though, and they flailed about, the heels digging into the backs of his knees and shins as he pounded away.

Rob watched his wife's legs thrashing about as Bunker Man fucked her. Their movements were incredible: looking just at them it was impossible to tell if they were waving about in fury and agony, or in the throes of ecstasy. It drove Rob crazy. Suddenly he realised he was on the point of coming, and had been for at least half a minute.

He got up on his knees, whipped down his spaver, and pulled out his cock. Two strokes from his fist and he ejaculated, spunk spurting out in front of him over the roof of the pillbox, and down through the smokehole.

A second later there was a roar from inside the bunker, and Rob knew, even without looking, that Bunker Man had come too. That was it. That was all he needed.

He tucked his seeping cock away, then got up and walked to the edge of the roof. He took the cleaver out of his pocket, held it above his head, and jumped. The landing winded him a little, but he got to his feet immediately, and ran round to the entrance.

Bunker Man was silent now, but Karen was still shouting and screaming.

I'm coming! yelled Rob, and headed down the zigzag passageway. I'll save you, baby! I'll get the bastard!

It was dark inside, and full of Karen's bawling, but he knew exactly where he was going, and what he was doing. Bunker Man was sprawled on top of Karen still, his face turned away from the entrance. That made it easy. Rob stepped over, raised the cleaver high, then brought the flat of the blade crashing down on the back of Bunker Man's head.

Got you now, you bastard! he shouted.

Bunker Man raised himself up on his elbows, tried to look round, but before he could, Rob smashed the chopper down on his skull again, feeling something crack and mush under the blow. Bunker Man tottered, then fell off sideways as his left arm gave way. His pale bulk thumped onto the concrete floor, and he lay there face up, eyelids flickering slightly, nothing else moving at all. Dark blood started pooling under one ear.

Baby! cried Rob, dropping the cleaver and kneeling beside her. I saved you! I saved you from the loony! The cunt had it coming, I told you, I told everybody. Maybe they'll listen now, maybe now they'll take me seriously.

Karen burst out greeting. You bastard! she shouted. You fucking bastard!

I ken, said Rob, He is. He's a bastard. But I've sorted him out for good.

You're the bastard! she screamed.

He shook his head. I wish I hadn't been late in coming, maybe I could've stopped the whole thing, but at least. . .

Rob, she said, struggling up into a sitting position. I saw you. What? I only just got here.

No. She was trembling. She pointed to the smokehole in the roof above her. I saw you watching, she said.

He started. What are you talking about?

You stood by, she said. You stood by and did nothing.

What? I saved you, baby!

She closed her eyes, held them shut for a second, then opened them and looked at him. I saw you looking, she said.

He nodded. I've always looked after you, he said. I always will.